STAR
WANDERER

CHRIS TURNER

CHAPTER 1

The dance club was centered beneath a high dome with a slightly raised floor. The see-through glass revealed a scene to a distant galaxy. The floor's surface was one big slowly-revolving disc, with RGB strobe lights veering down and dance beats echoing like a sound and light show.

The place was wild with people and surround-sound. A coed horde jived to a staccato synth-bass refrain, hair flying, hips twisting, an electro tango in motion.

Through the airwaves the hypno beat pulsed that seemed to reach in and pull out people's guts and take them for a ride—subwoofers which made the low-frequency oscillations go from sternum to plexus and out again. It enticed everyone to get in there and gyrate the body.

I had to give these architects and engineers credit for the multi-tech spectacle they'd created. The sound and light magic, the revolving dance floor, the cathedral ceiling...all were orchestrated to loosen people's pockets and inhibitions. We bouncers roved about the fray to handle any of the unruly clientele who might try to take advantage of the lenience of the management.

Gerry, the man who'd designed the layout, had an artistic flair. He shared a vision with a bunch of venture capital people who had pitched in money along with the mining companies to turn a profit and keep the blue-collar workers happy on what would otherwise be a dull planet.

My mind was drifting on the job, as it often did. I didn't notice the little redhead with silver headband until she slinked fingers along my arm.

"Wanna dance?" Her owlish eyes fluttered.

"Sorry, babe, I'm on duty. But catch me after two and I'll be available and ready."

She shook her head. "No way, chief. Early bird gets the worm." With an energetic, if not exaggerated butt wiggle, she sashayed up onto the dance floor to join the available fresh meat.

I flashed her moving parts a toothy grin. Her slim figure was lost in a tangle of moving bodies amid the smoky haze of dry ice.

Why I was reduced to eking out an existence as a lowly-paid bouncer, one of the 'Regulators', at *The Rocks*, was a long story. Besides being a happening place out on Perseus Way, it was one of the places on the main strip where all the glitter was. I practically had to beg for the job. Every grifter in town wanted a piece of something like this when labor was scarce. People wanted in on the action, to be in a environment where everyone was turning tricks.

I had some choices.

I could be working graveyard shift as a grunt security gunman patrolling the seedy warehouses, the shadowy yards and rusty gates of the industrial companies, looking for the usual two-bit cons who'd try to steal, hack, drill through to certain hordes of Sesim—that expensive, rare metal on Halroon that yielded high export value.

My hair was spiked purple. I'd acquired a fake ID, I had the moves and the looks and the streamlined physique that attracted the stares, especially when I performed gigs solo, and sometimes the admiration of wandering, drifting females.

How I found myself on that planet in that rain-soaked, litter-strewn alley a month ago, I won't waste many words on. I jumped a few freighters, bribed a few officials, landed without a mekh to my name. I expended a lot of energy and the last of my pocket reserves trying to grease the wheels to get half way to Pegasus. The jaunt to the space hub for a feeder flight to this backwater was dicey.

Once can detect surveillance. A place that has the all-seeing network of eyes. The deliberate staging: where everyone seemingly lounging around is a plant, where hangers-on are in places they shouldn't be, like bad, amateur extras in a low-budget movie. There's a suspicious air afloat...lingering, seeping into the very fabric of the background, giving everything a surreal normalcy.

That murky month ago, when I crossed into Ganganar space hub, I'd picked up a few tails. The beady eyes of a casual bystander straining too long on my unwashed hide. The out-of-place shifty look of a hobo pretending to be a grifter at an out-of-town spaceport. Almost too hackneyed.

Bounty hunters? Nerks? Spies? Ziddles?

Did it matter?

I knew I had to watch my back. I had to keep moving.

As much as the officials were encouraging immigration on this newly terraformed, frontier mining town, the local people of Nmoor weren't that welcoming to outworlders. Not my observation anyway. There was a healthy mix of races and folk from faraway planets, true. Mostly a younger crowd, bopping around, as could be witnessed here.

Why, one might ask? The old time migrants had bred a burgeoning population of young ones to run the service industries. Man the bars and casinos, the hotels and restaurants. Even certain peripheral industries had sprung up—sightseeing companies to bring an element of 'touristy fascination' to good old Halroon. If one were to call the mangrove swamps the other side of the open pit mines and the flowering terraterra trees and weird-ass grunting wombats, 'attractions'. For even the most gullible and enthusiastically-inclined, flat-bottomed skiff tours could be booked to explore the wetland waterways.

As a newcomer one needs a cover story. I didn't have one. So I spun a medley of yarns to amuse myself. People are curious, gossipy beasts. They have a compulsion to parcel everyone in a nice neat little box. I'd give the nod, do a slow four count, then dive into one of a dozen exotic stories about my being a god-fearing, down-on-luck runaway. It gave credence to my presence here on this world. Some tales played up to my lank-limbed mystique. Others didn't. The only common refrain being none of them came close to the truth of the fate I'd almost suffered at the hands of the cannibalistic Skurgs.

Even thinking 'Skurg' sent an involuntary shiver through my body. The memories were still vivid enough that I awoke in a cold sweat in the dead of night more often than I could count.

My new official ID was 'Jet Rusco', of Paranath World.

Never could be too careful. The kingpins of the Moon Temple and the Skurg muscle were out in force for my blood. Skel and I had busted up their slave compound some months ago and I was wise enough in my near twentieth year not to underestimate the ruthlessness of the Skurgs—or Gy-ar and his Moon Temple minions, and their dogged tenacity in hunting down dudes like me who they did not like. Personae non gratae. The ones who refused to join their club or readily hand over long lost artifacts, or who despised their tangled network of spies and informers.

Long story short, a month of long thirty-hour Halroon days have passed and I've managed to get myself relocated without getting my throat cut or kidnapped by Skurg slavers.

The Rocks was what visitors might call a one-stop shop. The casino with its rows of slot machines, dice, roulette and card tables sat off to my left in a pleasant murky haze. The meet-and-greet service was run by the barkeeps. A combo casino, live show and match-up service all in one. Males, females and non-genders could sign in at central control and the AI would play matchmaker. Hidden cameras would observe body language, personal engagement, group dynamics and while pinhead mics would listen in on conversations, voice inflections and catalog feedback loops, the AI did its magic of cross-tabulating. A kind of lightning-quick engine that was very accurate in its matching. Installed by the mining companies to 'inter-mesh' and 'socially engage' the migrant population.

Another proven gimmick, I thought with sour amusement. I was a bit of a purist, an old fashioned dude, one might say, who didn't go in for the AI angle.

All that to say, it got rowdy on the floor. Tempers flared, emotions ran high. Jealousies abounded. Fights inevitably broke out and required at least four bouncers on the floor at all times. Some males got miffed when their female picks, at least in their minds, got paired up with other guys.

Understandable...but guys, come on?

It was a low level stew.

Yet a job was a job was a job and I didn't mind being out on this backwater. Even in a mildly dodgy environment: it helped me to operate under the radar and out of the clutches of bounty hunters.

Up till now at least...

I did some occasional solo gigs here. The rock opera shtick at amateur hour on slow nights was entertaining, usually profitable. It was always a blast. I missed that old part of my past. The days before I acquired the artifact that threw me into this shit show and turned my existence upside down and sent me on the run.

The days of grandstanding on Hoag at Carnivale seemed like something out of dim history. The cheers, the high energy, the fringe benefits after hours—these were the rewards for our acrobatics on stage, belting out heavy music, the hoarse-grained lyrics, the wailing guitar riffs. Women were always throwing themselves at rockers. I didn't mind it too much. I'd take it while it lasted, at least before I was old, gray and bald.

It was the extra cash that was the incentive. Money to pay off certain gambling debts I'd racked up in my stupid haste to roust up enough capital to pay the rent. To finance the next jump to another haven, before I was made.

Rule #1: never indulge in a gambling binge on a foreign world. Get rich quick schemes never work out without an extensive knowledge of the gambling tables. Improvisations, accomplices, tricks and mirrors can get one's legs broken.

Moving on limber legs, I scoped out a table at the far wall with a 25-foot video screen. A pig-cheeked man jollied at a glass table with his two girls. He was making a jackass of himself. Climbing up on the table and doing his impression of 'piggly-wiggly' coming out of the swamp on hands and knees. He kicked glasses out of the way, shook his butt and grunted like a horny boar while his missies snorted with him. It seemed the AI had paired friend A-hole with a couple of girlie contenders.

I put a hand out and made a cut signal. "Okay, Grib, all's fun at comedy hour but why not save it for Friday? That's Karaoke and Yuk Yuk night. Your girls get a laugh, you get to take it easy and knock back a few beers for half price."

"Take off, Rubie," pig man snorted over the din. "This ain't your scene." He gave me an oily sneer, much drunken and Myscol-rich. "You should stick to the bar, or go back to being a two-bit rock junkie. Yeah, I saw you the other night. Woohoo. With the V and the Raggedy Ann hair mop boys. Better off with green hair than purple, methinks. Draws more attention. Sets off your eyes." He brayed out another heehaw of a laugh.

I nodded. "Thanks for your advice, Grib. I'll take that under advisement. Now please, off the table. Management gets nervous when clients smash glasses and fall on them and cut themselves. We get sued."

Jackass must have seen through my hockey mask disguise at the latest gig at the Talisman. Another liability. I felt the first warning bells ting.

He nudged the tall brunette at his side. She laughed on cue. "Hear that, babe? Rubie here is concerned for my health."

The chestnut hair at his other side let out a tired sigh. "You gonna let a two bit kid order you around, Grib? I'd say he's not a day older than sixteen."

"Yeah," the brunette chimed in. "Still got his peach fuzz and no doubt baby teeth too. Whose tune we dancing to, a man or a teenie weenie?"

My mouth curved in a strained grin. Ordinarily I don't go in for these rough and tumble beatdowns but Grib and his two gals were starting to get on my nerves. I was not what you would call traditional bouncer material. I was six foot, yes, and I could move like a cat and drop guys twice my weight, but Grib was still dangerous. Myscol had the effect of giving a clown more strength and stamina than his due, and his smiley-assed girlie-friends were due for a rude awakening.

"As I said, Grib, another strike and it's sayonara. Leb already flagged you for spilling beer on the ladies at the other table earlier this evening."

He let out a false squeal. "They wanted a shower. To cool down on account of all the hot lights and the sight of my sexy bod." He gave a high-pitched squeal.

Lebby, my bouncer partner, swaggered over. "Any problems here?" His brawny arms crossed his tattooed chest.

"Naw, Leb." I waved a hand. "Grib and me just having a little conversation, is all. Nothing I can't handle."

"Okay." His blueberry eyes narrowed, not liking Grib's fresh clucking chicken act. At a nearby table, one of the brides, what we called the 'female matchees', was having a meltdown so Leb was distracted. She was all tiny fists and elbows whirlwinding on another high-heeled woman in response to her 'go-to man' mooning over a new match. Leb jerked a thumb. "Gotta take this, Rus. Squelch the cat fight. Call me if you need me."

I gave him a salute and turned my weary gaze back to the tiresome threesome. It was getting on into the evening. A lot of gigs were still planned for tonight. It would not be becoming to prolong this little incident. In fact, it would look bad on my watch. Meaning docked pay. Plus it would inspire other comedians like Grib to try party tricks. It only took one wiseass to embolden the sheep to chalk up a few brownie points in front of their buds.

A whisper of movement caught my eye. The casino roller-roulette table to my left pulsed with a sudden activity. A flush-faced man flung a fist. Cal, our third bouncer, was having a tough time settling a disagreement. Fist-flinger was cut off from booze.

They say bad things come in threes.

The dim little chestnut hair I wasn't worried about. It was more the lanky brunette who looked like a shark out to take friend Grib for a ride. There was an animal cunning in those hazel eyes. Painted face, powdered cheeks, lips glossy blue, tinted to perfection. Lightly-oiled brow and forearms. Fake black lashes, not too long like the other cheeseheads floating around this joint, lingering in the reeds for easy marks. Yes, a shrewd intelligence lurked behind those eyes that feigned a bovine complaisance. I'd gotten good at reading people in my accelerated coming of age. Working this place had helped me size up the larks and the sharks. I could crunch the numbers.

Rumor had it that Grib worked the gambling tables around town and won more than he lost. The staff had eyes trained on him for some time, and up till now, he had the luxury of acting out with the extra cash in his pocket. We figured he was running a system but had no proof. Our shit-for-brains camera surveillance had come up empty. Our plants too. Grib was careful. He was also a lucky son of bitch.

But not tonight. He clearly was a class A asshole.

How much spice had he delved into? Maybe the pretty brunette'd spiked his mango lassi with double-fix Myscol. Who knew? It was a barbarous world.

Conjecture, Rusco. It'll eat out your brain. Just go with your gut instinct and spare yourself the extra agony.

So I decided to play a game, which I dubbed 'Figure out the mystery'.

Were both these women matchees? Maybe one was organic, just a cheesedog who dug Grib for the upstanding citizen he was.

That made as much as sense as salmon swimming downriver to spawn.

More likely the clever brunette was one of the meet-and-greets that Grib had picked up here at the bar. Grib had jumped, slavering like a pit bull. He had the face of a bulldog crossed with a baked potato, how could he score something as classy as that? He did have the physique of the regular gym-goer, but alongside it, the nervous mannerisms of a junkie and the subtlety of a street tram. But so what? At the very least he had no pot belly. Only thing keeping miss hot pants was some promise of money and maybe some entertainment along the way: gallivanting around with a show boater who could lavish money on her and take her places.

I stared hard at Grib who blinked back at me still doggy-style on the table with a silly-ass grin.

"Not going to let up? Okay, boss, have it your way."

I grabbed him by the scruff of the neck, my other hand on his designer sport jacket along the small of his back, and flung him off the table.

He rolled up badger-like. But in seconds he was on his feet, bouncing like a prize fighter. His fists balled, his red-churned face bunched in knots, clown-like. I had to smile. The Myscol glare in his cold eyes flashed as sinisterly as a pulsing signpost. It was almost comical.

Others had stopped to stare.

The man on street-experimental amphetamines can summon sudden bursts of energy. He can disarm one into fatal complacency. This was one such time.

Before I could react, his snake-fast hand had snatched out a stunner, palm-coin-sized from his imitation wrangler pockets and slammed me on the shoulder before I could block or dodge.

"Aw, motherfrike!" In agony I fell to my knees.

An electric zing rippled through my nerve ends. Son of a bitch! Blindsiding me with a cheap gadget like that. How the hell'd he get that past Jake at the door?

Chestnut-hair had paled, realizing this is not the party she'd signed up for.

I kicked at Grib's shin, sucking in a breath. I looped out my other foot which caught him on the fleshy part back of the knee. He tripped, landed hard on his side. Now it was his turn to cry out.

Out snapped a switchblade, ready to gut me or carve any exposed part it could find. I had the nasty feeling some blood was about to be spilled.

The blade was a mere inch away from my testes before the brunette kicked the blade away.

He gave a squawk of anger. "What'd you do that for, bitch?"

He slapped her hard and sent her sprawling into the arms of some standers-by.

Lebby was hustling our way—all sleeves rolled up and fists knotted.

Patrons were laughing. Bar flies pointed, others gawked. Look at the funny man with tall boy playing pattycake on the floor.

I was registering all this in slow motion. None of it making much sense.

I got out the way of his boot. A hard leather sole can break cartilage in one's throat. In other words, 'bye bye, Rusco'.

I turned and wheeled, deflected his other stomping foot and kneed him hard in the kneecap, hearing something crack.

He uttered a caw of pain.

Lebby came storming in, subdued his arms in a full nelson. Enraged, Grib squirmed and cursed but Leb dragged him away to the exit. He flailed some more and said some amusing things but Lebby only tightened his grip.

"Shut up, pig man. You're in a world of trouble here, Rusco," he bawled back at me, "you said you'd handle this one!"

"I was, until this fool pulled a stunner on me. What kind of secure door operation you guys running around here?"

"Happens all the time. Get over it."

Out of the corner of my eye, I saw a shadowy figure edge toward the exit. I'd seen pebbly eyes like that at Ganganar hub. Lera too. Come to think of it, on other worlds scattered through the star systems. Informers. Spies. Stooges. Reporting on something unusual, watching for certain telltale signs, like a long-haired youth demonstrating unique fighting skills.

Seems like my cover had been blown.

The brunette recovered from her slap and came over to help me.

I waved her off.

I owed her more than what I was giving her. I softened and muttered a grudging thanks.

"You okay?" She blinked, seeming genuinely concerned.

"It's nothing." I wiped the dust off my pants and flexed my aching wrist. My pride was hurt but I wasn't going to let it show. "Nice save," I complimented her. I gestured at the gathering mob. "Move along, folks! Come on. Nothing to see here."

"Don't mention it," she said. "You want to get out of here?"

I looked from her to Leb who'd returned after turfing Grib out on the street. The bouncer gave a solemn nod. "Take a break, Rus. You look all drained out."

The lady held out a hand. "I'm Areth."

"Rusco. Jet Rusco."

As Areth and I were making our way down the rain-splattered streets, I mused, why were these people putting so much energy into tracking a nobody down?

Even as I asked it, I knew the question was as naive as it was rhetorical.

I'd gone from potential poster boy at one of their domination cults to less than traitorous dirt and scum. Escaped death from their cannibalistic bounty hunters. I'd tossed up their crib, lost their precious artifact and I expected them to give me a pass?

You nutso, Rusco? People like that don't give a shit about expenses. They don't give up in any way easily. They have infinite memories...and even longer arms.

That familiar sickening feeling climbed up my spine. The heat would die down. It'd blow over. I'd just have to sit tight and...

The words sounded hollow in my throat.

Damn these scumbags.

CHRIS TURNER

CHAPTER 2

The yellowish half moon glimmered high in the sky as we made our way toward one of the late-night eateries in the downtown core. She made some overture of arching her back, showing off her shapely breasts and bumping her hip into me as we pretended to be a couple on a date. She glossed her lips with more of the purple goo they called 'Hot Lips' and clicked her tongue, "Damn that Grib, can you believe him lousing up the night? Where's a girl going to find a real man? Your computer matchmaking at *The Rocks* is way off, bro. Programmer better not quit his day job."

I grinned. "Preaching to the choir, babe." I gave her the once over—admiring the sultry eyes, lean of leg, slightly bowlegged, brazen strut. Ready, willing, able.

I checked the time. I would have been off work at 2. Already it was after midnight. Garth had called a meet with the other band members and a practice at the warehouse on Stella Lane. If we were up for it in the wee hours. Most of us were night owls so we'd probably all show up.

I did some quick calculations. Half hour to get over to my dim hovel under the magno tram, get in some drinks and serious flirting with the new lady with aim to get in her pants. No, not enough time, I told myself. I was not a big fan of rush jobs.

I could skip the meet. It was tempting. There was something exciting about this girl.

Plan B. Should I invite her along to our practice? It had its upsides and downsides.

When I dodged her idea of ice cream and dancing at *Bolos* farther down Pegasus, she seemed a little put out by my long pause and lack of enthusiasm.

"Listen, Areth, I've got some stuff on the go tonight. You're welcome to come to our band practice though."

There was a moment's pause as if the air suddenly crackled with ice. "Say what?" There it was again, the animal cunning in her eye. Five different thoughts coming in all at once in her pretty little head: convoluted possibilities computed on the fly in real time.

"Sure," she finally said, pulled out a vape, took a drag and looked away.

"You like that stuff?"

"I wouldn't be toking if I didn't. You?"

"No."

We turned up at the warehouse, me dragging my feet, kind of feeling off about this change of plans. I was wondering if inviting her was...well, such a good idea.

The guys were all there, lanky, lean, long-hairs sporting various colors of the rainbow. Some desultory sounds were coming from Beatie's amp. Our singer's high voice clipped overtop it all. Areth and I were latecomers. They offered us dull stares.

We'd renamed ourselves the *Startled Zombies*. Not bad if you go for teen title bands. Catchy and rebel. Not good if you take the name literally. I could think of better names. But Garth, our lead singer could be a little bitchy at times and he pushed the name. We knew if we didn't back his first choice, we'd never hear the end of it. It was easier to capitulate.

They were all my age, all eager to make it big: fame, stardom. Me, I pretended to want it—but I could care less. My pantomime of enthusiasm was all part of the act. To fit into this world with minimal participation. I was what bygone generations called 'one of the old guard', one of the few rare souls who escaped the fantasy-celebrity cult of addiction. Drummer and rhythm guitarist, Drodge and Beatie, were easy going, maybe not the brightest lights, but all round decent fellows. Geez, our bassist, had his moments. Garth was an uncontested pain in the ass, egotist, control freak all the way, a prima donna. Musicians could be like that. It was part of the trade. Hard not to be, especially in this cutthroat business, a front man no less. An overinflated arrogance the size of an airfield helps cushion one from the great fall and the parasites and the deceit...for a while.

So our personalities clashed, and sometimes it was all I could do to stop myself from smashing him in the face. Broken teeth don't look good onstage.

Truth is, it worked out I was playing both ends of the stick—a restless, young animal doing the band thing to keep me amused, semi-creative and in funds while moonlighting as a bouncer at *The Rocks*. None of the other band members knew about it. Not that it was such a big deal, but something told me it wouldn't be wise to bring attention to the fact. It gave the impression I wasn't fully committed. Maybe they'd let me go? Where would I be then? Hard enough as it was to get mekhs in my pocket and juggle two jobs without their knowing.

"Who's the girl?" Geez asked, hiking a finger.

"She's Areth," my date snapped. She sashayed in, casting him a look that set him back a few paces.

I grinned. "Friend of mine...met her at *The Rocks*."

"Oh yeah?" Garth muttered. They were all looking at her with the interest of wolves on the prowl. Too much interest. Geez, I trusted least of all. Fortunately we all knew better than to horn in on each other's dates, so they were on their best behavior. For now.

Garth had made some fool policy that no girls were to be at the practices. Too much chaos brought to the mix, he claimed.

Screw him.

"Areth, meet Garth," I said with a cheeky smile. "This here's Geez, Drodge and Beatie. This is our practice crib." I arched my arms high to the mouse-ridden rafters. Enough stone and plaster in these old walls to dampen the sound from the rest of the city, which was good. "What's the big deal with this sudden get-together?" I demanded. "Didn't we just do a four-hour marathon a few nights ago?"

"Special circumstances," Geez said. "Garth'll fill you in." He turned to Areth. "How'd you guys meet? You do that computer thing they have over at *The Rocks*?" Beatie had turned down the volume on his amp, unslung his guitar and shoved drinks in our hands. Mandrake beers.

"Nah, we hit it off," I said, "one thing led to another...here we are, right, Areth?"

"More like the guy with me turned out to be bore," she said. "There was a fight. I took up with Rus while he was working the floor."

"What do you mean, working the floor?" Garth said suspiciously, his heavy features creased into a sudden scowl.

I flashed Areth a warning glance. She picked up on it immediately. "I mean, working the room. Rus's got a sharp eye for the ladies. He picked me out right away."

"Damn right." I scratched my cheek.

Beatie and Drodge slapped me on the back. "Yeah, sweet. That's Ruskie, a good man. Never misses an opportunity."

"I called the meet," Garth said icily, "because I have important news to share. We have a gig."

"So?" I jibed. "You book us down at the pool hall?"

"No," he said coldly. "*The Rocks.*"

My jaw almost fell off its hinges. "Whoa, how'd you get a booking like that?"

"Cancellation. Gerry buzzed me at the last minute. Was looking for a replacement. I snapped up the offer immediately."

"Of course." I gave a morose nod.

I felt my mind drifting down pseudo-reverie lane. Rocker guitarist practicing in a rundown, mice-in-the-rafters warehouse playing dim smoky sets out in the dives for nickels and dimes. Rocker doesn't want to be a front man, relegates himself to first rhythm guitar, then lead. When Baxel the lead guitarist drops out—or rather gets kicked out of his band for his growing Myscol habit—rocker pretends to be Baxel and dresses up in a halloween mask—hockey mask with black-and-white polka-dot goalie shield over his face.

It was a big joke.

Laugh, if you like. But it was a gimmick that worked. Kept me incognito from wandering eyes looking for a certain Kip Rees—the early version of Jet Rusco who certain people wished six feet under. The fans called me 'Jason'—an old reference to a slasher from a cult series from ancient history.

I donned my mask. I worked to change the subject. "We ready to go?" I slung on my wireless, ruby-red flying V guitar and cranked the volume on my stack and let loose a series of discordant power chords.

Our gear was all set up: twin stacks of amps facing outwards, monitors in front, my pedal set on the floor—fuzz, reverb, chorus, delay, warble, arpeggio buster, and screech-howl for that extra layer of haunting underwater effect that I'd somehow made my trademark.

I dared Geez to come up with a bass line to those anti-melodic riffs I was pumping out fast and furious that reverberated off the walls and rafters.

Geez grimaced. "Rusco, you in a bad mood or is it just me? Maybe you're just a chicken shit about *The Rocks*, trying to sink us like a lead weight. Of course we're going to do this gig. We committed so we have to. We'll never get any decent bookings in this town again if we bail."

"Geez, it's just that I don't think we fit into that techno beat scene over there." Which was only part of the truth.

"Yeah, so we don't. Money is money and stepping stones aren't to be chucked away. We're doing it, end of story. Maybe take that goofy hockey mask off for a change. Getting sick of it. Are we running a hard rock band or a horror show here?"

Drodge stood up from his kit. "No way, Geez. It's his trademark.

Everyone knows Rus as Jason."

"Big fricking whip," Beatie noodled out a dark riff on his bass.

The fantasy all played out in my mind as I played overtop Beatie's nonsense, head swinging to my own cacophony. I'd spend the day practicing some nasty, ugly little solos in my cramped little hole below the tramway line in preparation for *The Rocks* show. The heavy dark harmonic riffs would just pour off the strings. To spite old Garth who deserved a comeuppance, I'd pull out the surprise at the last minute in the middle of our title song. Shock the shit out of them all. I laughed out loud. All of us'd been influenced by the old metalheads from past history...from way back in the stone age. They still had a cult following in these parts. Go figure. Yes sirree, anything's possible in this inverted world.

Garth waved his hands in a cut signal. "Knock it off, Rusco. You're being a goof. Let's work on our intros. The usual—'Fox in the Hen House', 'Toys in the Cellar' then 'World Engine' followed by 'Pain'."

I shrugged. We started to lay into our heavy riffs and rhythms with Garth spanning the range from low to high, doing his usual antics running up and down the makeshift stage we'd rigged up from long cargo boxes at the back of the warehouse. I'll give Garth that, he's got a superb voice and a way to mix his acrobatic stunts with the lulls and peaks of his song lyrics. Even has this thing going where he can do a backflip, then some killer cartwheels that wows the crowd before the dry ice streams up from under our feet. Then old Drodge does a mean drum solo on his double drum set, cymbals swishing to a rhythmic beat. All the while we chug away on our spangled, graffitied instruments, my purple hair flying, our heads bopping to the rhythm. We mop up the rest with the heavy sound that it is our trademark, along with my blistering leads.

I glimpsed Areth out of the corner of my eye in the back leaning up against a post. Her head was slightly moving to the beat. I admired her act. She pretended to look interested. Whether or not this was her style of music, or she'd rather be out on the dance floor schmoozing some rich guy, I was at a loss.

I was having trouble reading this woman.

Not to mention my playing was off. My mind was elsewhere. I screwed up the last solo. The fiasco at *The Rocks* had unnerved me and the girl was doing a good job at distraction. Still trying to peg her. I was missing something. Something very important and I couldn't figure out what it was.

Garth called a time out. "Rusco, you're blundering your entries. Your timing absolutely sucks. You're coming in way too late, or adding stuff that doesn't fit. You're making me look awkward over here."

"Yeah, well we've gotta lay off the edge, Garth. If we're playing over at *The Rocks*, half this shit won't work. Not a bunch of drunken truckers and miners that we're playing to. These are kids, teenagers, born and bred on tech disco."

"Screw that, man. They want heavy, they'll get heavy. Gerry booked us and he believes in us. He's seen us play. We'll even turn up the volume if we have to, to shake up some of those disco heads."

"No, you won't. Management'll turn it down. Right to off. You'll never get another booking again."

"Says the philosopher."

"We have to change our repertoire. Make it lighter to work in that place."

"Says who?"

"Says me. They're too mellow for this lineup we have going."

"I say we shock them."

"We can, but if we do it live on the fly, we'll get a better response. We gauge the crowd, we amp it up slowly, all the better to introduce more of what we're about. Last thing we want is the crowd to turn against us. Remember what happened at the *Forty-ohs* last month? It can get ugly over there."

"I remember that, but Rusco, you're a pansy ass."

I glared at him. "Just being practical, Garth. More than I can say for you."

He strolled over with a smile on his face, picked up his gin and flicked it in my face.

I slammed down my instrument and wiped the sting out of my eyes. "You useless, fricking tool."

I caught him a stiff uppercut on the chin. He had underestimated my speed and went floating back on his heels, scarecrow arms coming up to defend himself.

Geez hustled over. "Lay off it, guys. Damn it! We have to work together."

"No we don't. This sorry outfit's on its way out, Geez. I'm sick of this asshole's shit. This'll be my last show."

Geez's jaw sagged. "Aw, come on, Rus, you can't just up and leave us?"

"Can and will."

He shook his head. He slapped his palms on his thighs. "It wasn't supposed to end like this. We're going through lead guitarists like after-gig girls."

Garth nursed his swollen jaw. Made a few mewling sounds. It didn't bode well for his singing, but I could give a rat's ass at this point.

It could have worked out with the other guys: Beatie, Drodge, Geez. They were manageable. But not Garth. He was just a domineering little bitch. The chance that the other guys'd get rid of him over me was slim. No, I'd made up my mind. It was the end of the line.

"What about the show tomorrow night?" Drodge whined.

"Wing it like we always do." I gave a lukewarm flourish. "Knock yourself out, guys. I'm out of here."

And so it was a glum wind down as I gathered up Areth and we trucked out. Took our leave back into the rain-soaked streets.

"Jeez, that's tough, man. Sorry," Areth said while running a hand over my back. "I hope I haven't done anything to come between you and the band members?"

"Nah, forget it." I waved her off. "Garth's a jerk. Deserved what he got. This breakout was long in coming. Good thing I didn't hit him too hard, otherwise the *Startled Zombies*'d be out for good. I'm kind of relishing this gig tomorrow night and the shitshow it's going to be."

She stared at me as if trying to understand what kind of twisted mind would say that. She gave up.

"You know your business, Rusco. Your place or mine?"

I hesitated. "Would you be too put out if I took a rain check? Kinda bagged tonight. Let's say we hook up—" I glanced up at the angle of the sallow moon arching low in the sky "—sometime tomorrow. I'm just not in the mood."

"I understand. Leaving your band. It's stressful."

"Yeah. Other stuff too. I'll fill you in on the depressing details another time when we get to know each other better."

"Sure, whatever. I get it."

She didn't, and it was writ all over her face. The small puckered mouth, the tiny white teeth grinding over her immaculate molars. I sighed and dug my nails into my palms. I kicked myself for being a lame-ass. But it was what it was. Probably wouldn't see her again.

On the flip side I was getting a weird feeling about all this. I'd kind of got used to listening to my inner intuition. The night had already been weird enough without complicating it more.

CHRIS TURNER

CHAPTER 3

By ironic coincidence we were booked on the night of the 11th. While I was working floor—busting heads.

Convoluted, I know. But what part of this whole caper wasn't?

Areth came the next night. There were more people than could fit in the place. Could it actually be that the Startled Zombies actually had some fans? I'd worked it at the last minute that I could scoot out from duty and play the first set. I'd called in to Gerry's office telling him that I was still messed up from last night's fiasco and could I cut out early? Yes. Management had grumbled, but had okayed it.

"Grib?" I asked Kelly, the floor manager.

"Banned for life."

"Doesn't surprise me."

It would do Grib some good. Stop him from getting more cracked knees.

The hour was 10. We were on for the early show. A hot mugginess hung in the air. People were in high spirits, dancing to the warm-up music that pulsed through the quadraphonic speakers. Gerry'd taken my advice. He picked some harder, edgier tunes to ease the crowd into what they'd be getting from us.

Strobe lights flashed down on us from on high. Our metaller hair-dos were illuminated in brief millisecond bursts as we walked onstage—ruby red, parrot purple, yak yellow, gruesome green.

They'd put us front center in the middle of the revolving dance floor—a prime real-estate spotlight at the metrodome.

The floor was like glass: a funky projection film like a perfect see-through mirror which gave guests this eerie feeling of walking on the ice of a deep frozen lake. This night's image—a deep sea bay with tropical fish darting underfoot. Psychedelic.

As I took to the stage wearing my hockey mask carved into a sinister grinning face, I waved and made a big show of slinging on my guitar.

Garth wouldn't look at me. We traded no words. Fine by me. The other band members seemed dispirited.

"Come on, guys," I implored, "let's snap it up. There's no use staying in a slump. The audience can feel a Debbie Downer vibe."

"Yeah, no kidding," said Beatie. "We had some good times, Rus, but looks like Startled Zombies now becomes Dead-in-the-Water Zombies."

"Guitarists are a dime a dozen, Beatie, you know that. You'll find somebody else."

"But will it be a Rusco?"

I was touched by his sentiment but I couldn't dwell on it. Show time. This setup was circle 360. We were on a slightly raised platform about three feet off the revolving dance floor. It was about 30 feet in diameter. The circular stage revolved in the opposite direction, giving us the illusion of motion, so we kept up some good movement and everybody got a chance to see us. We played to a hopping crowd our first number, 'Fox in the Hen House'. Made for some fast maneuvering for Garth to keep everyone engaged. He had the toughest job: skipping about with his usual acrobatics, fancy footwork and dramatic gestures to keep the act all glued together. Though it was no small task for me to stay out of his way and tone down the harsh edge of the guitars, the way we usually played the song. Beatie was in sync, despite his earlier glumness. I was good with my moves. Years of working Carnivale on Hoag had paid off. Wireless guitar also made it easier to move about without getting hamstrung by my own wires.

Drodge had a foot switch. It made his kit revolve in either direction, so his gimmick was up and running. We hadn't had a chance to practice on such a wild stage before so we were basically winging it. Everything was running smoothly minus some rough maneuvering where Beatie messed up and almost collided with me, but we recovered. So far the audience hadn't booed us off the stage. Not even any blank stares. Areth seemed to be digging it. She was about three rows from the front and gave me a thumbs up and smiles. Our mellower renditions seemed to strike the right nerve with the crowd.

We were about half way through 'World Engine' when some high-pitched echo sounded in my monitor. I frowned, jiggled the gain. Maybe my pickups were getting some weird feedback?

No, now it sounded like an air raid siren.

It was definitely not interference. I looked over at Beatie. He was frowning too in his monkey face kind of way. He gave an anxious, confused shrug.

I saw them. Through the murky haze of dry ice...a conclave of four, black-leathered mutants coming our way up from the back.

Jake the doorman, was slumped motionless against the wall, his head tipped on his chest.

Decked in leathered armor, these creatures had rounded helms, black gloves and high boots. They were no less than seven feet tall. Me and Beatie were deftly playing away, belting out our power chords and heavy riffs when my hockey mask suddenly stopped bobbing to the beat.

The crowd went apeshit. They thought the monster halloween figures were part of the act! Fools! They cheered and gyrated and danced as more of the seven foot-monsters clambered in from the front doors...then onto the revolving disc. They headed toward the stage. Toward us.

My jaw dropped. How the hell—? Even now, their four foot electro goads clutched in mitted fists, started zapping people.

I saw Leb, his head cracked open, bleeding out on the dance floor. He was half way between the stage and the exit doors.

Serious shit was going down. No more jokes.

Pandemonium erupted.

Garth got cocky. He moved in to club the lead Skurg with his mic, but he got skull-cocked by it and carted off by another. A big bad mother. Toward the exit, to a slave ship waiting?

Beatie unslung his guitar. With a wild swing, he whirled it round his head. But the blow only grazed the arm of the creature that had brained Garth. The Skurg came hitching in at him, slamming him back into Drodge's drum set. He used his instrument as a shield to prevent himself from being clubbed to death. But he was knocked flat back into Drodge. I unslung my own flying V, used it as a battering ram to hammer at the Skurg nearest me. I swung it wide. It smacked face-first into the creature's jowl.

With a cursing roar, he staggered, his helmet smashed off. The marauder made a gruesome croak and sprawled forward even as his white albino head snapped up, budding horns bared. I kneed the pig-ugly face, breaking nose and cartilage and driving bone deep into his brain.

More of the Skurg's grotesque comrades came charging after me, gibbering roars of rage. Goads jabbed and swung. I scrambled back, backpedaling.

I was no hero. An insane person might try to take on these creatures with no significant blasters.

Not me.

The crowd went apeshit, now under no illusion that this was a stage act. Their dance gyrations had ceased, turned to an all out scramble.

Memories of my tooth-and-nail scrabbles with the Skurgs came back in chilling waves. In the prison camp on Skaldar, that den of stinking death. We were stuck in the middle of the desert. A horror beyond any person's comprehension.

Another giant planted feet before me. We faced off, guitar against goad.

There is a big nerve near the collar bone webbed with a network of bared nerve endings that have little protection of skin and flesh against a blunt, harsh blow. It was here that I directed my guitar bashes...whatever hybrid of anthropoid alien these creatures were, I hoped they had similar physiology to humans. My guitar went smashing down, hammering a wicked blow on his left clavicle between helm and tip of shoulder. The creature sagged, his arm hung limp.

I followed up with a boot to the throat, catching him under the helm and leather collar, crushing the windpipe.

I went ballistic, beating at Skurgs. The dome lent echoing screams of terror and anguish to all gathered.

And yet I was not faring well on the dance floor. A hard object came beaming down on my upper back. I went sprawling forward, the wind knocked out of me.

I caught the flash of a saber lumo-weapon as I crawled along the smooth glass floor, sucking air desperately back in my lungs. My nose slug-wormed on the cold mirror-like substance. The floor was still packed with people. A sudden wave of terror-stricken dancers swept by center stage and the squadron of Skurgs couldn't get to me right away.

I glimpsed another blow coming just as a familiar, fleet-footed figure bobbed into view.

She'd launched herself on stage as a Skurg's goad was about to short-circuit my nervous system.

Areth.

She did one of those fancy acrobat kicks and nailed the bastard in the nuts.

"Run, you fool!"

I lifted my head, forcing air in my lungs. Every muscle of my dead weight screamed in agony. I beat at Skurgs who advanced in numbers. The echoing tumult of zapping goads and limb smacking against limb pulsed in my ear.

I looked back. The tumbled drum kit was in ruin. Beatie and Drodge were nowhere in sight. I could only guess they'd been snatched. Snatched while I'd been lying dazed.

Areth and I jumped down off the stage. We joined the pack of unfortunate people scrambling for the exit.

But the front door was clogged with clawing, stampeding bodies.

"This way," I cried hoarsely. I beckoned her in the opposite direction. "The service staff uses the back exit."

She gave a wild gesture then followed my lead.

We staggered our way against the stream of people, me half-hobbling through the mobs. We squeezed through the steel-rimmed exit at the back. We made our way out into the street. It was near deserted. I stopped to catch my breath. Stooping like an asthmatic, I inhaled the muggy dampness of the air and tore off my halloween mask. A vagrant wind stirred the trash on the hardtop. Bits of debris and flotsam were there that hadn't been there before I came into the bar. I sucked cool air into my lungs. As I looked, my eyes stared up into a hulking shadow of death.

CHAPTER 4

A Skurg warship, all spikes and black metal, hovered above the street. Nothing less than a ghoulish predator if there ever was one. The local air militia was firing down on its armor-plated hull.

To no avail. Even the fearsome kite-like ships could not penetrate the enemy shields. The Skurg defenses were too strong.

Stray Skurg raiders ran about the streets, zapping unlucky citizens with their goads. They hiked the immobile bodies over their shoulders and hefted them back to the slave ship that had settled farther down the street. The Skurgs had coordinated an all out air attack with their slave convoy pickup.

There are some deniers who claim that alien invasions are not real. I would love to smash them in the teeth and plop them in my boots at this moment.

Get your legs pumping, Rusco, before they scoop you up like a jelly bean.

Areth sprinted at my side. She needed no prompting. Even on this backwater planet, the Skurgs had penetrated their defenses. No planet was safe from their molestation.

The local Nmoor militia was totally unprepared for a large scale invasion for which the lightning-quick attack of the Skurg was famous.

"We have to get to the spaceport," I wheezed, "or jump a ship. This town is going to shit."

We weaved amid the chaos in downtown Nmoor and my horror grew. It was a veritable space war. Two air militia fighters were down.

A Skurg ship was on its side, hull burning diagonal-wise across Tellis Street. Steel-framed apartments lay crushed.

Red and blue fire traces arced down the street. From both sides ships fought sniper-like on low sweeps.

I skipped nimbly aside, barely missing a blast that would have blown off my legs. The red Skurg traces intermingled with the blue militia guards' fire, both harbingers of death.

A dull crack smote the sky. Two kite-like ships flew overhead dropping traces in the streets onto some wandering Skurgs.

"We need to lay low!" Areth hissed. She pulled me back behind a pile of rubble.

I stared at her as if she was daft. "And get blown to shit?" I blinked at her in disbelief.

More red and blue fire traces whipped by, like long snakes.

"Follow me," she rasped. Her feet whispered cat-like on the hardtop as she sprinted down the street while there was an opening in the fire.

I shook my head. With a fatalistic shrug, I loped after her. She was hopping fallen girders and metallic debris like a gazelle, the wrecks still smoking and twisted.

We darted up some side-streets then came to a less ruined section, the Distillery District. A row of wine houses, restaurants, bodegas seemed semi intact.

She looked up at a half-leaning sign. "Mandrake Kitchen," she mouthed into her earbud communicator.

I frowned as I wiped dirt off my chin. "Who are you talking to?"

"Marcie, my roomie. She's going batshit. All these explosions careening outside her window!"

"She needs to get the hell out here. We all do. This two-bit town is going under."

She didn't answer. Her body language was strained. Something was off.

Was it shock? No. Something had pulled her out of her comfort zone. Almost as if she had undergone a personality change. This whole side excursion she'd led me down seemed less than real. "Come on, we have to move it."

I set my legs moving past the *Mandrake Kitchen* when all of a sudden she cat-crouched and snatched something taped to the inside of her left leg. "No one's going anywhere, rockerboy." She trained a four-inch R7 muzzle at me.

What? I studied her with mixed amusement and disbelief, then decided to ignore what I hoped was a bluff and kept moving.

She fired at my feet and chunks of tarmac kicked up, spattering my shins. "Hold up, Twinkletoes."

I stopped in midstep. The woman obviously was an expert markswoman, or she'd lucked out by just missing my left toe by half an inch.

I took the opportunity to examine her better. The traces of laugh lines bracketing her mouth now seemed brittler, deeper. Her mouth firmed up to show dry little wrinkles when under stress. Outlined against the ruined tops of buildings and the warships, she seemed slightly larger than life, with head held high and lip curled at me. I was the proverbial hare caught in her crossfires. Gone, the cutie of jet black hair with tinted highlights ranging toward the blue. The long legs, ample hips, a shamrock-cute face, stylishly light but shapely breasts, about three inches shorter than my own six feet. A juxtaposition to the cold clinical agent who stood before me, aloof and professional who trained an R7 at my chest. This was no fly-by-night floozy out of a B movie up for a cheap pocket theft. A calculated bounty hunter under orders.

She snatched up a fallen scrap of metal and smashed in the jagged glass of the restaurant's front pane. "Get in." She motioned me toward the dark opening. I shrugged, ducked under the jagged glass, being careful not to gouge my scalp or shoulders. Her fingers worked busily contacting a third party in her ear communicator. "Collection point, Mandrake Kitchen. Off Via Tellis. Repeat, Mandrake Kitchen."

"As slick as that, eh?"

The dots connected. Her willingness to fling herself at me at *The Rocks*. Keeping me away from the spaceport on this wild goose run. Her turning up so opportunely at the bar. Nmoor gets its ass handed to it by a horde of Skurgs. Coincidence? I think not.

My jaw clenched and a sinking feeling settled in my stomach. This was an evil dream come true.

I squinted around in the dimness. Tables to either side. A raised, eye-level aquarium containing lobsters and eels. My mouth quirked in a mirthless grin. The place I recognized as a hoity-toity seafood eatery whose delicacies included the sauteed Mandrake eel from the local swamps...it was now my handoff point.

Though the restaurant was deserted, closed for the evening, a dim light shone through the cracks of the kitchen door.

"Away from the windows," she said. Her boot nudged me in the direction of the kitchen. "This'll do. The meat locker for you, if you act out, Rusco."

In we went. Rectangular configuration, open concept, everything compartmentalized to conserve space. Stainless steel pots hanging above a long food prep island. Knives to the side with cutting boards. Sea-basin sink, dish and towel rack. Everything cleaned for the night. Spic and span.

"Why are you doing this, Areth?"

"Paid to do a job."

She busied herself tossing the cupboards, searching among the drawers and pantries for some way to contain me, maybe with some stout cord to bind my wrists? The faint dryness of skin and laugh lines around the corners of her eyes were accentuated under the harsh overhead lights. I guessed her to be about ten years my senior. Still sexy as hell. Don't get me wrong, she looked good.

Rusco, how can you think of something like that now?

My eyes flicked toward the selection of knives sheathed in the wooden holder.

She saw where I was looking and snapped, "Don't even think of it." She nudged me back with the barrel of her gun.

"Look, if you think—"

"I was recruited a long time ago. If I don't do what they want, they'll—"

"Kill you. Yeah, I know the drill. They let you live, but in fear. Then they let you look forward to living in fear for the rest of your days, but it's no way to live." I gave my head a sad shake.

"Nobody asked you." Her slender white fingers gripped the R7 tighter. I could see the central vein bulge in her high forehead. I recalled having Gy-ar in his space yacht give me a similar fireside chat not long ago.

In that moment Areth tugged her ear, a nervous habit. For a moment I saw the scared little girl in her—no mommy or daddy here to step up and look out for her when the darkness crept in. "This is going to end badly for you."

"What do you know?"

I studied her intently. "I know what I would have done."

"Yeah, what's that?" She snorted a dry, sarcastic laugh. "Is it going to be some pep talk on how I should—"

"Cut loose. Tell these pigs to bug off."

"Not possible."

"Anything's possible."

"I don't have anything against you, Rusco. You're a decent guy, talented and charismatic. In other circumstances, I might even have run off with you." She croaked out a laugh. "We could get on quite well. But, business over pleasure. The two don't mix. You understand?"

"I bet you perfected a heart of steel to be in the line of work you're in. How long's it been?" I had to keep her talking, give me time to come up with a plan.

She gave a careless shrug. "You do what you need to do. You turn your emotions off. Like being a star actor, spinning out a role at a moment's notice."

"Sounds fulfilling."

"My job was to bring you in, intact. Nothing more. The Skurgs wanted you slow-roasted on the end of a spit before they had you in their bellies. Gy-ar and the Temple people wanted you alive."

So, there lay the truth. How could I have been so naive? All along my instinct had been telling me something was off with her from the get-go.

"Enough gab—" A sound of smashed glass came from out front.

She turned, frowned. I bit back my anxiety. I was curious about how she'd pulled it off. "So how'd you go about setting it all up?"

She shrugged, as if realizing she lost nothing by telling me.

"I'd been stationed at Nmoor, part of Gy-ar's field team. I'd discovered a person of interest matching your description working at *The Rocks*. Everything fit but the purple hair. It was my idea to go in as a Trojan horse.

"Their instructions were for me to shadow you then disarm you. Get you softened up so I could bring you in without a fuss. I goaded Grib to make an ass of himself. He did. He's the one who gave me an angle to get close to you. You fell for it. Juvenile, I know. But I have a knack for this type of theater. It worked."

"Yeah, and how much they paying you for this little operation?" I could feel the heat of humiliation prickling my neck.

"100k mekhs is not a bad haul, don't you think?"

"100?" I croaked.

"More, if I brought you in unscathed. Seems Gy-ar wanted you alive for some twisted reason." She frowned.

I could feel my marrow turn to ice. "Bastards. How'd they coordinate you and Miss Chestnut Hair together?"

"The matching was faked. Rigged by Gy-ar's spies. They have access to the AI computer. I hadn't counted on Grib getting a second girl through his own extracurricular efforts. So I kinda had to operate on the fly and humor the girl. It was my idea to get him to act out and lure you over so I could work on you."

"It was a sneaky son-of-a-bitch plan."

She smiled. There came a rustling and light rap at the door.

"That'll be Cambor."

She went over to unlatch the door, keeping the slim muzzle trained at my midsection.

A thin, cauliflower-faced man entered. A low rider with straw-colored hair who wore a blue kevlar suit. A long black R1 was clutched in hands.

He nodded. A cruel smile twisted his pencil-thin lips. "We seemed to have hit the jackpot, Areth. Rewards are coming our way…"

She nodded.

"Any problems?"

"None."

"Good. We'll radio Gy-ar and make the exchange a few blocks from here. The Prime Ascendant will be most pleased—"

He skipped forward and without warning hip checked her, knocking her sideways while in one slick movement snapped the small R7 weapon out of her grip. It clattered to the floor as he trained his blaster at her chest. "I wouldn't do that," he warned as she started forward. His smile faded.

"As much as I'd like to share the spoils with you, agent Areth, I think not today. My cut becomes all the larger. Over by the wall. Now!"

He frisked her for weapons. She held up her hands in frigid silence. Satisfied she had nothing concealed, he gave her a shove with the back of his heel. Ignoring her hateful glare, he turned his attention on me. "The famous Kip Rees. I heard a lot about you. How's it feel?"

"You mean to strangle your wiry neck when I get a chance?"

He gave a chirrupy laugh. "Come on, Kip. Let's get real. I don't think so. I'm sure you understand there can be no witnesses." His tone was apologetic, almost patronizing.

Areth rasped, "What about you, you treacherous slimebag? Are you not equally expendable? When's it going to be your ass in a sling, your eyes looking down the end of a barrel?" Her mouth puckered and turned ugly. Obviously these two had a history and I wondered how many other things there were I didn't know about.

Cambor frowned. He paused a moment to assess the wisdom of her claim, just as a muffled boom came from the front of the building.

As he chewed his lip, I grinned. Sow the seeds of doubt in this shitbug. *Good girl.* Give me two seconds to knock the teeth back into his throat.

"Who could that be? Expecting visitors?" he grumbled.

"I called in for a threesome," I said.

"Shut your mouth."

I waved a jaunty hand. "Now that you're here, Camby, we'll be equally paired up, come on."

"I said, shut the hell up. Now get over there!" He kicked me toward the cold room—the meat locker that Areth had gone on about. "No more quips, or I'll rearrange your face. Good luck answering Gy-ar's questions then."

More activity came from without. The crash of splintering wood, boots shattering glass.

Cambor grimaced. He tossed his head back and stepped to the side with a pouty little scowl on his snub-nosed face. "You sure picked a substandard place for delivery, Areth."

"Whip me then," she retorted.

"Into the cold room," he ordered. "The two of you. Until I can figure something out. Hopefully if there are Skurgs about, they haven't detected us yet."

"Fat chance of that, bro," I said conversationally. "They can sniff out humans like bloodhounds."

"I told you to shut the hell—"

Their heads turned as another boom came rocketing from the front of the building. Ship fire? A deathly crack like thunder smote the sky. The dull vibration was enough to rock the building and with it came the crash of falling masonry.

"This Skurg thing..." Cambor rasped, a creepy trill that prickled the hairs on my neck. "Is nothing but Gy-ar's little surprise. I think it backfired on him. Some overweening Skurg maybe thought to skim off a couple ships of humans. I'll just be happy to get off this forsaken planet."

"Congratulations," I grated at Areth. "You helped bring about the invasion of Nmoor."

She shuddered visibly. "I had no idea that Gy-ar was involved in Skurg slave-mongering."

"We all learn the hard way," I said.

"Enough—"

The door exploded. Bits of wood sprayed against Cambor's face. His hand lifted with a cry to shield his eyes, but too late. A dark hulk clambered through the gap and slammed him against the wall. A Skurg captain who rose now to his full height about to execute a killing blow with his goad.

The distraction of the enemy spy was the Skurg's undoing. I lunged like a panther and kneed him as hard as I could in the groin. Cambor's eyes went white as the Skurg uttered a pig-wild squeal. In the same motion, I ripped the weapon from the spy's nerveless hands and trained it on the giant Skurg who hobbled toward me. The muzzle flashed blue, shot his face full of withering energy fire. He fell smoking like a Yule log.

"Rusco, to your left!" Areth was on the balls of her feet as three Skurgs came hopscotching through the gap. They were on us before I could utter an expletive or get more than two shots into their leather-armored hides.

One Skurg's arm was hanging half off before the other two swarmed me. They ripped my weapon away and clubbed me in the head with a goad. I went down in a slack heap, seeing stars.

"Rusco!" Areth's scream came from faraway as from an underwater dream. She was snatched up in a pair of black-mitted hands and hurled over a shoulder. They took me out in like manner in the street behind her. To where? The slave ship?

CHAPTER 5

The pig-monsters hauled Areth, Cambor and me through the smoking, debris-strewn streets toward the enormous oval-shaped ship which hunkered like a leviathan on top of a small rise.

Through slitted eyes, I pretended to be dazed. I noted the breadth of the ship's creepy menace. It was much as I'd remembered them from months back. Eight-foot spikes protruding from the hull every few yards. Everything inside would be black and cold, metal laced with edges, stark, brutal, with prickles like thorns.

They'd set down in the middle of a construction area, a northward extension of the downtown tram station. A night crew had been still working on it—backhoes, cranes and dyno-loaders—or at least had been working even up to this hour of invasion. Some engines were still idling, indicating the crew had taken off.

While I played possum, I let my arms dangle limp as the muscled brute dropped me carelessly in a cart along with other unconscious figures. Then he wheeled us up the cargo bay's ramp and into the darkness of the hold. I had no recourse but to go along with the pantomime. To attack these brutes head on without weapons would be suicide.

A rough gangway led to the cramped holding area little more than a slave quarters where Areth and others from *The Rocks*— Drodge and Beatie and Jake—were dumped unceremoniously. No sign of Garth. There was a foul reek of sweat in the air. I saw Beatie staring dismayed at my crumpled form. Four guards stepped back, with luminous green goads lifted on the ready to snap at any of us who were bold enough to try anything.

Areth hunched in the murk, sunken-cheeked, grime-faced, like a ruffled rat with shiny eyes. A look of incredulity framed her shamrock features as if she couldn't fathom that this had happened to her.

Squinting out through my own bloodshot eyes, I felt every muscle in my body strained and bruised. I'd been through this hell back on Belruus. It was no less terrifying the second time round.

Grib trembled uncontrollably in the murk, cowering in the sweat-stinking hold on his hands and knees. He'd aged, looked ten years older. Likely they'd picked him up in some dive, a tensor bandage still wrapped around his left knee where I'd clocked him. The man was incorrigible. Even injured, and banned for life from *The Rocks*, he couldn't stay away from the gambling pens and the cathouses.

I heard the rumble of an engine. A cold stab of fear hit me. Not much time before this bird took off. Then it would be game over for us all. The Skurgs'd work us to death in their mines somewhere and we'd never escape. They were cannibals. We'd be used as playthings in their blood rituals under the naked sun. When they tired of our feeble efforts to stay alive, our limbs would amputated one by one, replaced by robot parts, while they gnawed our freshly-hewn limbs slow-cooked over fires to slake their repulsive gluttonous appetites.

There would be no better chances than now. With blood pounding in my ears, I made my move.

Cruel hands came to dump me from the slave cart to the floor when I surged up in a burst of rage.

I came lunging at the first Skurg, fingers and thumbs locked on his eyes. I hooked my left thumb into his eyehole and elicited a roar of rage. I ripped the goad from his belt, ducked the strike, caught only a grazing, mitt-fisted blow below the left ear. Dazed, I swung his goad and smacked him on the side of the head. He staggered back, disoriented. Enough for me to jab him with my full strength. I knocked out his front teeth and felt the weight of the goad slide down his hideous gullet.

I saw Areth claw at the eyes of a Skurg three feet away in a last desperate struggle to live.

It became a chain reaction. At least fifty captives from all quarters surged forth. With nothing to lose, they swarmed the Skurg guards in a snarling mob. Many people were caught by a fresh wave of Skurg muscle racing from the interior, sizzled by volts of electricity, but enough of us got past their numbers to overwhelm them. The frenzied mob tore off their helms and ripped them to pieces.

Areth and I raced out of the hold and skittered down the ramp pell-mell into the street away from that prison pen.

Already one Skurg slave ship had lifted off into the sky with a hold full of fresh humans never to be seen again. The one we'd emerged from shuddered a few inches off the ground. She was aiming for the refuge of the clouds as the cargo door clanged shut. The engines raced to get up to impulse speed and I turned my back on the horror and started my legs moving far away from there. Across the litter-strewn street, I saw ship fire arc into our dwindling numbers.

Where were Beatie and Drodge? A sinking dread welled up in my gut. I almost doubled over on the spot as cold guilt made me feel nauseous.

It would be an act of cowardice to leave those innocent souls trapped in there. Yet it was desperation and lunacy to attempt a rescue. But I had to do something. Why do you torture yourself, Rusco?

My skull still rang from the Skurg boxing my ears. That same underwater sound that made one feel dizzy. I shook my head. I just wanted to get the hell out of here. Easy to flee these ruined streets and make for the spaceport and rid myself of the treacherous witch Areth who'd gotten me in this mess.

Was I developing a conscience?

"You can't do anything," she cried three strides behind me. The air wheezed from her lungs as she efforted to catch up with me.

I risked a look back.

"Are you crazy?"

She was right. For a brief moment I sucked in a breath and thought hard about whether I could sleep at night, knowing my friends who hadn't escaped, Beatie and Drodge, were carted off to nowhere land. Something in me snapped. I couldn't abide another human getting eaten by those inhuman monsters.

My eyes roved over the construction site. My mind set to work, an unconscious animal intelligence working in the background, hoping to save its skin and those of others.

It was in these creative moments that the best came out of me.

The two dyno-loaders which sat parked near the half-completed entrance to the new tram station were still idling. Heavy, squat industrial machines which had ample horsepower to lift girders and haul heavy building supplies. If I could—

Areth's eyes flashed and followed where mine were looking. Flames were eating at a ruined air car by a dumpster that the Skurgs had fired upon. "No way!"

"How long would it take you to divert the Skurg gunners?" I rasped.

"What are you talking about? What diversion?"

"Anything! That airnaut over there. The one not burning."

She stared at me in disbelief. I could almost hear the gears in her mind calculating the odds, the how-to-break-in permutations and getting it airborne.

I ignored her hesitation. I'd already turned my attention toward the loaders. I'd barely heard her cluck of frustration as she ran to the open air car abandoned on the street side. I scrambled to the first loader. It was too small for my purposes, but the second had a massive open scoop in front. The rumble of the idling 3rd generation motor was music to my ears. I hopped into the cab, jammed the shovel's forward lever up, leveling the blade in line with the ship's rear thruster. With the added bonus of two inches of tempered steel protecting my hide at windshield level, I'd be safe from Skurg fire.

Relatively safe, I thought.

Speed was of the essence. I slammed the machine in gear, got it rolling, jerking forward like a lumbersome juggernaut. A low roar of three tons of moving metal. There was a heavy tire iron on the seat beside me. I swiftly dropped it on the floor and used it as a wedge to clamp the accelerator while maxing out the engine's rpms.

The loader lurched forward on a crash course with the ship's rear thrusters. Twin ship cannons came swiveling at me. I ducked. Lethal red beams came arching at the shovel end.

Metal melted. Sparks flew. I caught from the corner of my eye a small green and yellow airnaut shape. It came whizzing across the ship's line of sight.

Areth!

Momentarily she distracted the port gunner's attention, taking the heat off me. But the second gunner resumed his fire with full intensity. Before they could roast me, I tumbled out of the cab, grabbing the tire iron, rolling onto the hardtop, taking several layers of loose skin with me.

The Skurg's fire had virtually melted the shovel, but it had come too late. The ship was too slow in getting off the ground.

What was left of the shovel rammed full into the rear thrusters, smashing the delicate ion screens and machinery within. No way was this bird getting off the ground. The loader's left side had swerved and impaled itself on one of the spikes. Smoke and sparks belched out of the ship's rear end.

I gave a grimacing chortle of triumph. I snatched up the tire iron I'd chucked out with me. One good deed done for the day.

I limped to my feet, blinking in a daze.

Areth came around on a wide loop in her battered airnaut. It was green and yellow with tinted windows and twin passenger cab. The small civilian vehicle had escaped the Skurg fire unscathed, but for the right port side that smoked where a black hole had been blasted in her panels.

She landed beside me. I hopped in with a lopsided grin. The airnaut lifted and Areth sped off into the indigo night sky. The engine sputtered a few times but was, touch wood, hanging in there. The craft was on a limited lifetime. Areth banked and her thin hull vibrated. The craft threatened to drop out of the sky. I groaned. But she held.

The city was in shambles. Blackouts, fires, buildings in ruin, crumbled, smoking. Figures scrambled down the littered alleyways, escaping the clutches of the monsters hell bent on capturing them. Too bad this ship didn't have a gun mounted on her front, otherwise I'd be chasing them and blasting down these filthy vermin where they stood. As it was, we were in a civilian craft with no weapons. Limited range and speed. We were lucky to be alive. The Skurg ships had enough going on than take out one small civilian craft with a twin passenger cab making a getaway. They let us be. The militia air guard was still firing into their midst.

Areth headed toward a small airstrip looming to the south beyond the city limits. It appeared to be a small industrial landing pad.

Ships were taking off from the tarmac. The pilots, perhaps seeing the lay of the land, had decided it was a foolhardy risk to stay any longer on this doomed planet.

CHAPTER 6

Time seemed to slow and my pulse with it, but my mind was still a beehive of emotions. At least we'd grounded the second Skurg ship. My heart went out to those who'd been captured early on, like Garth probably in the first ship who hadn't managed to escape and get out in time.

I recalled my last glimpse of him at *The Rocks* before he'd been taken: slumped, doll-like, a face white as milk. It was not a way to remember someone you'd worked with. Most had been there in the hold with us, but not him. We'd not been friends but it was no wish of mine for anyone to undergo the horror of the Skurg rituals.

Areth snapped her fingers in front of my nose. "This thing have radio?"

I shrugged.

"Patch me through to sub-frequency 6.23AZ, if you please."

I flipped a dial and tapped on the fine tuner. The connection cut in and out, but the message was clear.

"Yisabel Areth, you are a remarkable lady. Small wonder I recruited you."

"Go to hell, you bastard! What's the idea of shanghaiing me back there?"

There was a long pause and my blood ran cold at the lilting and patronizing voice I heard from the recent past.

"For this little inconvenience, you have cost yourself dearly."

"Yeah, what?"

"Your daughter."

For a moment she stared blinking then spat out a defiant laugh. "Nice try, Gy-ar. No one knows where Slevana is."

There came a mocking pause. "You mean Miss Horst? The young raven-hair who works down at the dance school on Pegasus Way out on Ares II?"

Areth blanched. "Wha—? How? Leave her out of this! It's between you and me."

"If it were only that simple, Areth, we would have no issue." There was another deadly pause. "If you are there, Mr. Kip Rees, then listen carefully. I am coming after you. We still have an important reconciliation to settle."

I felt creepy crawlies in my gut. An ache to jump through the wires and throttle that dirtbag's neck. But wisely I kept my mouth shut. No need to give the scum any more leverage than he already had.

Gy-ar's smarmy laugh came over the speaker. "Maybe we won't have need to kill your daughter, Areth. I offer you this consolation. We'll put her in one of our lodges, to participate in the rituals of the Snake, part of our planetary tribute tours in honor of the great Zalahad. Does that sound better? Which would you prefer?"

"I'd prefer your head on a stake, you scumwad. I served you loyally for five years!"

"You did...But you are not serving them very loyally now. You killed Cambor, my distant cousin. Even you must know that blood is blood, even distant."

She rasped in grainy voice, "Cambor was alive when I last saw him."

"He was slain in the slave stampede you helped instigate. He was subsequently devoured by Skurgs. I hold you personally responsible for this travesty."

"There's no way—" She trailed off, her throat and face beet red.

Gy-ar's voice was controlled. "I have a beef with these feckless Skurgs. Our 'allies', but that is another issue, to be dealt with at a later time." His words ended in a strained hiss.

So, Gy-ar was on a vendetta. Revenge, a dish better served cold.

Areth inhaled a tortured breath. "Your spooks of nepotism can go bone each other up the ass for all I care."

"Tsk, tsk, Miss Areth. Your daughter gains nothing from these crass remarks."

"Go to hell, Gy-ar. You're a skull-sucking scumbag!" She reached out a white, trembling fist and cut the channel.

I raised a brow. "Was that wise?"

"Wise what?" She glared at me, her eyes pools of venom.

"Egging him on."

"I get a little emotional. So what of it?"

I looked out the window where I saw the floodlights illuminating the sprawl of the invasive zinc and nickel strip mines to the north. As far as the eye could see, a dragnet set before the foot of the line of low rounded hills. Other metals were extracted there too: proponents of the rare batteries for airnauts—NiMh based—and for the star cruisers and the million other gizmos that the human race had produced in the last few centuries.

The fact that we were able to communicate with Gy-ar without lag, implied that he must be somewhere close. Maybe in orbit around Halroon? Or perhaps even within the city itself. That thought gave me new chills. No trans-light communication could be had along the hyperdrive channels in a meager airnaut like this. Maybe the few high end models could link to varwol server-ships in the city and relay messages at FTL speeds, but not this one.

Areth had somewhat come out of her shock. Her voice was a low hiss. "We've got to get to her."

"We can't. We're light years away. We're in an airnaut on its last legs. We are running out of juice. Company at 2 o'clock. Look—" A Skurg warship was advancing out of the glow over the city. Or maybe it was one of those gun-ridden space yachts that friend Gy-ar was accustomed to riding? Did it matter?

She rapped her thin, white-knuckles on the dash. Bright tears streamed from her eyes. "We can't let her die. We can't let him get to her."

"The only chance we have, Areth, is to get off this planet," I said calmly. "Maybe we'll be in time to get to your daughter."

Her hands were shaky and I guided the airnaut myself via the co-pilot controls to swerve down over some trees. I landed her battered hull in a small clearing. It was a few hundred feet from the road and the airstrip that looked promising. I hoped to hell that the enemy ships hadn't seen us. Either way, they'd search the area. We had a limited window. We had to get the hell out of here and come up with a plan before it was too late.

If I read Gy-ar's hints correctly, somewhere along the way the Skurgs had gone rogue. Maybe they'd gotten greedy. For slaves and blood in their carnal games, they'd likely broken their pact with Gy-ar.

"Cambor would have killed me," she murmured. "Made it look like an accident, a casualty of the Skurgs. You heard his innuendo, about no witnesses. I owe you my life."

"It was mutual self preservation."

"No, you saved my sorry ass," she croaked idly. "Why? Even after I'd betrayed you." Her eyes welled with tears. "Help me to understand all this madness."

"I'm a stand-up guy—maybe not who you think I am. Vengeance is not in my blood. The philosopher Drojen, says it is the lowest of human impulses. I wouldn't be able to live with myself if I let them cart you away and eat your flesh—cheer up, sport, you're too cute to be eaten."

Her lips parted and she sat motionless for some time.

"The price for failure," she said, "was that someone close to me would die. Gy-ar told me even worse than my own throat being cut, I would have to remember the consequences I'd brought on my loved one—for the rest of my days."

I could see how a punishment like that would be an endless

torment.

"They will kill my daughter." Her lips quivered at the image and her voice broke. Hers was a world of bitterness and rage. Sorrow wracked her slender body as fingers grasped her hair, knotted it in bunches. "I will fight them to the end." She spat out a gob of phlegm. Her face was the color of snake venom.

Anger is good, I thought to myself. "At least we are on common ground."

She gnawed at her knuckles and her face took on a ghost-like hue. Her beauty had diminished into a wan, scarecrow-waif oblivion.

We were under enormous pressure. We could not stay on this planet. We had to hop a ride. Skurgs were everywhere. The Temple of the Moon people were out for our blood.

We set off across the ditch, stumbling across some muddy water and hopped the fence, careful not to get cut on the barbed wire. There'd been a tool bin in the back of the airnaut which included a winch, tire-iron and pincer-snips which cut the wire looped along the fencetop quite handily.

With grim apprehension, I slunk toward the airstrip. Areth trailed at my heels.

Beyond the empty crates set on skids, several ships sat parked. We crouched behind the crates, eyeing three potential vessels parked in front of a warehouse. The tarmac was lit with arc-sodiums. A damp night mist mingled with the smell of oil and grease. The craft, second in line, was being loaded by a gang of workers near a loading depot.

"There, that one looks promising," she said.

I cast her a bland look. "You sure?"

She shrugged, a tired diminutive movement.

I gave a weary sigh. "Your guess is as good as mine. At least that one's going to be moving soon."

Little did we know in that single choice the hellish fate the universe had in store for us...

CHRIS TURNER

CHAPTER 7

The vessel, labeled in bright red characters, *The Vipra, Kaladar Enterprises*, was docked by the depot doors and ready to ride. She was almost fully loaded of her cargo. The craft, ample enough with her triple rear thrusters and twin forward blasters for defense, was as much an anomaly as her strange construction. Wide flat dorsal fins splayed like a dolphin. A tall shark-fin piked high like an overhead rudder. What was its purpose, an amphibious vessel?

It made no sense.

I saw the five crew members loading the last of the girders of hyper-radonized metal. Building struts? Hollow light tubing, silver and mauve, for an elaborate, hi-tech construction? Probably heading to an affluent port of call. Good for us. If civilization and infrastructure awaited us, it could work to our advantage. If we weren't discovered first. But I didn't see how that could happen, if we were careful.

Areth went to say something but I held up a hand. "Listen."

Words were spoken by the loading crew, traveling across the open space.

"Get it moving, Spiff. Skurgs are laying waste to Nmoor. Orders are, if Remus' shipment gets waylaid, our heads are on the line."

"Rolph, there's no hell way am I going to be part of any head-splitting."

Grumbles. The sound of feet scuffing as men heaved and hove with better efforts to load the tubing.

We had one opening. Between the time the loading crew were closing the cargo door and the work crew headed back to the warehouse, it would be possible for a lean-limbed, fleet-footed runner to scramble up that ramp and hide in the darkness. A slinking meerkat like myself could do it. I'd made sneaking aboard freighters my pastime from a young age. I grabbed Areth's arm. We beetled out from behind the stack of crates.

She hissed at me, resisting my clutch.

"Pick it up, Areth! Time's a-wasting."

We dog-tailed it for the cargo bay door. We leapt into the shadows, crouched down, hardly daring to breathe. Just in time. A straggling stevedore chanced to catch a whiff of movement, perhaps a gray blur. Areth sat hunched at my side, glaring breathlessly at the men outside.

"Hey, Rolph, did you see that?" The worker tugged at his companion's arm, a dark-haired man with sweaty face and heavy jowls.

"Naw, you imagining boogeymen again? You need to lie down, take a pill. It's getting a little early for your drunken hallucinations, Spiff."

The other shook his head like a dog. "You think?" He snatched off his cap, stroked his balding head. "I'll lay off the rotgut tonight."

"Good."

The ship jolted into the sky and we were thrust back into a half stack of tubing. I glared around the murky hold, nursing my aching shoulder. Another bruise to add to the hurts.

The ship tossed and turned some more, heaving wildly, sent us crashing into each other. We clasped each other in a not so casual embrace. There was an awkward silence. We unwrapped ourselves from our points of contact and hints of steamy possibility. Areth's blush deepened.

I grinned, my blood quickening.

Dull thuds racked the hull. The Vipra seemed to be taking evasive action. Likely eluding the Skurg ship that had stalked us from Nmoor.

The stakes had risen. We were now two fugitives stuck together in a weird symbiosis—with a common enemy.

"We'll get your daughter back," I told her as I set to searching the dim cubbyholes.

She bared her teeth and shook her head. "Gy-ar is a meticulous planner. I'm afraid my daughter is lost."

I looked away. I could not deny the possibility.

We prowled around the hold's perimeter, each nursing his own private thoughts. The shipment of girders that sat piled in the center, flush to the rightmost wall. gleamed in the dim glow. The steel door leading to the interior of the ship was locked from the outside. Two inch steel plates I guessed. No other exits or entrances. The air vents were too small for a man to slip through. Even Areth couldn't wiggle through with her wiry frame. No way we were getting out of this crib. Our getaway chest had become our prison. A problem come landing time.

I cursed my luck and sat back on my heels. I rubbed my temples, trying to think of a way out of here.

No ideas.

Which was unusual. I was usually creative and wild brained.

We were going to get awfully thirsty here after two or three days. Curse this dim place.

"What are we going to eat?" Areth grumbled.

"Probably some rodents. We can flush them out of the corners."

"You're kidding, right? What if we have to go?"

"There's always the corner." I pointed.

"You're a real card, Rusco. This was a bad idea from the start, getting us boxed in here like crickets."

"Getting stuck on Nmoor would have been worse. With them after us, we'd have been caught and dumped in a Skurg camp. This way, at least we have a chance. If only we can sneak off at the next port."

She snuffled out an acknowledgment, but she didn't sound convinced. She stood akimbo, staring down at me as if I were the cause of all her problems.

I knew what was going on in her head. Her daughter was probably a goner. She might not make it herself. Everyone in a terrible bind has the need to lash out at someone. To vent a great universal hatred on some enemy or some devil and feel better about himself. A voice promoting justice. I was the closest and easiest target. No one ever wants to point fingers back at oneself and admit to a screw up.

After a time, she squatted down beside me and apologized. "That was uncalled for. Sorry."

"It happens."

I felt the tug of the varwol disengage. The ship gave an almost audible sigh, almost as if it pulled back on itself like a steel ball under the tug of a magnet. The steady whir of impulse engines vibrated the hull. Say what? Such a short trip for such a big ship and cargo? Was she making a side trip? Pit stop? Maybe she suffered engine trouble? My mind tripped over all the possibilities, each one more disturbing than the last.

It was none of the above. The ship made the jump back to light speed.

Many long hours dragged by and Areth slept the sleep of the dead, curled up in a half ball in the murk, her long, slender back to me, head resting against the tubing. I almost envied her. I wondered about her life pre Gy-ar. Her hopes and dreams. I knew so little about her. Did she ever get bucked off a horse? Did she cry for ice cream at the town fair? Was she conned into worshiping the same gods as the Moon Temple people or was she a closet agnostic? What was her childhood like? Did she get on with her mother? Did she have a lot of friends? Had she ever made love in the rain?

I brooded over all this and many other things, pondering our stark predicament, doggedly looking for any solution that would ease our worries.

None came.

I paced back and forth with hands behind my back, mumbled, drew tic-tac-toe lines in the grime, played against myself. Anything to stave off the boredom and my restless, caged-tiger energy. It was the soul-sucking thoughts that were the killers, the ones that needed to be dealt with pronto.

After a time Areth came awake.

"Wha—? Where am I?" She did a face palm and groaned. "Please, universe, let me go back to my dreams. Lying on a beach with a lanky tanned pool boy massaging my back with Argan oils. Pina colada in hand. A deserted island out to sea, gentle surf lapping the white sand. Dolphins leaping in the waves, oodles of warm, delicious sun and soft stringed music streaming from a nearby cabana."

"Sounds lovely," I said. "Sorry to disturb your reverie." I looked at her through bleary, bloodshot eyes.

Her fine cheekbones bunched and her face took on a dour cast. "What have you been doing?"

"A whole lot of nothing."

"Why does Gy-ar want you anyway?"

I attempted a disinterested shrug. "They thought I had something to do with an artifact they lost and tried to recruit me into their clique. I didn't have what they wanted and I didn't want any part of their eerie old boy's club. They tortured me when I wouldn't give them either. They threw me into a Skurg camp to rot and die. I escaped with the help of some very courageous friends. Let's just say the Skurgs running that camp didn't fare too well."

Her eyes widened and she licked her lips. "You did all that? I mean—" she smoothed out her cheeks. A rueful sound struggled from her mouth. "It doesn't seem so strange now when Gy-ar—"

"When Gy-ar what?"

"Well, his weird behaviors for one. Certain sadistic proclivities and voyeurisms and worse. He's an odd duck. He keeps company with sinister folk." Her face pinched in a frown.

"You're telling me all the stuff I already know, Areth."

"You don't know everything. My fellow agent in training, Katra, confided in me. We were invited to be part of an initiation on a mystery world. We'd been bumped up the ladder for 'good services rendered'. Up-and-coming agents. We were slated for a higher pay bracket and more dangerous assignments."

And for 'good looks' too, I bet, I thought dryly.

"It was in some temple somewhere. All secret, all hush-hush. They even took us aboard the space cruiser and sequestered us in the lounge. We weren't allowed to wander anywhere or find out where we were heading."

"Not surprising."

"When we got to the temple, everything was formalized. Ritualized, as if some hallowed costume party. It was as if we were back in some ancient civilization of Old Earth. Everyone masked, robed or wearing gaudy, medieval garb."

"Sounds like fun."

"It wasn't. There were a hundred or so of us there. Two were chosen to be heraldic figures of beauty, Katra and me, for our impeccable figures. Both of us were dressed in butterfly outfits. There was a vote as to who would be queen. Katra won, and it irked me, but it's maybe what saved me. There were a lot of female agents there. All were required to wear masks and costumes like everyone else. I didn't like them. I felt hot and sweaty in mine and couldn't breathe."

"Sounds tough."

"Two of those monster slavers, Skurgs, were there guarding the door. Massive double doors with gilded bas reliefs. Of extinct, prehistoric birds. Serpents too. Flanked by bronze gongs hung from iron chains. In the hall, gigantic pillars towered fifty feet high and rose up to meet the dome inlaid with the purest red gold. After dancing and socializing, they gave us wine to drink from heavy chalices. One sip and already my head started to swim. Off to the sides sat comfy couches, divans, leopard skin rugs, arranged with trays of grapes, figs, jugs of wine."

I was starting to get more intrigued now.

"A figure with bull horns approached me. I recognized Gy-ar."

"How'd you know it was him?"

"I knew it was him," she growled. "The eyes were pale blue. One's grayer than the other. Opalish, a birth defect."

I grunted.

"He was different, taller somehow, as if he were on raised boots. His gestures were more programmed, as if he were possessed. It could have been just the wine which'd been laced with something bad which made me hallucinate. The horns on his head were a foot long, curved, ebony, shining like stars.

"The evening passed in a blur of sweating, buck-naked nastiness. I got lurid snatches out of a graphic dream. Grunting, heaving, spread limbs. Slack and tautened until I was sick of the sight of orgiastic embraces and intimacies of which I derived no joy and hold no pride in saying I participated in. Come to think of it, my memory seemed to be mysteriously erased after the debauchery. We were trundled off back to our home planets. It took me a week to recover. Only a burning sensation in my loins, a throbbing in my skull, a dryness in my throat, a foul taste in my mouth, limbs heavy as lead. My mind was...strangely disjointed as if it were flashbacking to some disquieting scenes which my subconscious tried to block.

"The only lasting image I had, was the horned man reaching for Katra. His blue-black shadow fell over her like a pall. Her defenseless as a doe, her eyes wide and staring, barely blinking in her butterfly pose and costume, pure white and saffron yellow.

"When I blinked and looked again, both bull and girl were gone. In a wash of fog, all to a backdrop of low, throbbing music. I never saw her again."

I looked away, refraining from a grimace.

"I don't know why I mentioned it. It was the first thing that came to my mind." Her eyes misted and flicked away from me. She looked down at the floor, confused and distraught.

I thought of my previous experience with Trix at the chapel of Xi-ar's 'moonlit orgies' at the Temple of the Moon on Riga. Areth's account did not seem that far off from what we'd have been subjected to, but I didn't tell her any of that.

"Do you mean that, what you said about helping me get my daughter...and me being cute?"

"I don't lie about stuff like that. A lot of other stuff I have, Areth, but not that."

She hitched in closer and stretched a tentative hand round my shoulder. She stroked the back of my neck, in my favorite place. How did she know?

After a time she pulled me down beside her so close that our faces were inches apart.

"If we're going to get mauled by Skurgs or die of thirst, we might as well make the most of it."

I couldn't fault her for her logic.

I got up and pulled off some rumpled tarp from the nearby tubing. I spread it out and gently lifted her to slide it underneath her.

"Wow, Rusco, you're a real gentleman. You sure know how to treat a lady. Quite a romantic bed."

I grinned. "Glad you approve."

We unpeeled our layers and I gazed into her hazel-cacao eyes with pupils a shade on the amber. Not a ounce of fat on her sleek body. I trailed my hand from the round of her hips to jut of angular shoulder to the soft warmth of her breasts. It was slightly cool in this stuffy, must-ridden hold but both of us were sufficiently heated up to overlook that inconvenience.

I pulled her in close and she clasped me in an eager hug and rolled up and over, opting to take the higher position. She was a lady who did not waste time on foreplay.

It was a strenuous event. There was some domination at play. Each of us vied to take the lead and break the other. Finally I broke through and flipped her on her back and had her moving in sync with my own steady movements. Her head was angled back in tigerish husky throatfuls of pure abandon.

As is wont to happen, good things never last. In bad places, most of all.

I froze when a thunk came at the steel door. The metal creaked open with a vacuum whoosh of cool air.

"Heard some moaning and snuffling going on in here on the audio monitor," a gruff male voice said.

"You're crazier than a coot, Spiff. Last time we went to check, we found three mice and a were-dillo. Unless mice start moaning, I think you'd better let up on the Alkili ale."

The other snarled. "You're one to talk, Crobe. Worth it to take a look. Remus will have our asses if we allowed some rude-assed stowaways aboard. Let's flush them out."

"Right. Knock yourself out."

Bootfall. Scuff of steel-toed ankle boots on metal. At least two mouthbreathers had come to interrupt our festivities.

I scrambled up to my knees, pulled on my denims, reached for my leather shirt. Areth groped for her skin-tight leathers. Her eyes gleamed, droplets of sweat beading her neck. Her breath was still labored. I didn't like the looks of these two bearded grifters. Thugs, most likely. Cretins at best. Areth's chances were slim with a couple of mutts like these, especially in her flushed, bare-naked condition, with the spoor of sexual completion on her skin. I pushed her away under cover of some tubing just before all hell erupted.

I was in the process of zipping up my fly, chest bare as a babe when one of them, the squatter one, came tripping over to practically stumble on her.

"Hey, ugly!" I called, distracting him. I waved my hands. "Come to dadda."

At first his jaw dropped, then he gave a fluting call. "Jesus Murphy, Crobe. Look what the cat dragged in. We got ourselves a freak boy. Likes to pleasure himself in the corner." His abundant belly heaved in laughter. "What's a matter, freak? Doing yourself in your mommy's basement not good enough? You got to get off in exotic places?"

"You got it, cowboy," I grunted. "You want to go for a round?" I batted him an eyelash.

His partner nearly keeled over in laughter. "Looks like you got an admirer, Spiffy. Your boy's got the hots for you."

"Shut up, Rolph." The bald man's jaw clenched. He lifted his blaster.

I slow-sauntered over to the wall away from Areth. The mouthbreathers may slip up any moment, which would give me an opportunity to clock them into la-la land. As I feared, I didn't like the looks of these two and things would go ill for us if I didn't come up with something quick.

CHAPTER 8

The two stooges shuttled me out of the cargo bay. The door clanked shut, leaving Areth sealed in her tomb.

They marched me down the hallway with little or no formality, offering me a few kicks and bruises along the way. Seems these fellows were not fans of glow boys.

Before we got to the bridge, I put my hand out to the wall to keep my balance as the ship rocked to enemy fire. "Looks like you guys got friends."

"Come on, you!" Baldy fisted the door unlock mechanism and forced me through into a cramped pilothouse, dim-lit and smelling of sweat and unwashed bodies.

Through the single small viewport on the far wall, I saw an aqua-colored planet encircled in white cloud.

A small command center for a ship of this size, I noted. The bridge was minimally equipped: weapon-wise and gadget-wise. A single weapon's grid low to the ground on the starboard side. A sweating gunner sat glazed-eyed staring at the controls. Dumbfounded. What this ship lacked in firepower it made up for in cargo space. Engine power too, judging from the size of her twin dual ion harvesters.

"Caught this rat skulking around the hold," Crobe called.

"And? What do you want, a hero's medal?" the captain growled.

"He's a smartass. Cocky as hell." He thrust me at the feet of the captain. "Bastard was trying to proposition us."

"With what, mekhs?" The captain frowned.

"No. He was bare-chested and catcalling, if you get my drift."

The captain wheezed out a smoker's cough. "Get him the hell off my bridge. Why'd you bring this carny boy up here?"

"Thought you'd want to see—"

"You thought wrong, Croben. Now get back—"

His eyes suddenly strayed to new movement on the holo feed. "What—? Shit, two more? These Skurgs are hovering there like wolves...we're not five minutes out of light drive then *boom*...all hell breaks loose as if they were waiting for us."

"They were. Any fool can see it," I said calmly.

The captain swiveled his steely gaze my way again. "What's your name, wiseass?"

"Rusco. Jet Rusco."

"What kind of stupid name is that? Jerkoff Razass. Jip Rimpa. You picked the wrong time and wrong ship, friend, to play stowaway." He balled a fist and took a murderous step my way—a brown-bearded ruffian with heavy jowls and only half a head of hair. His beady eyes bore down on me like knives then darted to the five enemy vessels fast approaching—apparently we were one of the three of our small convoy of cargo haulers moving at near max impulse toward the blue planet below us.

My heart sank. More rogue Skurgs? Why were they everywhere at once? Couldn't they just piss off and die? The gears in my mind worked. They couldn't have followed me and Areth, could they? No, this was something else. Gy-ar had even hinted that the Skurgs had broken ranks. Dissension among bloodthirsty scum like them was a part of the empire-building process that shaped planets.

The gunner, a lean-shanked man with a thin face, oiled mustache and matching goatee, pointed a finger at the tactical holofeed. His fleshy lips gave way to a soft, desperate moan.

The helmsman who was at his side, a red-bearded man with

pencil-thin brows and lips curled in a perpetual snarl, flipped dials and turned levers. He struggled to get the ship moving away from the advancing fighters. Under the circumstance, this was not a good plan. We were outgunned, overpowered, meaning the Skurgs would chase us relentlessly, enslave us or worse.

Better to fight.

"What the hell are they doing this close to Oranthe?" the helmsman cried. "I thought Cyr appeased the mongrels?"

"Always some new mystery," the captain said. "Keep your eye on the target, Rolph."

I recalled the damage that had been done to our shields. The gauge was dangerously low for a ship of this capacity. Old memories of Skurg terror resurfaced.

"You'd better coordinate your efforts with your convoy or those Skurgs'll make mincemeat out of your ship."

"You a backseat driver? Shut him up, Spiff," the captain growled.

Spiff grinned evilly. "Righto, Remus." Just as Spiffy was about to clock me, there came a red alert warning as a stray or calculated blast penetrated our shields. A blue electrical arc surged through the dashboard and rainbowed to the adjoining console.

"Aargh!" The gunner's eyes smoked. He jerked like a marionette for a brief second then slumped face-first on the console, deader than a doornail. The captain and the helmsman both stared. Gunner boy was fried, electrocuted on the spot.

"Jesus!" cried Spiff. "What now? Gully was our best gunner."

"Kreff can sub in." Remus gestured. "Go get him."

"Wait, I can navigate this," I said, stepping in.

"You?" The captain guffawed. "You look like a kid who just got his first joint and nooky out in the schoolyard."

"Trust me. I can do this."

"Couldn't navigate your way out of a paper bag." He glared at me slantwise anyways, mumbling, but for a brief moment those bloodshot eyes, rivets of iron, seemed to dare to believe in me. "You better not be shitting me, boy, or you're dead. I'll skullcock you myself." He whipped out a snub-nosed blaster and aimed it at my ear. "Before they atomize this vessel or tow it to Kingdom Come, you'll feel the fire of my R2 in your ear."

I pushed away the electrocuted body, what was left of Gully the gunner, and clomped down in the weapons' chair. I set to familiarizing myself with the controls. *Let your fingers skim over the dials, Rusco. Tilt, yaw, fire, aim. No different than flying with Skel on the XL3 Vigon out in Tildara. Remember? Taking target pot shots on Moon Base, thinking you were some damn hot shot?*

It had been a recon vessel with twin EA scopes, deep range cloakers and power to burn. Ample weaponry. This one was even better equipped. My earlier assessment had been wrong about this ship. On the surface, it looked primitive, but under the hood she was tricked out with all kinds of gadgetry and sensors. More modern too, with some fancy scanners and hi-res holo grid racks. Nothing I couldn't figure out.

The captain pushed the muzzle closer against my ear. "You'd better not screw up, flyboy, or you're going to get a blast of ion tickle sooner than later."

The helmsman whined, "Cyr's going to be pissed if this ship and expensive cargo don't make it to Aquatown."

"Expensive cargo? What about our irreplaceable hides?" Spiff moaned.

Remus gave a wolfish bark. "That old sly-dog Cyr could give a shit about our hides."

The ion fire came without warning. Shields were hit hard. The Vipra skewed sideways and we started in a downward slide toward the planet.

"Crap!" Rolph bawled. "These Skurgs don't waste time. Aren't they—"

"Get out of their zone, you imbecile!" Remus staggered over to the weapons' console. "Fire on them, damn it!"

On sight of the enemy, the two other cargo haulers in the convoy took evasive action. Each impulsed toward the planet's nightside while they readied their cannons. It seemed they hoped to stave off a blitzkrieg attack by getting to ground first.

The Skurgs had been anticipating just such a maneuver. Two ships headed off the runners and fired at will. A storm of death—they came screaming in head on in a brutal ship-to-ship attack.

The haulers split into opposite directions. Skurg ships pursued each of them, maintaining closest possible proximity. They were not going slow.

The first of the convoy was unlucky. Maybe its shields were low? Had it not been recharged properly on Nmoor? The hull turned a dangerous orange then flared to red, its main power sucked dry. The Skurg vessel hovered over its prey like a quilled vulture. It could easily just blast the doomed ship to oblivion, but it did not.

Now that it was incapacitated, the Skurgs wanted to hijack its cargo and enslave the crew.

The other convoy ship fired blindly, but fared no better. Two Skurg vessels were doing spiral loops around its silver hull, dodging its stern fire. Damn, they were good! They were ever weaving an electro net around the Kaladar vessel itself. A spidery web of blue and yellow as it came hitching in, whirling toward their ship like an alien parasite. The net flowered into an ugly grapple then of fine bright stars, curling malevolently around the ship like a dragon's claw. Didn't the pilot grasp what they were doing?

I'd seen such butterfly patterns on Belruus during the Skurg battle in the forested hills of my youth. The memories crept back to me like a black widow in the night.

There was a flash and a flushed trail of dusky light that arrowed into a speckled line which stretched off to infinity. The Skurg ship and its cocooned-wrapped victim disappeared into a spray of hyperdrive as the varwol kicked in. Cyr's precious cargo and its crew went with it, on their way to Skurgdom. How long before it was us?

CHRIS TURNER

CHAPTER 9

I thrust the doomed ship from my mind. New enemy traces were raining down on us from above.

Rolph turned and hissed through his teeth. "Damn bitches! They're all over us."

I let my fingers move over the weapons' grid with grim purpose. The man deserved a pat on the back for the evasive maneuvering he'd done thus far, credit be given, even though he was a grumpy, nitpicking bastard.

"We got to get to planetside," Remus snarled. "They can't fire on us underwater."

I jerked my head around. "Underwater?"

"Yeah, in case you haven't noticed, this is an amphibious vehicle."

"I noticed," I grumbled. "Just hadn't connected the dots." Nose out of joint, I sighted on the Skurg craft that came skimming dangerously close to our starboard vane. My ion fire went wide. By a foot.

"You missed, ace."

"Work with me, Rolph!" I rasped. "No chicken-shitting around. You got to get close. Not deking around like an old maid."

"You're an overweening little—"

"Go straight at them! Then lurch away," I cried. "Give me a chance to plug some atomic ruin up their ass."

"Shields are at 34%," he hissed. "A few more direct hits and it's game over."

"Shut it! If we don't nail them, you, me and this whole crapbucket of a ship are toast."

The captain snarled. "He's right. Do it!" Remus lurched over and watchdogged us like a bloodhound.

"Okay," said Rolph, "you guys want death, so be it." With hopeless, fatalistic energy, Rolph jammed the impulse to max. The craft veered in on a kamikaze course, straight for the Skurg vessel.

I aimed the digital crosshairs on the lead runner. It was a harrier of stunning proportions. This was it, either strike or we were dead meat. With quick fingers, I locked on the leviathan, a big black hexagon bristling with devilish spikes, rods, or whatever they put on these ships as their customary trademark. Legend had it that the Skurgs of old would fly their spiked hulls straight at the flagships, breaching their enemies' hulls, rendering the rest of the cargo fleet vulnerable to their scavenging. It had the ring of truth. The pilot was a sneaky mother and fast. He'd spiral in an impossible trajectory then he'd impulse back out of our sights at the last minute, trying to draw us out.

I'd had a lot of practice with Skel out near Tildara. Fighting the Skurgs aboard Goliath too in orbit around Argentile. I knew what strategies they liked to employ. Having been thrust from frying pan into fire, I recalled everything I knew in the art of dogfighting.

I loosed all she had.

A section of the Skurg's stern broke off. I chortled in glee. The ship flipped sideways and went spinning off down to the planet like a toy.

Rolph gave a wild shout.

"Good hit, Rusco," the captain crowed. He stood behind me staring intently at the viewport. "We're not out of the woods yet though. More at 2 o'clock." He slammed a mallet-hand on my shoulder. "Quick, lay into them! Rolph, get this crapbucket moving."

"Aye, aye, sir."

The captain was not far off in his assessment. No less than three Skurg fighters tried to wrap us in their blue weave.

A flash came from the nearest ship. No ordinary flash, but another of those spidery webs of death as it came spinning in toward our hull like some form of alien growth. It flowered into an ugly grapple of fine bright points, spreading over our hull.

I'd seen spider wreaths like this on Belruus engulf whole flagships like a jellyfish's streamers before it carted its prey off to some slave planet.

Horrors of misery spent in a cramped Skurg hold. Trundled off to a prison camp to chip rock forever, or worse. Become a cyborg for the rest of your life. Skel and I had barely broken out of one of those camps by the skin of our teeth. I did not wish to repeat the exercise.

Just as I thought all was lost, a sleek Vargon lightfighter, some new ship with ample guns, had come out of hyperdrive to land in the chaos between us and the remaining marauders.

My eyes narrowed in confusion. Did I recognize that ship?

It had four tapered-back wings and long, twin-barreled cannon mounted port and starboard.

It couldn't be. What were the chances?

Another ship arrived in its wake...a big mother three times its size, light trails fading as it stood battle-ready with cannons aimed aside its smaller peer. An XT6 cargo ship, if I didn't miss my guess. A class B war vessel.

And all too familiar...

I had to blink. Krake?

No, not possible. But then again, he and Skel had made it their missions to hunt down Skurgs galaxy-wide on the frontier worlds.

The two ships impulsed toward us right into the heart of the Skurg free-for-all.

"We got a rogue posse at oh two hundred," Rolph cried. "Hot damn! Seems as if this party of two's bent on giving the Skurgs hell, Captain!"

"We'll take it Rolph. Who are they?"

"Hailing frequency's blocked. Maybe reinforcements Cyr sent up? Don't look like any reinforcements I remember."

"Radio in anyway. Tell them to take the left flank. We'll take the right. Blast this shit vanguard to smithereens."

"Right. Consider it done."

"Captain," a vaguely familiar voice came from the Vargon lightfighter. "Steer your ship alongside ours. We'll go in as a team. We'll batter them into buttermilk. You distract them while I take out the weaver intent on wrapping you in a cocoon and towing you to Skurgon."

"10-4, Vargon," the captain chimed in grimly. His face had creased, as if he were miffed to be superseded by an unknown, but he was humble enough to let it ride.

"XT6, cover me," the Vargon pilot said. His voice was unmistakable. Skel's.

"Roger that."

"Who are they?" Remus murmured again.

"Friends of mine," I rasped.

"Yours? Jesus, this day is full of surprises, Rusco. You and me are going to have a long sit down when this is all over."

"Look forward to it, captain."

Rolph brought us close to the tail of the enemy.

I went on firing, a maniacal spree of staccato bursts at their ugly spiked hulls. Rolph was getting into the spirit of it. He brought the ship in on a tight, reckless loop.

"Attaboy, Rolph. Momma would be proud!"

Skel came busting in like gangbusters.

While Rolph charged on, I fired as many shots as I could. Skel took the bulk of the hits. Damn the man was fearless! But I already knew that, having been in close contact with him for some weeks. A bit of him had rubbed off on me. I girded my loins. Whether that was a good feeling or not, who was to say? Let's say it was good. It would be a lie to say I wasn't pumped by the joy of battle.

As Skel's Vargon and Vipra swept in, it became clear that the second hauler of our convoy was incapacitated beyond saving. But Skel's side fire lashed against the spiky hull of her oppressor. The Skurg scout ship escorting the spin-weaver was knocked out of its flight path. It came slipping into the squeeze zone of its own spin-weave. Now it was cloaked in heavy multi-colored spidery thread, with engine and weapons' systems defunct. In the confusion that followed, the scout ship and the auxiliary Skurg vessel rammed head on. A ball of flame erupted where they collided. Super-charged metal spattered against our hull. Multiple concussions pounded our port bow.

We swerved out of control for a few dizzy seconds. There came a deafening boom on our port side. Dark smoke trailed from cracks in the overhead panels. We'd been hit—by pulse waves, or cannon blasts—I did not know.

I coughed, sputtered, swept a frantic hand out to clear the air around my nose.

We had suffered enough damage that we wouldn't last long.

A jagged ray suddenly shot out from Krake's XT6, grazing a Skurg's hindquarters that was zeroing in on our side. The enemy vessel went spinning out of formation.

"Holy crapola. We've got angels," said Rolph.

"One gun left, Rusco," the captain wheezed. He clambered to his feet, heaving himself up from the dusty floor. "We lose that gun and we're finished. Your neck is mine if you bungle."

"That a promise, Captain?"

"Yes."

Through the smoke, I saw Rolph blink and moan. The Skurgs were on us and it looked very grim indeed.

But in the seconds that followed, a battle cruiser came impulsing up from planetside into our midst. A searing white flare came from her starboard cannon and sent the Skurg team leader—the one who'd caused us so much trouble—spinning on its side. Krake and Skel's fire joined in the assault to harry the bewildered craft.

The Skurg who'd fought us so valiantly tried to limp away, but

Remus would have nothing of it.

"Fire on that bastard, Rusco!" he roared. "Send the team leader to purgatory."

My hands clutched for the weapons' sighter. Like Remus, I yearned for sweet revenge on those pricks who'd punished us so dearly.

But the giant warship impulsed in and cast its mountainous shadow over our damaged vessel. Such was its imposing weight that my hand paused. This ship was much larger than Vipra and more stately, with the same odd rudder-like fin protruding from its spine and dorsal wings flared back on a 30 degree angle which made it look like a massive whale or some ocean-going leviathan. At least four cannons sighted aft and fore.

A strong male voice crackled over the com. "Captain Remus?"

"Sir," said Rolph. "Starship Narwhal hails us."

The captain croaked. "Here, admiral. You are a sight for sore eyes. We're—"

"Stand down. I repeat, stand down, Remus, do not fire on the Skurg destroyer."

"But sir, the vessel's—"

"A sitting duck and crippled. She can do no further harm."

"Sir, she's caused us undue—"

"I wish to have words with these cretins who defy me."

The captain's shoulders slumped. "Roger, admiral." He looked over at me, his eyes glaring.

I held up a palm. "I had nothing to do with it, Remus. Don't look at me like that."

The captain spoke in between clenched teeth. "Sir, with all due respect, we almost had the crap beat out of us and trundled to Timbuktu. We deserve to shoot them to Kingdom Come."

There was a pause. Cyr addressed him politely, "The captain of that vessel is a rogue Skurg. I will have words with him. He will be worked over by my agents. If there are any more upstarts in this vanguard who would hinder my operation, they will all die."

Remus grunted. "Message received." Sweat trickled down his hairy cheek. His lips curled into a sullen scowl. It seemed as if he'd had personal experience with Cyr's torture programs. I stared anew at Narwhal's snub-nosed gray-blue snout, her streamlined silver hull and pipe fish-tapered stern.

"Captain of the Vargon," Admiral Cyr's voice boomed, "that was some impressive shooting back there. I'm inviting you to a meet. At the beachhead at Tyramin Bay, coordinates 32.1 o 43.02e. We have some business to discuss."

Skel acknowledged the invite. A cheeky 'Aye, aye' was all he said. It was good to hear his voice.

Vipra was still on red alert. Klaxons bleated while smoke gathered in the bridge and drifted down the hall as we limped planetside. The captain left Rolph at the helm and assembled the rest of us amidships—while Crobe and Spiff scoured the ship to gather the rest of the crew and prepare for a quick debarkation. I broke away from the procession and headed down the half-lit hallway bathed in emergency-lamp amber to the port bay.

"Rusco, where you going?" Remus said, taking a step after me.

"Gotta hit the loo, Cap'n. If I loose my bladder it isn't going look pretty."

"Make it snappy. Cyr wants to talk to both of us. It seems you've made an impression."

"Peachy."

"We're going to make it to Oranthe but the ship isn't safe until we're on dry land."

"Captain, you're a wealth of practicality."

"Lose the lip, Rusco."

I gave a somber salute and scurried down the hallway to the place I remember seeing the communal head. There was also a locker room or some storage area there. I was glad to be out of Remus's scrutiny. The man was a pain in the ass. This might be time also to form some plan of action regarding this wounded vessel. First I had to get to Areth. She must be going out of her skull with all the buffeting and careening, locked as she was in her dim crib.

With fumbling fingers I rummaged through the open lockers and snatched up a soiled robin-egg blue technician's uniform, a pair of scuffed black boots, and a hokey rumpled gray cap, then I hurried to the hold.

I encountered only one crew member on the way down who glanced at me curiously before scurrying toward the landing bay. Everyone seemed eager to get off this boat. I jerked open the heavy steel cargo door and wedged the nearby block of wood in the door jamb so I wouldn't get locked in. It seemed other crew members had suffered from this same fate...

CHAPTER 10

Areth popped out of the shadows like a jack-in-the-box, a bedraggled scarecrow with hair askew. Her voice was a grainy hiss.

"Rusco, you're a sight for sore eyes. Where the hell've you been?" Her voice scratched at my ears. "I've been going out of my tree here. Didn't know whether you were dead or alive, if you'd taken over the bridge, or were riding this bird roughshod." She paused and frowned. "You look rough."

"Thanks."

"God, it was horrible. Buffeted and rocked. Groans. Bruises, creaks of tortured metal. I thought we were goners."

"Let's just say the gods were on our side."

"How'd you get—"

"No time. It's a long story." I pushed the uniform I'd grubbed from the locker room into her hands. "Put this on."

Her black brows knitted. "Officer Stags. How nice." Her eyes flicked off the name tag to my impatient scowl.

"Get it on you."

"Right here?"

"Where else? Modesty has no play here unless you're worried I'm going to see something I haven't seen before."

"How flattering of you."

"My pleasure. Now hurry up. If you're lucky we can get off this tub without being noticed. We can be on our way to help your daughter."

The idea inspired her. She picked up her pace, uttering fewer words.

I tossed her the gray cap. "Tuck your hair under this. Stags is supposed to be a service guy, judging from the rest of the gear in his locker."

There was a pause then a jolt as I heard a clank of ship's landing gear on cement. "Man, we're here already. Not much time."

We bumped into each other trying to get organized and there passed another one of those awkward moments of heightened sensual awareness. I think each of us just wanted to tear the other's clothes off and make love on the spot.

A bad idea.

The cargo doors were opening and she'd just managed to get her overalls on and hair tucked away when two dockhands stood blinking in the sunlight, gaping at us.

We staggered out, down the ramp and I trudged past them with Areth on my heels. I gave them a salute. They opted not to offer any resistance.

I squinted under the wan light. Vipra was smoking and sizzling. Some score marks cut deep on her port side. There was a slick gooey stuff caked in the ruts: yellowy-blue spidery strands that dripped onto the asphalt. It had a sulfurous smell to it.

Areth wrinkled her nose and grimaced. "What's that?"

"You're better off not knowing."

"Rusco?"

"How do I know? Maybe elasto-spidey goo...with electrostatic properties that the Skurgs find ideal for cocooning ships."

The captain, Rolph and the others had debarked, formed a tight-knit group assembled on a rude, serviceable tarmac. A small spaceport or landing pad. If I didn't miss my guess, Remus was peeved. He caught sight of us and shouted, "Hey!" and beckoned his henchman, Rolph, too.

More ships were coming down on the landing pad: Cyr's, Skel's,

Krake's.

A gray-yellow haze hung in the air which stung my eyes. I smelled smoke in the air, the odor of burning compost or campfire logs smoldering. I looked around but I could see no bonfire or flames.

A faint briny tang of the sea drifted to our noses, intermingled with the smoke. The sound of surf played on the beach farther up beyond the ships. Seabirds wheeled in the briny air beyond the first white-tipped swells. Massive blackstone cliffs towered at our backs. Cut in the middle was a sand-bottomed gorge that pushed out like a hammer from a fist into the rock at right angles to the shore.

The ocean was a limitless plain of aquamarine azure, the same color we'd seen from space.

I motioned to Areth. "Walk with me, pretend you're one of the crew. Look as boyish as you can."

She gave a skeptical grunt. "Are you the secret agent now giving me advice?"

"Just follow my lead."

No way we were going to escape Remus's notice. I figured it best to meet them head on.

The captain marched briskly with Rolph in tow and a big man who'd emerged from the whale-like ship. Cyr? It was he whom I fixed upon as he approached, a hulking figure dressed in bottle green and blue khakis. Black boots rose to knee. A matching beret crowned his brow. He turned to Remus.

"Who is this?"

"The stowaway, sir. Jet Rusco. The man who took over when Gully was killed at the controls. I put him to work. He showed promise."

Cyr gave me a shrewd inspection. It sent tingles down my spine. His gaze was like a knife. He stood at my height but had a hundred pounds on me. My first impression was a bear, a hulking mountain bear. Curly brown hair. Straight cut sideburns. Wide face. Frank, deep set eyes the clearest sky blue set under thick, furry brows. But the most striking feature about him was his presence. A figure of authority. A man who was used to getting his way, getting people to do whatever he wanted.

"And the woman?" Cyr asked, more gently.

"An associate of mine. Miss Areth." I said.

His gaze softened as he drank in her abundant figure and the round of hip under the uniform.

Remus's head shot around. "You sneaked her aboard?"

I coughed. "We were in a bit of a jam back on Halroon so I—"

"You miserable piece of crap—" He surged forward and dug fingers into my shoulder, another hand angling for my neck.

Cyr pulled the captain off me with a force that sent him reeling back. "Control yourself, Remus. Under the circumstances, I think we can forgive Rusco's indiscretions." His cold blue eyes took in the breadth of my heaving chest, muscular frame. He laughed. "You're a resourceful fox, aren't you, Mr. Rusco? The two of you, this Skel, captain of the Vargon, quite a pair. However did you cross paths?"

I looked past him at the air field. Skel's ship had landed alongside Cyr's, the one I'd flown in with him some months back on Tildara. I gazed at the long, sleek breadth of her. "It's a long story, admiral."

"Of course it is. We'll hear about it all soon. I am Admiral Cyr. For now, I have a proposition to make." He paused. "But I forget my manners. Lady Areth—" he bowed. "I'm pleased to make your acquaintance."

Before she could react, he reached out a palm and kissed her hand. It was like one of those debonair chivalrous moments from back in history.

I rolled my eyes when she did an eye-flutter. She blushed. Could this get any more maudlin?

"Remus, get Vipra repaired," Cyr's said sternly.

The captain turned with scowling face and lifted a hand to Rolph. "You heard the man! Hop to it! Once you unload the piping from her, summon the crew to bring her over to the service bay." He jerked a thumb up toward the gorge. Rolph and the two cargo hands jumped to attention.

Cyr shifted impatiently from one foot to another. "We need Vipra protecting our air space as quickly as possible." He gave an exasperated grunt. "What next? Attacks by sea on my underwater complex?"

The rogue Skurg ship was brought down on the tarmac, towed by one of the admiral's tugs he'd sent up.

Cyr looked upon the invading vessel with the beginnings of a hostile face. Its long, black, spiked hull seemed to cause hateful waves to surge in him. "Crack the miscreant hull open like a can. We'll deal with the rebels inside, as need be. Remus, we lost good men up there and a custom-built ship and expensive supplies." He turned on his heel to brief others who'd arrived. I heard them talking about the supply shipment on Vipra and the remaining hauler.

Krake's XT6, a black blockish brute of a cargo sloop, dropped down beside Skel's lightfighter, sleek and silver.

From a distance I saw those I remembered from the rebel base on Tildara emerge from the ships: Skel, Krake, Lisse and five others. Skel and Krake shook hands. They slapped each other on the back, laughed and exchanged jests.

They came over, blasters at their hip, Skel sauntering my way like a rangy cat. He gave me an ear-to-ear grin. Skel was a tall man, my height with well-worked sinew on arm and leg, a sun-browned face from our trials in the Skurg open-pit mine on Skaldar. "You keep turning up like a bad weed, Kip. When I am going to get rid of you, mate?"

"I could ask you the same thing."

He was the same as ever, jaunty, ever the rogue, frank, with a bushy mane of carrot-red hair held in place with his thick white headband. He caught me up in a bear hug then beamed brightly before his gaze settled on Vipra. "I thought I recognized that ace gunner up there." He shook his head in mock wonder at the score of ruts on its smoky hull. "Getting careless in your old age, you rascal? Pushing it a bit too much to the edge?"

"Not really. We were just lucky to survive."

"Sure you were. Hey, I dig the new hair-do by the way. You going for the retro look?"

"How did you get over here? We'd barely been out in space for two days."

"Lisse'd been monitoring the underground channels and caught wind of Skurg mobilization on Oranthe. Many of us were keen to investigate. I was eager to kick Skurg butt. We hyperdrived out to where the action was. Sure enough, we picked up a mayday signal near Oranthe. Here we are." His teeth shone brightly in the sunlight.

I dared not believe how the wheels of fate kept us all intertwined.

Catching some of this latter conversation, Cyr stepped over, smiled, nodded. "A moving reunion. Two friends showing their appreciation for each other." He lifted a comradely hand. "I am Cyr, admiral of this sector. Any friend of Rusco's is a friend of mine. You must be Skel. The brave man who fearlessly defended our convoy with his crew."

"I am," Skel said, offering a small dip of head. "This is Krake, Lisse, Jerome, Baskra, Comby and Quassa." The crew nodded their greeting. Sunbrowned faces crinkled.

Krake stepped forward and shook Cyr's hand. He was a rusty-haired, stockily-built freedom fighter about thirty some odd. He had a pronounced limp ever since his 'accident' at the Skurg camp. One of his prosthetic legs had short-circuited when hit by a Skurg's goad. Lisse, quiet and dark-haired, stood at his side, a scrapper capable of a fierce inner fire. I'd come to know her personally during the blood games of the Skurgs. She gave a demure nod. She had a robot foot courtesy of the Skurgs.

"The pleasure is all ours," Cyr rumbled. "Over here is Captain Remus of Vipra—and this is his first officer, Rolph, who stares so curmudgeonly upon us. I thank you once again for coming to our aid." He cleared his throat. "It is for this reason I came in private to meet the lot of you. You are an exceptionally rare breed in today's world of spineless citizens content to suffer their dues and eat their gruel in the cityscapes of the settled frontier worlds. I wish to invite you to my complex...to be part of my personal guard in building my militia."

Skel's brows lifted. "What militia?"

"A land-sea base."

Skel stared. "You mean this scruffy patch of beach?"

"No." Cyr laughed. "The jewels underwater—what is not seen." He thrust a proud hand out to the sea, beyond the beach. "What do you think all these building supplies are for? The work crews that toil up the gorge?" He jerked a thumb toward the bluffs. We all looked up the narrow crevasse between the towering cliffs into the shimmering sun. Cranes and small diamond-shaped air-drays bustled from the sheltered lee of the canyon where various warehouses were dug under the cliff and sheltered supplies. Such supplies were transported seaward by amphibious vehicles similar to Vipra but smaller and more compact in shape. "As you can see, I am building an underwater city."

Skel's eyes widened no less than mine. "Incredible. What duties would you require of us?"

"Keeping guard. Dealing with intrusions, saboteurs causing me delay and financial hardship. There are a lot of jealous factions on Oranthe. Conflicting interests that would see my enterprise ruined. For example, eco-freaks from the Yesmian forests who think the sea is not meant for humans. Corporations inland that wish to preserve the status quo, for risk of losing their land-based commerce. Enough detractors for me to button my lip and leave it at that. You will get a generous stipend. Bonuses for good work done, naturally."

Skel bobbed his chin, as if this were something he could buy into.

"It will be a full time position," Cyr added, "demanding long dedicated hours."

Skel scratched his brow. "My job or purpose in life is to hunt and kill Skurgs, not play fiddle to some militia."

There came a dark scowl on our host's face. He paused while he tugged on his beard. I got the impression of danger, that anyone who questioned his authority trod a perilous path. A chilling feeling ran up my spine and with it that uncomfortable feeling that there was much more to Cyr than we were privy to. He had the look of the classic warrior: affable and charming but capable of violence and bloody deeds when needed.

Surprising us all, the man just grinned. He clutched Skel's shoulder in an eagle's grip. "You'll have plenty of opportunity to bust Skurg skulls, young stallion. I have another parallel project on Oranthe's moon. Solas will also need protecting. If you show promise on Oranthe, perhaps you will have a job up there to fulfill too. Remus and Rolph currently oversee the protection of my underwater asset but are overextended. You will be part of their guard unit."

I frowned. "Remus doesn't seem too pleased with the arrangement."

"Remus has no say whatsoever. Your first assignment begins in Yesma on the morrow. I hope after some celebrations this evening you will be rested and ready for action."

"Naturally." Skel gestured and asked, "We will use our own ships?"

"Nothing but."

Remus grumbled some more but Cyr paid no heed. "I will be exporting this technology to many frontier worlds. There will be plenty of Skurg opposition as it will trample on their slave trade. Do you not see how revolutionary this all is? It will alter the landscape of terraforming!"

Skel considered. "What kind of money will we be getting?"

"Upwards of 1000 mekhs per week."

"For the bulk of my crew?"

"Every one."

Skel looked pleased. "I will consider your offer. As an independent contractor it appeals, but not full time. Too much of a commitment."

Cyr gave consideration to this remark. He gave a crisp nod. "And you, Jet Rusco?"

"Me?"

He arched his brows in feigned impatience. "Did you not think you were part of this venture?"

I shrugged, caught slightly flatfooted. This was all happening too fast.

"One thing." Cyr frowned, his eyes narrowing. "I'll be paying you both handsomely for this endeavor. Do not fail me. Any destruction or disturbance to my underwater complex will be punished in equal measure. To fail in your duties has consequences much worse than being captured by Skurgs. Let us say that gallivanting about a Skurg encampment will appear as a walk in the park compared to the punishment I'll bring down on you, if harm or loss comes to Aqua Rex." His face returned to its charming cast. "Lady Areth, I hope you will be staying on with us?"

"I'm afraid not, admiral. I have other business to attend to—my daughter, she is in trouble."

"Oh?"

"She—I mean Slevana, has been threatened by a powerful man. He—" She trailed off, her face ashen. She wrung her wrists.

Cyr's brows arched. "Does this person have a name?"

" Prime Ascendant of the Moon Temple, a certain—"

"Gy-ar?" Cyr held up a hand of authority and gave an odd cluck of tongue. "I am familiar with this little fellow. I shall have a talk with him. Your daughter will come to no harm. Never fear. I hope you will stay on with us for at least another day?" His expression was hopeful, even avid.

Relief suffused her face with a rose-colored flush. I had never seen such a transformation from the gray to the glowing, no less a complete trust in a man's luminous charm. "That is most gracious of you, Admiral Cyr."

"Think nothing of it."

"I—I think—I could stay for a day or two longer," she faltered, "if I can have some guarantee of Slevana's safety."

"You shall have it."

Krake and Lisse opted to join us on the tour. Baskra and the others stayed aboard the XT6 to watch over it, to be on the ready in case Skurgs decided to attack the beachhead.

Cyr made a casual motion of hand. "Caution is always prudent, friends, but defenses are adequate on the ground and we've had no advance report of Skurg retaliations. But that could change." He gestured to the two ion-displacer anti-aircraft cannon poised at the mouth of the canyon. "Supplies are coming in from planets all over the star systems. It makes this a prime hub for thieves. Your crewmates can occupy themselves on the beach. We have sports and other activities: volleyball, surfing, hacky sack to amuse everyone. Also a quaint restaurant up the way in the shade. Let them enjoy themselves at my expense!"

Skel gave a satisfied nod.

I noticed movement at the far end of the beach. Past the ships, a score of figures in green-and-blue uniforms similar to Cyr's were practicing defensive maneuvers. Also hand-to-hand fighting. Both men and women, curiously androgynous in figure and form.

Cyr noticed where I was looking and swept out an expansive hand. "My recruits. Marines, if you will. But come!" He encircled an arm around each of us. He drew Skel, Areth and me toward the Narwhal, his amphibious flagship. "Let us make for *Aqua Rex*. We will dine there." Like a king of a realm he escorted us up the ramp of the waiting submarine ship. "There are many details to iron out. We will speak more of this later."

CHAPTER 11

We assembled aboard the Narwhal, Cyr's famous underwater starship: twice the size of Vipra and more than twice as impressive. We made our way to the bridge. A place richer, more spacious and equipped than any I'd seen. Through the wide viewports I saw the ship lift several feet, before it glided out about a quarter of a mile to sea toward a nearby island then dip under the waves.

The ship, now quasi-submarine, produced a giant screw of four blades where normally the rear thrusters would be. We followed the coral-ridden shelf parallel to the beach through a turquoise underwater gloom toward mysterious depths. The way was lit only at shallow depths by the sallowing sun Phaedra of this fruitful world. I was amazed at the ease of our transition from space ship to submarine. I'd never been in an underwater vessel before, let alone a spaceship submersible. The giant screw, Cyr explained, was of special design, powered with significant torque to propel the craft forward at impressive speed.

About two miles along the shelf, the first major mounds came into view: curious transparent domes. Enormous.

The Narwhal approached the first of these domes with a caution born of a timid crustacean that evoked the puzzlement of Skel.

Cyr lifted a proud finger. "The terradome."

Through the watery expanse I could see more domes laid out in neat double lines. These were impressive tiers of intricate order along the multi-colored coral shelf. Perhaps fifty to a hundred of these domes were cleverly connected, the lower ones twice as high, fitted to perfection as the sea shelf dropped to the blue-gray depths.

Even through the glass and the water, I could make out human figures near the closest dome's summit. Dozens of divers assembled connecting reinforced pipes with the help of only a single underwater gantry. Similar to the ones we'd seen earlier practicing military drills on the beach, they worked with a tremendous team-like capacity, like schools of fish.

"My workers, loyal and strong. They are fit and dedicated," Cyr exclaimed.

I squinted into the gloom, noticing the speed at which the divers could swim.

Teams of them, outfitted in light black neoprene wetsuits and long matching flippers used the buoyancy of the water to fit girder extensions on the northern wing of the complex—the same girders that Areth and I had been confined with in the Vipra's hold.

"Don't they come up for air sometime?" I gasped, lips parted, noting their lack of oxygen tanks.

"They are a new breed," Cyr explained. "The Aquor have been engineered to withstand high pressures of the sea and have the ability to go for long periods without air. An alert eye will see tiny slits on their throats. Gills."

I narrowed my eyes but even if I could see through their neoprene I would not relish verifying anything close to Cyr's claim. The concept of gills sent a shiver down my spine. Nor could I look any longer at the Aquor, Cyr's workers in the same way.

My eyes settled on a particularly robust woman, taller, sleeker, faster than the others. She was manhandling a stretch of pipe along the newly-fitted glass with three workers.

"That is Makala," Cyr exclaimed, "my most prided aqua-woman."

I had trouble deciding if she was a woman or not.

Cyr read my look and gave a soft exclamation. "Do not be

deceived. Her androgynous air is misleading. She is quite resourceful and fit. Capable of enormous energies."

"I don't doubt, but—"

Cyr held up a firm hand. "Save your excitement for later, Jet Rusco. Look—"

Even while I recovered from my shock at the divers, I could make out the forms within the adjacent dome. Thirty-foot-high fountains, sprawling park lands, garden paths, streets, towers, some stationary vehicles which looked like air-scooters within.

"What do you think of our greenbelt under the sea?"

I had to blink to see whether I was seeing correctly. A whole swath of deep-green trees were growing in the dome above.

"They are dendrons, like those that carpet the inland leagues of Yesma. We grow trees under the sea. To resemble parks with trails. Citizens can still feel connected to nature, if they ever get homesick or to missing the outdoors. Over there is the astro-dome, a veritable miniature zoo and menagerie that contains, or will contain, hundreds of breeds of indigenous wildlife."

"A clever idea."

"It is not just an idea, Jet Rusco. It is ingenious. The idea of the century. It is my brainchild. I call it *Aqua Rex*. A complete world unto its own!

"We've got generators, varwol link, air purification systems, water desalination systems, port access east and west, tunnels connecting every dome, parks, pathways, kitchens, fishing ports, everything one could want in a self-contained community: activity sections, learning labs, games room, sauna and spas."

"All in one dome?"

"Spread across domes."

"Does everyone have access?"

"Mostly everybody. Privileged citizens have full access."

I refrained from asking who a 'privileged' citizen was.

As the ship glided alongside the underwater constructions, Cyr pointed to the blossoming fountains, the park lands, the old architecture, reconstructed cathedrals from the renaissance of old Earth. "Here you see hints of Venice, Paris and Prague lurking within each subsequent dome." His voice rang sonorously, stentoriously. He spread an arm with easy ceremony. "This is a prototype. As you can see, I have not stinted in cost, quality or imagination."

"I can see."

"People can take tours by submarine, in ships like Vipra but smaller. They can enjoy the coral and the aquatic life. We can recreate all elements under the sea as on land."

I looked at him blankly. "Isn't it just as easy to enjoy them on land?"

"A question indeed. Do you ever wonder about the potential of land and the dwindling planetary resources?"

"Sure." I shrugged. "But what of it?"

"Back in the old days, the ruling powers opted to create smart cities. Cabals that oversaw shadow governments that controlled the people, economics and culture. They failed. Even though they liked to think they were making bold strides, they did no such thing. I have come up with another solution—the underwater city. Preserving nature to retain the vitality of the ecology while offering humanity a salubrious place to live."

"You really think humans will want to live underwater?" I asked frankly.

"They can live anywhere, Jet Rusco. They can live in holes in the ground for all we care, if that is their fancy. As long as they are provided artificial light. Humankind is a most adaptable creature—more adaptable than any in the universe."

"A very bloodthirsty one too," added Skel, "with cruel and tyrannical motives."

Cyr ignored the comment. "The continents can be spared humankind's rapacity. They can be tapped for many purposes, ecological in nature, even to make commercial profit if it is needed, for the greater good."

Cyr's words somehow didn't ring true. His dogma was a little grandiose. His smile was too broad, his mouth too full of big words, his gestures too dramatic, as if to mask the cruel and uncompromising hints I'd perceived earlier.

"I see you are skeptical, Jet Rusco."

I shrugged. "There will always be resistance to such ideas."

"There are always ways of dealing with that. Whole volumes have been dedicated to the subject." He let the idea hang ominously. "Implemented by minds greater than my own. Let us enjoy the vistas, gentlemen and ladies. There is a time for more philosophical discussions later."

I was wondering why Cyr kept deferring such conversation and queries. All of it was maddening. A part of me wanted to reach out and smack him. Perhaps he had something to hide. Or he wished to avoid uncomfortable topics or opposition.

Areth's eyes had fixed on the improbable forests. Her eyes rounded in wonder. "How did you build Aqua Rex?"

Cyr chuckled. "That would take half a day to explain. The short answer, it is an engineering feat beyond description—on par with the science of terraforming itself. But I will say this, the domes were built section by section. They had to be built to perfection. Then came the painstaking efforts to pump free the seawater, a period of months, using state-of-the-art machinery. Then there was the gigantic pressure to consider: a sea a gargantuan weight folded upon the glass and metal surface. I have devised an ingenious method of creating a geometric pattern, an inverted double helix of struts, to withstand such stresses, reinforcing the glass. Alloys composed of super-tensile metal, three to ten times stronger than normal metals, some of which are manufactured on Halroon."

"It seems you have selected a very convenient planet for your experiments," Skel remarked.

Cyr gave a resounding sigh. "Oranthe was not always hospitable. In the last century she has been terraformed beyond recognition. Her climes have undergone numerous changes. Now she is tropical. Before she was mainly tundra. Her land and seas have been remolded, stocked with innumerable species. Mackerel, bonito, albacore, tuna, too many to name. Thanks to our automated fishing technology and our robot harbor sensors, we can enjoy the finest seafood at little to no cost. If we are lucky, we will see moray eel and manta rays as we descend. Look! There's one there."

I turned to behold a monstrous, six-foot rose-colored manta sweep by us like a gliding kite.

Areth blinked. "It's all so overwhelming. I cannot even imagine how it is possible to build an underwater city, let alone terraform a planet."

"The manpower and machinery, it is enormous. There is the temperature and salinity of the water to be considered. They must be overhauled. Young species and fragile specimens must be transported by ship across the light years, or bred in situ. Biologists must research habitat ad infinitum. Chemists, geophysicists, astrophysicists must study structure and form to the nth degree—an army of thinking minds. The cleverest, most agile brains of the universe engaged. To overhaul an entire ecology is not for the frail of intellect."

I gave a troubled nod. "My mind balks at the air chemistry alone that must be modified to support organic life. It is on the scale of something unfathomable."

He peered at me with interest. "Have you seen the terraforming machines, Jet Rusco?"

"No."

"They are vast metal towers. Weather stations, if you will—with tanks and blowers on the lowest tier; on the upper, mixing and manipulation technology which must be shipped in and assembled from scratch on sometimes inhospitable worlds. This hardware must be manned and maintained for a period of years, sometimes decades. Only then can the plant and animal species be brought in and survive. Whole ecologies must be studied, tabulated, cross-examined. This involves a massive feedback loop with efforts by both human and machine like never seen before."

The ship plunged deeper into the gulf with a cetacean's sureness and headed straight for the base of the largest, closest, dome. We came to a concrete jetty and docked Narwhal next to an entry port carved into the side of the lower port section near the tallest dome. There came a loud hiss of air pressure being released as metal clamps secured the hull to an airtight rubber seal. A flood of bubbles rose to the surface.

Our company passed through the decompression chamber and Cyr led us into a spacious hall. Twenty foot ceilings rose above a glossy tiled floor set in a mosaic of sea-creatures: squids, crabs, whales, many others. The walls were thick glass, but the lower levels were richly shrouded with creepers and vines and flora of many species—green dendrons, deep-jade-mauve mangalorn trees, yellow yossup bushes.

The place resembled a vast parkland. Tiled walkways snaked through the islands of shrubbery.

The first thing I noticed was the quietness and contained-ness of the atmosphere. The smell of tropical fragrances filled the air: bamboo, coconut, eucalyptus, flowering azaleas. The air was cleaner than the smoky haze we'd gotten used to, the place we'd left behind.

Liveried attendants greeted us as we drew near. An older gentleman of refined qualities and manner, in a golden gown and silk top hat, clasped his hands together and graced us with a genteel bow.

"Lord Admiral Cyr, it is a pleasure to see you again so soon. What are your wishes?"

"They are as you can expect, Elengskar. Provide these gentlemen and ladies with cocktails, then private lodgings in the Tide Quarters." He turned to us brimming with pleasure. "It is our most elegant venue within the guest wing of Aqua Rex. We meet in two hours for dinner. A veritable banquet! Do not stint, Elengskar. We have numerous toasts and much celebration before the day is done."

"It will be as you wish," Elengskar said simply. The attendant bowed low and escorted us through the maze to our accommodations.

Cyr had not exaggerated. Glass chandeliers hung from high

ceilings, opulent brass and gold fittings graced even the most mundane, or ordinary fixtures: bathroom and sink. An unusual richness for such a place whose every square inch of real estate must be beyond precious.

Before long we sat down at Cyr's elegant table to an excellent meal. A seemingly endless variety of succulent fishes, one by one. A cathedral ceiling soared aloft in this dining hall. To the north, a wide oval port overlooked the bay, framed in between a pair of sprawling mangalorn trees. All the time our host floated about, making grand gestures like the entertainer he was, the odd time making moon eyes at Areth. I did not care for his exuberant inspection. His bright blue eyes twinkled with an intensity that seemed more than friendly.

The attendants brought dish after dish: various lightly-seasoned scallops doused in butter, baby shrimps, sea turnips, bread-battered swordfish, octopus fingers and many more delicacies with white and blue caviar and wine, iced buckets of it, served by liveried waiters, served dry or fruity in clay jugs like the old days of Rome.

"Lady Areth, you look quite contented," Cyr said after a time. He lifted a glass. "How do you like our delicacies?"

"Sumptuous." She smacked her lips and batted her eyelids, green eyes roving past Cyr's imposing bulk to the schools of goldfish darting beyond the port glass. Krake and Lisse murmured their own praises.

The only other female present was Makala, who said not a single word during the entire meal.

Cyr beamed. "Caught in our very nets this morning, Lady Areth, in the bay yonder—" he waved a casual hand to the darkening blue waters.

"By your friends, the aquamen," I added languidly, arching my brows.

"None other."

Skel grinned, not adding to my facetious comment. He drank in excess and I daresay, became a trifle drunk. He spoke out of turn, which seemed to annoy our larger-than-life host. All of which would have been amusing, if it were not our first day out and newly hired on the spot. Skel seemed oblivious to maintaining political correctness or making a good impression.

Areth sighed. "I am happy in knowing that my daughter will be safe in the hands of an influential and powerful man."

He nodded sagely and made a diminutive gesture. "Think nothing of it. Speaking of the Prime Ascendant, his holiness has instructed me on some new ideas to accelerate my enterprise. Quite revolutionary. He will set up lodges in the new settlements undersea. We have arranged a partnership."

I huffed out an astonished breath, rising slightly in my chair. "Gy-ar?"

"None other. Does this surprise you?"

"No, I mean—I really don't know what to think."

Cyr seemed amused at my confusion. "Are you unnerved, Jet Rusco? For one who appears to be so tough, it seems out of character. As if your virgin ears could not quite handle the name 'Gy-ar' mentioned casually at the same table where you dine. Is the name of a magnate such a discomfort to you?"

"No."

"There are many powerful players in the commercial world. Gy-ar being only one of them."

"On a superficial level perhaps," I said stiffly, "but this man…" I trailed off, not finding the words. Part of me knew that whatever I said would have no impact whatsoever.

Cyr moved on. "Almost ten thousand of us will live here by the next moon of Osguluth. It is the wave of the future. Think of it! Underwater cities sprouting up all over the settled worlds. Wherever there is an ocean, there will be an Aqua Rex. Humans will no longer have the need to live on land."

"You're going to have to build an awful lot of these sunken cities to migrate whole populations under the sea," I said, my mind still troubled at the mention of Gy-ar.

"Not necessarily, Jet Rusco."

"What's that supposed to mean?"

"It's a question of population management, as I mentioned earlier. Also planetary allocation of resources."

I gave a doubtful squawk. "That again? What are you going to do, fly billions of people in on dolphin helicopters? Get them to eat fish food in the underwater cities for the rest of their lives?"

"Survival of the fittest," he said. "Not all are destined to survive the coming age, a dark one that is fast coming upon us." He chewed with more concentration.

"Again, what is that supposed to mean?"

"Exactly what I said."

"Are you implying only a few tens of thousands of people will be left on any one planet?"

"You said it, not me." Cyr drank generously from a jeweled goblet. "There will be only Aqua Rex, and the chosen ones to populate it."

"I find that fanciful and disturbing."

"Let's put it this way, the only protected, safe haven humans will have, is under the sea—away from floods, pestilence, war, cyclones, earthquakes, climate change and a dozen other natural disasters that will smite humans around the galaxy. Even now, fires rage over the inland forests of Yesma." He gave a vindictive snort, shook his head indulgently. "People will not survive; they cannot die fast enough, Jet Rusco. Rapid expansion and industrialization has changed the face of our living space...the entire ecology of the planet is at stake. Mother nature is angry. She is flaming mad. She will rise up, friends, and smite...and her vengeance will be fierce."

Skel blew air out his cheeks. "A nice concept, Cyr, but I think not. You've been delving in too much pseudoscience."

Cyr gazed at him for a long moment. "Have I now?" His fingers curled like crows' claws, pulling at his left cheek. It was a nervous tic of his. Whenever his pride or vanity was pricked?

"There's change, yes, atmospheric changes," Skel agreed, "waters rising, falling, but not to the degree you describe, that the globalist fearmongers who hoard and control all of the planetary resources, push down our throats every day to scare us into submission. Their problem-action-solution modus operandi that rapes the worlds of their resources and gets the masses to jump like lemmings into whatever trap they have set, is getting tired."

Cyr shrugged. "Perhaps." He shot me a cool glance. "What do you think, Jet Rusco?"

"You both make interesting points." I set my fork to work on a pile of excellent scallops and chewed thoughtfully.

"A wise man." Cyr smiled. "Guard your thoughts. Gather facts before jumping to conclusions. You are a man of an earlier generation, Rusco. You don't huff and squawk over every little conspiracy theory out there, as many people I know." There was an imperceptible facetious flick of eyes toward Skel. "You will go far working here at Aqua Rex."

"I daresay," I murmured. I smiled as I could see Skel grinning sourly to himself across the table.

CHAPTER 12

As the meal wound down, we each wandered around the dining hall and the adjoining shrub-bushed footpaths that led to other views of the bay. Skel took me aside with a squinting look.

"What's with the Rusco bit?"

"I've got guys after me. Unpleasant ones."

"Same ones tailing you from before the Skurg camp?"

I gave a crisp nod. "What happened to Captain Masty and his daughter Trix, who were aboard the Goliath?"

He shrugged. "They split. They weren't into it or couldn't hack it. You decide which."

"I figured as much. The old man was a trader. Not cut out for the life of a vigilante. The girl, well—I worried about Trix—a waste of a life to be chasing Skurgs so young, in my opinion."

Though I felt relief that she'd skedaddled away from Skel's outfit. I had these bad dreams about her ending up in the greedy grasp of the Skurgs.

"Still got something for her?"

I licked my lips. "I'm disappointed she didn't break loose from daddy, if that's what you mean."

"What, and end up here with you like this?" He gave me a mocking grin.

I felt a stab of cold annoyance when really I should be chuckling. "Anything wrong with that?"

"Rusco, this is the problem with you—you're way too sensitive. You're wound too tight. You miss the obvious. You don't see the forest for the trees. But don't worry. Looks as if you already have another hen lined up." He gave me a nudge and wink-wink and pointed to 'Lady Areth' who had chosen to stroll with Cyr down one of the secluded paths, obviously taken with his charm.

I scowled. "Looks are deceiving."

He gave me a laughing prod. "Any goof can see you and she have a thing going. You have some competition though, bro. Looks like the lady's got the hots for old sea dog—"

"Hold off. Someone's coming."

The eerie aquawoman, Makala, approached. She barely gave us more than a passing notice. There was no poetry in the sway of her hips or her slate-blue eyes that remained unblinking mirrors into nowhere.

"How'd you like that for a dinner date?" Skel asked after she'd passed. "Ice queen dike of the century."

"Not much," I said.

While Skel admired her sleek boyish butt and her tall sinewy form, I dropped into one of my plaintive reveries, seemingly a bad habit of mine these days. Long ago while I had some psychic power bestowed on me by an alien artifact, I'd had a vision. Of Skel and his scrappy freedom fighters perishing in space at the hands of the cannibalistic Skurgs. It hadn't happened yet. The artifact's powers had been remarkably accurate. Did that mean maybe the future was not carved in stone? Were we masters of our own universe, our fate, beings who could change destiny on a mekh?

It made my brain ache to ponder such concepts so I dropped it.

"Not sure how much I trust this Cyr fellow. His vision and delivery seem off. He seems too absorbed in his philanthropic rhetoric and brainchild than the greater good that it might offer humankind. He's too sure of himself. I've seen plenty of such qualities in Gy-ar and his bum buddy, Prior Xi-ar. It's disturbing. There's something about this whole project that seems off. I'm getting queasy feelings about this employment deal we've agreed to."

Skel lifted a hand. "I hear you. Preaching to the choir. It is what it is, Kippie. Relax. We got this. We'll do Cyr's little gig for a while, as we rack up some mekhs. We decide where to go from there. We might even be able to recruit some of his fish boys and girls for our cause. How'd you like Makala for a workmate?"

"You sure about that?" I frowned. "These aquamen seem a hop-skip from robots."

"We need grunts for our war against the Skurgs."

"You still on about that war?"

He pierced me a look of daggers. "If it hadn't been for me and Krake busting in when we did, you'd be chipping rock in a Skurg camp right now, or toasting marshmallows over a Skurg bonfire. Maybe even with a couple of robot legs to go."

He was right. I grimaced, lowered my head.

"Forget Captain Crook, Kippie. He's no more evil than any of the other industrial moguls out there. Trust me."

I shook my head. "Getting a bad feeling about this, Skel."

"You're always getting a bad feeling, dude. If I had a mekh for every time you said that, I'd be able to buy a ship."

"Just saying, seems as if it goes hand in hand with you being around. Something's off with the man."

He shook his head and scowled. "The 'man's' paying our wages."

"There's more to life than money."

His face reddened. "So where were you, hotshot, when I offered you a chance to hunt down Skurgs? You tucked tail between legs and ran off like a whipped dog. We could be cleansing the galaxy of those pig-scum, instead we're here playing errand boys for some rich bastard."

I looked away with my own scowl. Skel had a way of putting things that shunted out all shades of gray and nuance. He kept bringing that bit up about the Skurgs which bugged the hell out of me. When would he ever give it a rest?

He went off in a gruff mood to join Krake and Lisse and catch up on news, maybe brief them on something or other, while I stayed at the port hole, musing darkly. The glass was weaved with a metal wire helix pattern arranged in foot wide loops. The fiber-like metal was lit up in blue to illuminate some of the surrounding sea.

I stared through the pattern at a new school of majestic rays that had come to feed on some smaller fish. They blinked disparagingly at the wall of glass barring them from gliding further. I was feeling overwhelmed, uncentered. Too many new happenings in the past while.

Cyr caught me staring out the porthole. He laid a heavy hand on my shoulder.

"Rusco, you've got the best seat in the house!" He motioned to a newly arriving school of blue dolphin that had come to chase the rays away and frolic and ogle.

He droned on at length of the dolphin and their merits, how they'd evolved over millions of years to be graced with such sleek, playful bodies, how they'd been brought here across the gulfs of space when the planet had been terraformed so many years ago.

"The only memorable indigenous species on Oranthe are the dogfish and the yakfish. You don't want to come across either, Rusco—" he made a brief comic sound "—even in these shallow depths."

I noticed the pace of his words increased as he chattered on about anything about the sea. A flush of healthy color would suffuse his cheeks. It seemed the only time he became truly passionate about anything was when he was referring to Aqua Rex or his pet child, the sea.

"Isn't it wonderful, this view?" he said. "Breathtaking? The sea cucumbers, the seahorses, swordfish, the anemone, the great blue dolphins, the whales."

I gave a slow nod. "You obviously love the sea."

His bear face crinkled into a brimming smile. "I've always loved it. Even as a young child. You cannot know the depth of her even if you've spent decades exploring her expanses. My passion has always been for the underwater mysteries, the life she nourishes below."

"Ever worried about one of these port holes imploding?"

Cyr tapped the six-inch glass with confidence. "It would take a pretty big bomb or a major hit to do anything like that, what with the custom helix reinforcement I've installed. And even then, it would at most leave only a hairline crack. My engineers could plug the leak and repair it."

"Forgive me for saying, Cyr, while beautiful as all this is, it seems improbable that one man could have come up with all this. Am I missing something?"

His whole body tensed, and for a moment I thought I had insulted him.

But he exhaled a long drawn-out sigh. "I cannot expect you to understand, or have any idea who I am. But I will try, Jet Rusco, because I know we have a lot in common and an important path to share. I grew up in the gutters of Parinossus, a scum world off in the hinterland frontiers. Full of tyrants. Warlords. Smugglers. Bully gangs ruled by street thugs. I was kicked around like a stray dog. They didn't like my bear looks, or my size.

"But that was when I was younger and less knowledgeable in the ways of the world. I learned to defend myself. I learned to outwit my oppressors. I become slier and craftier than all those fools. Now I am stratospheres above them and here with a glass eye and a prosthetic leg. But my body is immensely strong. As strong as three men. I've had implants. I use hormones to augment my physical condition. My mind...as far as I know, works like clockwork—I have read only the most cutting edge journals, studied the most advanced sciences of the age for decades. Every source I can get my hands on, I read. And I read them over again."

"Very admirable, Cyr. You are the penultimate renaissance man."

"I sense you are not impressed."

I made a vague motion of hand. "I'm impressed by deeds over words."

He laughed at this and his blue eyes twinkled with such mirth I could not believe it was the same man who'd spoken so solemnly just a moment ago. "Rusco, you speak like a crusader." But Cyr's leaden eyes soon bored holes in me. "You and I are not much different. We have grown up through hardship, I can tell this without knowing the intimacies of your background. I survived. You survived. I may have twenty years on you, but we are of the same breed, the same ilk. With your friend, Skel, together we will go far."

"I have heard such words before, Cyr. So you can understand my skepticism."

He gave another brittle laugh. "Of that we will see. Relax, Jet Rusco. You are too tense and serious for a man of your age. You should be out chasing that young skirt, Areth. My, what an exciting, adventurous woman. Why are you leaving her to an old codger like me?"

"'Lady Areth seems quite content to go on walks with you."

He tsked his tongue and shook his head. "For one so perspicacious in the ways of the world, you seem to be a bit green with women. Areth only did that to make you jealous. Typical female behavior to get you to pay more attention to her."

I had to laugh, a wry one at that. "It seems to be working."

"She is a remarkable feline."

"She is that."

He called for his attendants and we were taken to our lavish quarters for the night.

Odd that each of us was assigned our own private quarters. Though simple in configuration, the elegance was outstanding and the rents alone would have been in the thousands of mekhs per night in so exotic a locale. I marveled anew. The porthole view out to the marine life at sea was something that few souls would ever experience. I had such quarters, so did Skel. I imagine Lady Areth had two, judging by the way Cyr doted on her.

I lay in my queen-size bed, on the freshly-starched white sheets, hands clasped behind my head, gazing out at the timeless panorama. Colorful fishes roved the gulfs. An immense silence permeated the place. A bluish light from above illuminated the waters and the fishes' unblinking eyes and multicolored scales as they drifted by. It was an awesome sight. I'd never really been under the sea before so it was a new and overwhelming experience.

Whiskered butterfish, speckled sea trout, yellow-green jellyfish floated by. I saw crustaceans, bunches of cauliflower coral, fluted rays, goldfish, yellowfish, groupers, rainbow violets, oranges and deep blue. A dozen other tropical fish. Whole schools come to gaze upon the invading construction that disturbed their natural habitat.

I took this all in with mixed feelings while the more practical part of my brain contemplated a surprise, nocturnal visit to Areth's chamber. Yes, one should follow Cyr's sage advice.

Yet I discovered to my chagrin that the silver-steel door was locked from the outside.

What the hell? I pulled on the handle only to get the slightest rattle. I sat back on my haunches in sullen displeasure. Cyr was a cautious, suspicious man. For a moment I cursed him. I couldn't hold back on my earlier premonitions that there was something off about him, and anger at being a prisoner in his underwater domain.

Skel's breezy conviction, be damned! I felt cold misgiving once more about this communal venture. Should we have accepted it?

CHRIS TURNER

CHAPTER 13

The following morning dawned too fast. A watery, surreal light streamed in from the porthole.

A brisk knock came at the door. A key turned. Servants already? I rolled over, groaning. Couldn't Cyr give us at least two more hours to enjoy the pleasures of deep sleep?

No. We were hustled to the dining hall. To Skel's and my cold inquiries, our esteemed host seemed unusually curt. "The doors are locked for security. Part of Aqua Rex's protocol." I looked over at Areth to see if she shared some secret joke with Cyr, perhaps a tryst, but I could find no evidence of it.

After a light breakfast, all delicious—poached sole, braised eel, anemone-bread dipped in cod oil—we made our way to Narwhal's bridge.

The trip back to the beachhead was brief and uneventful. For myself, verging on the edge of a stiff silence.

We glided from a height of a hundred feet and I got a better perspective of the gateway to Cyr's futuristic underwater city. The gorge was marked by flanking boulders. The 800-foot-long canyon met the sea at right angles at its widest point, about 100 feet, ending in a crevice two feet wide. The impregnable face of limestone, 200-feet high, was its curtain of protection from the inland forests and any dissenting locals.

The harbor at the gorge's mouth was a natural seashell shape. The gorge itself, a repository for the necessary equipment and materials needed to construct the fabulous city, was protected on all sides. A beehive of activity now. Loaders, lifters, various vehicles were transporting massive piles of reinforced tubing seaward, the ones that would shape the skeletal framework of the dome. The engineers had tunneled into the rock up the gorge to extend the storage and the work areas.

I marveled that Cyr's hidey-hole was well off the beaten track, inaccessible by land. No road for trucks or supply vehicles to any civilization that I could see.

Cyr turned, as if reading my thoughts. "I picked this place because I needed a site away from prying eyes, Rusco, so I wouldn't be spied upon. Or my ideas discovered or publicized. At the worst, my project could be sabotaged. So far I have succeeded in avoiding all three, but perhaps not for very long." He gave me an airy wave. "These wildfires have made the eco-freaks antsy. They are fueled by zealotry. They have become dangerous and unstable, vandalistic and unpredictable, turned to looting and murdering. Perhaps they wish to take their frustration out on me?...on those who govern the sea?"

I shrugged, baffled by the militants' behavior.

As soon as we'd landed on the tarmac, Makala had gone off to join the marines who trained in the field. A team of Aquor, women with no hips, vestigial breasts, and the men, hairless with no noticeable groin, were working hard. Sleek, fit with emotionless eyes and coordinated movements.

Cyr made a sound of fond admiration. "In order to protect my interests, I have gathered a small army of mercenaries— hybrid men and women, as you can see. You'll be able to watch them drill and train under the direction of Savas and Makala. That woman is formidable, as I have mentioned. A taskmaster with endless energy, not to be trifled with. I am always looking for new recruits such as yourselves. Fresh talent to augment my team."

Skel turned to Cyr in amusement, "If you think we're going to grow gills and do races underwater, then you're looking at the wrong people."

"Hardly," Cyr said tartly.

"Just to verify, we pilot our own ships?" Skel demanded.

"Naturally. As agreed."

"Let's—"

Cyr held up a hand. "Skel, one moment. I was pondering last night who will go with you."

"What do you mean who will go with me?"

"Makala. I mean, Makala."

"Why her?"

"Because she's trustworthy. The last time I sent a brigade into Yesma, my marines never returned. I can only assume they were slaughtered by the rebels. She will be my eyes and ears. Makala will report to me and ensure that all is proceeding to plan. I do not entirely discount Captain Remus's qualms about you, though you've fought bravely in my interests."

Skel only grumbled.

"Guerrillas move in on half-tracks. They resent my buying up all the forest real estate, to buffer myself and protect my investment. They claim it is their land, not mine to buy or sell. Fine, I can respect that, but it's a mercantile world. Ruled by the wealthiest. The fires have inflamed their spirits. Now they come in numbers to badger my ass and take back their lands, and for some strange reason, sabotage Aqua Rex."

I frowned. "It seems unreasonable."

Cyr sighed. "Much of this world is governed by unreasonable people and fanatics."

Recalling Gy-ar and his zealotish moon cult people, I had to agree.

"Only two days ago I lost contact with a team of Aquor, who, as I said, had set out on land rovers to intercept a band of desperate Yesmian rebels bent on destroying the beachhead. They were carrying explosives and incendaries shipped in from the war-like

Rdelnarians. To sabotage my beautiful complex. Perhaps drop divers to install bombs on Aqua Rex. I fear the worst. That my team has been ambushed and taken prisoner or slaughtered. That's 25 good men and women. Your mission is to go out there and get them back, or find out what happened to them."

Skel nodded grimly. "We will find out what happened and what the Yesmians' plans are."

"Good. Use stealth, guile, force, any means necessary. Much is at stake here, Skel. Billions of mekhs and the future of the frontier worlds."

Remus came trodding in and handed Cyr a stack of black-and-white satellite images. "We just picked up this spy footage, of a convoy of armored vehicles heading north on the forest road. They're trekking in through the wetlands. Making for the mouth of the gorge. Possibly to make an assault on the beachhead."

"Or some other mischief we cannot yet fathom," mused Cyr aloud. "The same eco terrorists and dissidents I have been talking about. See the insignia written faintly on the sides." He stabbed a finger down at an image. "People's Army. PA."

Remus growled, "My guess is they switchback down the bluffs to the east where the dendrons are sparse and the cliffs less steep."

"If they are allowed," said Cyr.

"They will not be allowed, admiral, with me on point."

"You will remain here, Remus. I need you to be defensive guard, in case the beachhead is breached. The moment Vipra is up and running, you will captain her and join the brigade."

Remus's mouth dropped. "And you trust these ragamuffin hoodlums over me to lead an exp—"

"Yes."

Remus's face reddened. He stomped off in a huff.

Skel frowned. "Who pissed in his porridge this morning?"

Cyr sighed. "Remus is a temperamental man. He'll get over it soon enough. He's got Rolph to vent on." He gave a humorless laugh.

Makala had returned to the landing pad and stood waiting, arms at her sides, silent as usual. Her brow was lathered in sweat from her exertions.

She was six foot one and a half inches and I did not relish one such as she looking down at me so confidently and indifferently. I don't ever recall any woman that tall, or for that matter who could look down at me so incuriously. It didn't appear as she cared one way or another. I don't know why I was so wigged out.

Tight gray-blue pants fit around snug mannish hips. Muscular shoulders. A long, square-cut nose. Short black mane of hair close-cropped at ear. Oily brow, sweaty and gleaming in the sun. Slightly tanned skin at throat and wrists where bare skin showed. A regular bronze Adonis.

Areth initially balked at the sight of her, and I could understand why.

Cyr briefed her on her new mission. He looked to us for acknowledgment.

Skel approved and gave her his usual breezy look over, "Sure, Cyr. You're the Admiral. The more the merrier."

Cyr gave a curt nod. "There will be time for jokes later, Skel. See to it that there are no bad feelings aboard your vessel, and proper cohesion in your group. There are a lot of outsiders, including Remus and Rolph, who do not like the Aquor."

"Now, why would that be?" I mumbled.

"What's that, Rusco?"

"Nothing. I seem to have a frog in my throat."

Cyr shoved the satellite images into our hands. "The coordinates are marked. Follow the route as the crow flies—south. Find the lunatics and root them out." He turned and moved off to tend to other matters, the movement of supplies to the sea.

As we stood waiting to decide who would go in what ships, I stumbled forward to give Areth a brief hug.

"You coming with us?" Skel glanced at her, some amusement writ in his eyes.

I looked at her awkwardly, as if half expecting Areth to turn around and march off and I'd never see her again.

But she didn't. She traced a slow circle on my lip with her finger. "I go where you go."

I made a wry face. "I'm flattered. But you don't know what you're getting yourself into, Areth, when you get mixed up with Skel and his schemes. You should seek out your daughter, despite Cyr's promises."

"How be I decide where I want to go?" she snapped, "and what I want to do with my life?"

"Suit yourself."

Skel cast me another cheeky look which made me want to hit him.

He shook off his amusement. "Krake, you and your crew, including Areth and Makala, take the XT6. Kip, you come with me. We've got butts to kick."

Sure, let Areth, Krake and the others deal with Makala. She barely spoke, so she'd probably cause no problem.

Skel skipped off to the lightfighter and with a grim smile, I hopped in the cabin next to him. When I was in the copilot seat I looked at the row of pads, grid layouts and sensors. My hands moved gingerly over the weapons' grid—range finder, crosshair sighter, amplitude control, enemy AI tactical as I re-familiarized myself.

"Just like old times, eh buddy?" he said.

"Just like."

CHAPTER 14

Skel got the engines whining to life and lifted us into a clear sky. The Vargon circled and shot southward over the bluffs, following the razor-edged line of the gorge for a mile or so before we blitzed the treetops with the XT6 trailing behind us. We ascended to 3500 feet, staying high to get a panoramic view of the lands.

A wall of faint smoke billowed far to the east. Behind it a glowering glow that backed to the sea, obscuring the tranquil arm of bays and inlets that curled southward around the Yesmian wilderness. How much greenwood had burned was another question—how greenwood could burn in the first place boggled my mind. All I knew was there was a lot of smoke drifting westward over the lands and north to the sea, poisoning the air.

Our lightfighter rocketed southward skirting the smoke and away from Cyr's precious underwater complex.

The dendron and mangalorn spread endlessly east, west, south. A vast garden of cauliflower-like treetops intermingled with long-needled fir. From what I understood, the satellite images showed a natural greenbelt 200 miles long and 400 wide with seacoasts to north, east and west. The ancient mangalorns loomed majestically in their lordly fastness. The dendrons, distant cousins, crowded in between their brethren, broad green leaves wavering in the humid gusts. I imagined what it would be like being lost or stranded in that knitted tangle below and I shivered, shaking off the thought.

A foolish notion. How could we ever get marooned, with the XT6 at our backs, and the megawatt firepower at our disposal?

We kept eyes open nevertheless for our quarry, the assault vehicles. The fast-flowing Umena stayed to our left. The avocado-green waters flowed south to north, forming the east-west divide of the Yesmian forests. Also marking the front of the fire zone. From what I could see, no flames had yet crossed the river.

We were getting closer to the area marked on the satellite images so we dropped to a few hundred feet above the forest.

The road was a broken ribbon, snaking north, like a torn earthworm as the treetops curled overtop to obscure it at times.

Not far long along this path I saw movement in the distance: mini copters powered by a single rotor engine. On closer inspection, the crafts were camoed, scout vehicles manned by a single pilot. On the red dirt road below stormed a convoy of half-tracks with machine guns and heavy wheels, heading north.

"There's our sugar plums!" Skel said, "and a bonus, skybirds—four of them." The copters came arching toward us with utter fearlessness.

"Are they fools or what?" I croaked. "We could blast them out of the sky on a whim."

"We could. But I'm not worried about them. It's the half-tracks that are the real problem. We get rid of them, Kip, we end this little rebellion here and now. Hang on to your butt, buddy!"

He dove the fighter toward the convoy on a breakneck angle while I clutched the guide strap. "Hold up! Shouldn't we scope them out first before charging into—"

Skel grinned. "What are these pissants? A couple of armored trucks grunting through the bush like hogs. They make growly little noises with their antique gas engines and pretend to take on star fighters."

"I don't know, Skel," I said.

The back wheel treads were riveted steel and continuous like those of tanks. The front wheels, normal and fat-bellied, could weather heavy terrain. There were howitzers mounted on the flatbed at the back: conventional, yes, but could pack a hell of a sting. I counted twenty one of the brutes, each combining the off-road hauling capabilities of a tank with the conventional drive power of a military truck.

Skel banked like a daredevil. Howitzer muzzles swiveled and hot metal shells flew at us and fireflied off our shields. I saw our shield strength capacity needle down. As we skimmed over the treetops and buzzed the convoy, I set to work on the crosshairs and sighted the middlemost vehicle. I laid fire into my target, sending it leaping off its path into the overgrown ditch and bursting into a small ball of flame. Skel shot up for a second strike and I re-sighted but a menacing movement caught my eye: a flash of silver metal on the rearmost truck.

"Watch out!"

My warning came too late.

A loud searing blast came from the rear vehicle. A smoke-trailed RPG came skating up at us on an impossible angle. Before Skel could dodge, it smote the tail end of our ship.

The Vargon lurched. The missile hadn't penetrated her shields but it rocked the hell out of our ship enough to lose a few dozen feet then precious momentum. And soon enough, another fifty feet.

"I can't stabilize," cried Skel. "Shit, we're going down!"

My heart quailed. Time seemed to slow to a freezing halt. A wall of hard treetops came rearing up at us way too fast.

The Vargon's port wing smashed into a high-rising mangalorn, clipping off the tip of the wing and spinning our ship around. A shudder came from the stern. The lightfighter slewed sideways, pitching out of control. Broken wing and ship came careening down toward the interior branches of the giant mangalorn.

Krake's voice crackled through the com. "Jesus, guys, get the hell out—"

But the radio went dead. Our craft went nosediving and the ejectors failed but we hung in mid tree in the swaying branches locked in the smoking ruin of our ship.

I lay on an awkward angle, half in and out of my seat. My head hurt. I moved a leg. Winced. Stiffness, bruises. Nothing broken.

Skel shifted beside me, let out a mournful groan. The creak of metal strained under our weight but our lightfighter was held in the giant mangalorn's branches. How long it would last was another question. I kicked with my boot but the starboard cabin exitway was seized shut. The port glass was too thick to smash.

Luckily, emergency power had kicked in on the console and the hatch on my side was operational for a few moments. With my persistent kicks I managed to wrench it open. I crawled out of the crumpled cockpit.

Skel was in a daze. Fingering his blaster at his hip, he licked his lips and made efforts to crawl across the seats. He required coaxing. I clung to the tree trunk and got him out clinging to my back, our combined weight wedged almost flush to the massive tree trunk between the hot metal of the hull. Other trees had caught the lightfighter's hull otherwise we'd have fallen and been crushed.

Clutching the rough bark we shimmied down the trunk in jerky spurts before the half-track people found us. I hoped to hell the giant weight of the ship wouldn't crush us. It was not a reassuring sight. The creaks where its broken fuselage sagged in the branches were getting louder and the swaying of the branches and cracking of its trunk were ever ominous. At last, the tons of steel started to slip. With horrified cries we leaped the last twenty feet and rolled out of the way before the massive weight pancaked us.

We lay there in a trance, eyes blinking in the dappled light, heaving air into our lungs. We'd landed in a bed of ferns and creepers, verbally thanking whatever gods exist in the universe that we hadn't met our maker right there and then.

Through moments of my own daze I guessed our location about a few thousand yards from the place they'd shot us down. The road and the half-tracks were somewhere beyond the thick tangle of trees. Not a long distance as far as the crow flies but a distance not easy to access.

All around us the sound of stillness lay in the forest. A jungle like no other. Only the stray, faint warble of a forest bird. *Woo-hoo, woo-hoo.*

Skel stood staring at the wreck, his eyes strangely unfocused. The hull lay on its side, twisted under the low-hanging branches.

"She was a good ship. Too bad."

"We've got to get out of here, Skel."

He nodded, tongue stuck between his teeth.

"Yes, we do, Kippie boy." He smiled at me as if he were on Myscol.

I pulled him by arm and elbow and we stumbled along a faint animal trail. Wild boars? I could hear the sounds of growling engines above us.

Those damn copters. Where was the XT6? I caught a glimpse of a camoed fuselage as one of them passed over the gaping hole we'd left in the trees.

Skel snapped out of his daze after a time, shaking his head, wincing. "What was I thinking back there, Kip?"

"You were in shock, buddy, is all."

"Give me a kick in the ass if I do that again."

"Gladly, my friend."

CHRIS TURNER

CHAPTER 15

We couldn't wait for Krake and the others to rescue us. A couple of the copters had poked their blunt-assed noses through the gap in the treetops and were buzzing around looking for the enemies who'd blown their half-track off the road. We'd have to double back when the coast was clear. How long would it take to rendezvous with the XT6? What a screw up! We hoofed it down the path, leaving the growl of the roving engines behind us.

I suddenly realized why such miniature craft were favored by the rebels. Maneuverability was king in thick jungle like this.

The mangalorn reared around us like ancient sentinels: tall corded bark, sprawling branches and thick knotted trunks. We were cat-footing our way down the forest path, picking our way over fallen logs, mossed with green, when I had this weird feeling of deja-vu: of being here in some time in the ancient past, running in some other body: a lone, naked warrior, with sweat dripping off my bronzed muscles, clutching a ceremonial torch, with enemies right and left at my heels, shafting arrows. The closest I could come to describing the feeling, was like an intense deja-vu or one of the vivid visions I had with the I-TERA. Maybe I was having a flashback? Or some withdrawal from the evil thing? Who knew? The side-effects and lasting implications of the alien technology I'd swallowed, were unfathomable.

I thrust the visceral feeling away. We booted it past still pools, hanging moss, snaky vines drooping from thick, leafy branches while the warble of birds echoed in our ears. The air was still and moist. A paradise almost, but for the violent circumstance of our landing.

The gray-yellow haze of smoke hung low in the air and had me coughing. It had my eyes watering.

The call of a tree creature startled me from nearby. A marsupial? I could hear the tinkle of a hidden stream. Quietness? Safety?

No. My sixth sense said danger was about. I sensed a lurking menace nearby, waiting to spring.

Flup, flup, flup. A copter's rotors beat at the air and zeroed in on our location. It buzzed back and forth trying to get a read on our whereabouts. Why did they care so much about us? We'd fired on them, true, but we were down and our ship was destroyed. We could not retaliate against them.

We were not brave enough to bushwhack straight for the road. The dense thicket would have been impassable anyway. Instead we followed the bank of a small stream in a direction vaguely eastward, if my sense of direction was correct. There was a downside: it gave the copter a chance to hone in on us.

Given the swath of branches the Vargon had taken out and our open course along the edge of the stream, it gave the skybirds enough for a sighting. As one of the scouts spotted us, bullets came whizzing from the machine gun mounted on its bow, shredding the ferns and foliage around us.

"Jesus!"

We ducked and scrambled away.

"Those bastards are vicious."

"And we aren't?" I croaked. "Let's get the hell out of here, Skel." I motioned him down the trail.

We crossed the stream and took some short detours in the bush until we were almost hopelessly lost, but I thought we'd ditched them.

I could hear the faint roar of the XT6 roving above us too, somewhere beyond the treetops but we were invisible to the crew with the tree cover and the smoke. I also heard the thunderous echoes of destruction of shattered trees and rocket fire and ion blasts from air and ground. It was not too distant. I wondered how Krake was faring against the half-tracks. I considered climbing one of the monster trees and waving my hands in the air but realized that would be futile. About as effective as washing clothes in a sand storm. The chance Krake and his crew could see us was zero. I'd probably slip and break my neck on the fall 60 to 100 feet below. I sucked back a wave of hopelessness.

It was then that a herd of twenty to thirty black-striped creatures, half monkey and low-riding lizard came at us. They hissed and crouched on all fours a stone's throw away. They'd found us—or rather had sniffed us out. The closest thing to describe them would be one of the giant monitors of East Timor of Old Earth. They roved back and forth like herd animals as if inciting us to a showdown. Their teeth were bared and throats snarled with a premonition of violence to come.

Skel and I backed away on cautious feet.

One of the smaller orangutan-sloths we'd sighted earlier had failed to get out of the herd's way fast enough. A mad scramble ensued and an obscene tongue shot out from a wide gaping mouth and ingested the hapless creature whole.

My jaw hung slack. These monsters trumped Cyr's yakfish and dogfish as far as indigenous predators went. What others roamed this enigmatic planet?

Could we scramble up the nearest tree? No, these lizards could climb those too.

Skel lifted his blaster. He fired shots into their midst, dropping the lead two. We ran to where the trees thinned, hoping that the stalkers would back off.

No such luck.

If anything, Skel's blasts had only provoked them to further violence.

The sound of engines whined overhead somewhere upstream.

The same copter had spied us, the nosy one with the jade green camo that we'd sighted earlier. I heard the pound of heavy flat feet at our backs, and for once Skel hesitated, not sure of what to do.

"Better run, Kippie," he called. "I can't shoot all these monsters at once!"

I put on a burst of speed while he held his ground. He fired rapid shots into them, dropping a dozen. Why the hell hadn't I grabbed my own blaster when I had the chance? Shock? If I had known the weird fauna we were to face before dropping out of that tree, I wouldn't have been so dozy.

At the edge of the ravine, I could hear the water gush eastward toward the sea. Skel had caught up to me and we passed close to its edge, crowded by foliage.

A dense patch of large purple bell-bottomed plants wedged us closer to the precipitous drop. I frowned as my eyes took in their gangly numbers. The tops were like giant closed tulips with four tight-knit petals. The bulbs, drooping slightly, rose on thick, green-gnarled stems at about rib height. They had a sinister look to them. No other plants or creepers seemed to grow in their vicinity. Why was that?

Just after we'd passed the last eerie flower, one of those stupid lizard-monitors caught us by surprise. It dropped from an overhanging branch almost taking out Skel's head. He jerked aside at the last moment and blasted it. The thing dropped, sizzling and smoking in the middle of the purple bell-bottoms.

They seemed to awaken all at once. Stems swayed and petals opened like lotus flowers. One dipped down and snatched up the maimed creature head first into its bulb. Petals closed over it. Only the tail showed while the whole bulb quivered and shook violently.

Skel froze spellbound for an instant. It was a deadly mistake.

Attracted by the motion of its feasting comrades, the nearest bell plant grabbed Skel's foot. He cried out. His blaster went skidding out of his hand and went clinking down the ravine as he fell. I watched in dismay as it plunged into the rippling water below. He lashed at the thing with his fists.

"Get it off, Kip! Agh! Quick!"

I ran over and pounded my fists on the tough, rubbery hide.

To no avail. The petals just clasped him tighter. The tips came tickling another few inches up his leg closer to his knee, making soft squelching sounds.

I reeled back in horror. Skel groaned and seemed to be in a world of pain.

While the plant-creature was occupied with his leg, I tried grabbing it by the stem and uprooting it. No give at all. The roots were tunneled deep. I had no knife. Others of its kind started to bob near and I crabbed back in horror, afraid of getting petal-sucked myself.

A nightmare!

Now the low grunts of the monitors we'd left behind were growing steadily louder to add to the terror.

The copter burst through the trees and came at us at a dead run following the line of the ravine.

The pilot dipped low, fired bullets into the lizard creatures' hides. Half a dozen of them dropped where they stood in sprays of orangish blood.

The herd scattered, panicked at the noise of the vehicle and the bloodshed. The pilot set the craft down on a bed of ferns near the bell-bottoms. A slim figure hopped out of the cabin. She wore a tattered smock, goggles and wielded a long R1 weapon. A woman, as I saw—with shoulder length hair, auburn, of average height and compact frame.

"Get back!" She hurried our way, rifle raised.

I got out of her way. With quick fingers, she brought out a salt-and-pepper shaker from her pouch at the belt. She sprinkled what looked like a pepper-like substance on the petals that grasped Skel's leg. The tough fronds curled and relaxed. The stem retracted like a snake and within moments there came a sharp whistle-like hiss of petals unfolding.

Skel pulled back his leg, scrambled back crab-like to safety.

His left pantleg was shredded, dissolved by plant secretions. Underneath his skin showed raw and red.

He could walk, but limped. His face was pale and his language foul.

"You were lucky," she warned. "A few more hours like that and your leg would have been putty."

I studied her. She seemed unfazed by the plants. The monitors and the danger of enemy ship fire were incidental concerns.

"The victim goes into shock," she explained, "while the plant ingests the decomposing meat."

"Nice," I quipped.

"Just one of the many surprises you'll find in this jungle." She leveled her blaster at us, a curious hybrid of R1 and miniature uzi of an older generation.

"I thought you were firestarters so I had to come and check you out. We've got a lot of those here. You don't look much like firestarters. Who are you?"

"Just McGoo and McGuy," Skel said, grinning through his pain.

"Very funny." She turned her attention back to the purple, bell-bottom flowers. She licked her lips in distaste. "Nasty creatures. I should have left you to them, or the mondrian, those lizards over there. Dalree and the others'll want you for questioning. Maybe even use you as leverage."

"How thoughtful of you," I murmured.

"You've got a smart mouth for someone caught in between a rock and a hard place."

I gave a grinning half bow. At the same time I realized without this lady's timely appearance, Skel and I would have been plant fodder.

She stared with curled lip at the scorched bell flower. "The moral of this story is—"

"Not to go traipsing in the forest-jungles without a friendly guide's experience," Skel finished.

"Something like that. The fact that you yobos survived more than twenty minutes in this place is a miracle in itself. You should be in some Guinness Book of World Records. You'll only find leeches, spiders, snakes, scorpions here."

"How charming."

A male voice crackled through her radio unit strapped at her chest. *"Razen, you there? Where are you?"*

"We're at the ravine, Dalree. No worries. Coordinates 67.45 e3405. Situation is under control. Bring in a team. I'll meet you half way."

"Roger. Bring the hostages to the holdout, Razen. They're our insurance policy."

"Over."

CHRIS TURNER

CHAPTER 16

Our captor was garbed like a vagabond. She wore a ragged rust-colored smock with many holes and scuffs that had seen better days. My eyes took in the sight of her, her lithe contours, cat-quick movements. Everything in sync—no wasted energy. A compact moving machine, fit and efficient. Green eyes wandering toward amber. Slightly tanned face. No-nonsense type. I pegged her at about five years older than me. Concentrated. Hardened by the hostile environment and the choices she'd had to make in life to play GI-Jane in this rough brigade. Capable enough to fly one of these mini copters and rescue fools like Skel and me from the jungle. A heavy good-quality leather belt hung at her hip with other goodies—bowie knife, bear spray, first aid kit and another vial of stuff like the powder she'd sprinkled to save Skel's ass.

He seemed to admire the young rebel. "Nice rig you got," he said. "Turbo rotor?"

"Two stroke, hybrid electric and running on abascus oil."

"Sweet."

"Had it ever since my uncle Rainer died last year. It was a gift."

Skel nodded in understanding. "A bit small for an air vehicle, I think."

She shrugged. "They need to be small to navigate these forests. You can't touch down if you can't squeeze through. No point in being sky-locked with only option to land on the road or the odd clearing like this." She scowled, suddenly aware of Skel's intention. "That's close enough, bucko. Back off, slow and easy. Let me get a better look at you."

"What are you fighting for? Land? Oil?" he asked. "The thrill of the chase?"

"Justice."

An ironic smile touched his lips. "Yeah, the best reason of all."

"Come on, move out. You too—" she motioned her weapon at me. "This is no gab fest or charity picnic. Serious shit's going down. You're smack in the middle of it."

"Geez, you think?" I said.

Her square jaw tightened. "You guys have some nerve firing on a rightful convoy. Meddling in affairs you have no concept of."

"Rightful?" I scoffed. "You fired at us, remember?"

"That wasn't me. That was Belhed, the idiot. Shoot-first-ask-questions-later Belhed in the sea-blue copter. A hothead and a border-line redneck."

"That explains it then," I said. "Let's forgive and forget—" I bowed "—and sit down for afternoon tea."

"Shut up. You've got a smart mouth." Her grip tightened on her R1.

"Not smart to rile the little lady," Skel warned.

"I ain't a little lady." She leveled the muzzle at his chest.

He held up his hands. "Okay. Just joking around."

"Yeah, well, don't."

I studied the copter—it was about twelve feet long, half as wide, with a single four blade rotor and a smaller guide rotor at stern. "You play a risky game flittering around on this hop copter with starships buzzing about ready to blast you to bits."

"Goes with the territory," she said coldly. "I see your starship mangled to shit and it's you two grounded not me with a gun pointed at your heads."

It was not a good lead in for further conversation.

I turned to Skel. "How's the leg?"

"Sore. Feeling better. Thanks for asking."

She scoffed. "It's nothing. Don't be a baby. Just a little chicken scratch."

"So, let's go back there and slip your leg in some tulip mouth then we'll sprinkle some pepper spice for good measure."

She laughed. "You guys are a couple of larks. Could even get to like you—if not for the fact that you shot at Kestrel, nearly killed him—and you took out one of our trucks. Got word from Dalree that Kestrel made it out. Hair singed, some minor burns on his left side."

"Maybe Kestrel shouldn't be driving armored vehicles ready to take out beachside cities then," I said.

Her face colored. Her hazel eyes flashed and I could see that she was ready to either belt me or whack me with that heavy muzzle. But she clammed up. "We'll talk more about this later."

Oddly she left the copter where it stood. With weapon trained at our backs, she prodded us forward down the dense path with no gentle persuasion.

We followed the vague trail while the smoke gathered. Whether animal path, human or both, neither of us could say. The overgrowth was heavy. Skel and I swatted at flies, coughed at the smoke, we cursed, stumbled on roots. At times I thought to hear a hostile rustle in the hanging branches. But Razen was a capable markswoman and she brought the mondrian down that lurked in the leaves. We heard the creature crash through the brake with a dull thud.

"I'll get Kal to come back and fry that one up," she said proudly.

I licked my lips, the sardonic part of me feigning hunger for some mondrian. By the look of Skel's brooding and darting eyes, I divined that he was contemplating a plan to storm her while her gun was lifted but I shook my head and showed the whites of my eyes. She was too fast. She followed at a safe distance a yard or two behind us. It'd be suicide for the two of us to try anything.

I sighed, riddled with frustration. Just sit back and enjoy the ride, Ruskie. Life's an adventure.

I hated these dumb little voices that whispered sermons in my head.

The mangalorn were a lot like banyans. All sprawl, bunches of snaky, knobby branches, gnarled twisted trunks. She saw where I was looking and waved a hand at a massive trunk. "This forest is a thousand years old. That it's burning to the ground farther east of us is a sick tragedy. Like Cyr coming in and buying up all the forests and pushing us into his underwater cities. A ridiculous insult to the creator and her people. Damn this smoke." She batted a hand in front of her nose.

Little did I see what the wildfires had to do with these rebels attacking Aqua Rex, but whatever. I just held my tongue.

We met up with six charcoal-cheeked marines dressed in camoed fatigues and R1 rifles slung over their shoulders. Tough-looking bastards with day stubble or full beards and longish, shoulder-length hair. They wore black army-grade boots. All wore flat-brimmed khaki hats.

Dalree, the commander of the outfit, flicked his eyes over us. He was a lank-limbed, lean-jawed stocky man with sun-browned hands. He made an instant appraisal. "Couple of new young recruits of friend Cyr, I don't doubt. I don't know where you boys got the heroic idea and the fancy ships, but you picked the wrong people to mess with."

Skel shrugged. "You win some, lose some."

"See, Dalree," Razen hissed. "This is what I've been dealing with ever since I picked up these two. Gets your blood up and your mind spinning."

"Yeah, well maybe not for long. They're just a couple of hothead punks itching to get a bullet in the back." He waved her off and she went trudging off to fetch the copter while Dalree and his commandos bunted us along.

CHAPTER 17

While keeping to the cover of the bush, we passed the charred wreckage of the half-track we'd blasted. The vehicle was on its side slumped in the ditch. One of its back tracks was in the air, the other dug deep into the soft soil.

The rest of the trucks were nowhere in sight. Only a wasteland of shattered trunks and smoking brush along the roadside. I pieced together a likely scenario: the XT6 firing roughshod on the half-tracks in search of us and the lost Vargon. But the trucks had beetled up ahead under cover of the trees making it impossible to flush them out without tearing down half the forest for 50 miles.

Turns out the rest of the convoy had moved about three miles farther up the road where the tree cover was so thick that their upper branches arched completely over the roadway screening all of us from view. Convenient and clever.

From what I remembered, this heavy tree cover persisted for many miles, so it would not be easy for Krake to pinpoint our location.

We came to the first of the armored vehicles, well off the road on a 45 degree angle in the ditch. The others were in a vague crescent-shaped formation on both sides of the road. One of the trucks looked like a fuel carrier. More figures emerged from their vehicles and peered at us with ever-rising unfriendly looks.

One drifted over and lifted an accusing hand. "We should plug these flyboys with lead like we did those last marines of Cyr's moving in to take us out."

Dalree looked on stonily, stroking his black beard. The buzz of Razen's copter grew as she blitzed over our heads and landed amid the straggling semi-circle of half-tracks.

My eyes were drawn to the deadly muzzle of the first uptilted howitzer mounted on the nearest half-track. Rocket missiles could be fired from such a cannon. The riveted armored plates gave ample protection.

I was sick of all this silence and the sullen glares and could hold it in no longer. "Murdering marines a pastime of yours?"

Dalree turned on me with smoke-colored eyes. "If you're talking about those quasi-human thugs of Cyr's, it was them who drew the first blood. You did too. Yes, we slaughtered those fools. But nothing they didn't deserve. You'd strike back too if an invading army came to destroy your way of life."

I pointed to the PA, People's Army Freedom Fighters Liberation Group logo written in faint letters on the back of one of the gray-green armored vehicles. "Sabotage part of your freedom-fighting agenda?"

Dalree grumbled out what must have been an oath. "That's what your belief is, hotshot, what your employers'd have you believe?"

"Sure, why not?"

"It's all bullshit, boy. You've been listening to too many fairy stories written by propagandists. You don't know anything about anything."

"I say we should cut these bangers' throats," said a greasy thug with blue bandanna and crooked teeth. He grabbed me and slung a wicked bowie knife near my throat. "Where there's one, there's more."

Dalree interceded and grabbed the man's wrist. "Hold off, Belly. We're not butchers or wanton murderers here. Just trying to get some justice."

Belhed pulled his arm back, snarling. His weapon was clutched tighter, within striking distance of my jugular vein. "Call us what you will, O hallowed leader," he grumbled, "but war is war. It means a lot of killing which you're not going to pretty over with jabber."

Razen had glided in between us. She had her back to me. Belhed backed down, obviously respecting her enough not about to slit her. "Blood spilled yes, Belhed, but unnecessary blood spilled is on our consciences. You want to stoop to their level?"

He grunted out an oath.

There were some grumbles of approval, and so Belhed was not without his sympathizers. I looked about grimly. It was a raw, bad mix of people, and we were in the middle of it. I opened my mouth to speak, but shut it, my spirits descending into a sullen gloom.

"So what's the truth here?" asked Skel.

"You don't know it?" grumbled Dalree. "That the fires are made my man and that Cyr's feeding you a bunch of frontier-expansionist BS?"

A sudden sinking feeling hit my gut.

"Never thought of that, did you?"

The man's conviction was like iron. Had we lashed out against the wrong enemy? I suddenly remembered Cyr's words spoken back at Aqua Rex: about the revolutionary ideas of Gy-ar's to accelerate his enterprise. In an instant I knew that we'd been played. I felt less and less content about my firing on that half track from the air and nearly killing the man. An asinine act, or misguided murder? How much blood had been spilled in the countless wars fought through the ages where each side righteously thought it was fighting against an evil oppressor?

"You have proof of this?" Skel asked.

Dalree ignored him. He motioned. "Radio up to the big ship, Kal. Tell them to hold off their attack on us, or their friends die."

I felt some relief. They weren't going to kill us—at least not immediately, and there was some hope they'd turn us over to Krake rather than face a standoff. I turned my attention to the armored vehicles.

The half-tracks were souped up with a snowplow-like attachment for driving through thick brush and clearing mounds of earth. At the end of each blade, I saw wicked serrated-tooth, chainsaw-like attachments for cutting through fallen logs and felling trees.

"Looks as if you're well equipped," Skel said with a satirical edge.

"When trunks are too close, we can't make it through," one the drivers said. "But for the most part, the mangalorns are nicely spaced apart. They fan their boughs out like willows, forces them to make room for each other."

I saw that the trucks, even with their high clearance, were squat and low enough to slip under sprawling boughs.

I could hear the roar of Krake's ship hovering nearby still looking for us. Good. But they could still not see us through the tree cover and where they'd cleverly hidden their half-tracks under the canopy arched cathedral-like over the road.

The winds had taken an unfortunate turn. Smoke circled and had our eyes stinging. Our throats were raw. Bad enough that some of the liberation army were wearing masks. Big, complicated, snorkel-like jobs with black hoses running to air tanks on their backs, as if they were fighting some mustard-gas war.

Skel jerked a thumb. "You think you're winning this tear gas battle with those?"

"No time for jokes, friend," Dalree said coldly. "This is war. People die. Justice is as far away as Solas." He touched finger to chest, brow and pointed to the moon, which sat somewhere up there past the smoke and the tree cover.

Skel only grunted.

"Kestrel's not looking too good. There he is," one of the drivers growled. "Doesn't look much like a 'kestrel' anymore."

It was true. I saw the bald-headed man limp out from behind one of the half-tracks. The one I'd fired on. His hair was singed off, face fire-blackened, an arm hung in a heavy white bandage. My head dropped in guilt.

I knew Makala had been given orders to make contact with Cyr every few hours and provide updates. Our mission's standing orders were to knock out the rebels who'd destroyed the last batch of marines using any means possible. I wondered how that was faring as Krake rode around the skies, impotent as he was. I knew he would never abandon Skel, but what could he and the crew do? Blast whole swathes of the forest, section by section, until they found us? Even now a thunderous crack boomed half a mile distant, smashing trees and sizzling brush.

CHRIS TURNER

CHAPTER 18

The agreed-upon hand-off point was farther south where the dirt road widened and some brush had been cleared at a T-junction. A small ramshackle wooden rest area lay tucked to the side by an artesian well. Enough room for Krake's ship to land, maybe squash a few trees and possibly part of the rest house. No big deal. The T-branch wound straight down to the eastern shores where the sea wrapped its aquamarine fingers around the cape which connected to the beachhead many miles away.

The XT6's engines grew louder and her massive bulk set down in the middle of the road. Smoke rose from her armored plates where she had caught rocket fire. Her forward guns swiveled on the ready. She looked like a big angry black sphinx.

Dalree, Razen and five others marched us out to the parked ship where Krake, Areth and Makala had disembarked to fetch us. Blasters hung at their hips. The ship's guns swiveled our way.

Areth came running over to give me a rib-squeezing hug. "You're alive! We thought you were dead."

"Not just yet, thankfully."

Skel arched his brows. "Don't I get a hug too?"

She looked at him and his raw-red leg, tattered pantleg and somewhat grinning, leering look. "No."

"Okay." He shrugged, unfazed.

Areth put a hand to her mouth, squelching a cough. "Let's get out of this smoke."

"Nowhere to run, love," said the jeering man named Toemlin. "Your own people fire these woods to blow smoke over the populated areas and poison the Yesmian people. The fire and smoke kill animals, uproot our way of life."

"Why would they do that?" Areth scoffed.

"To corral all the people like lemmings in the underwater cities— safe from fires, and other 'disasters'."

Skel frowned. "You have proof of this, or is it just some fiction you've cooked up to justify your war games?"

Dalree bared his teeth. He motioned to one of the commandos. "Go on, fetch the prisoner, Iwan."

One of the Yesmians, a broad-chested man with wiry mustache and R1 rifle slung over his back, strode over to one of the half-tracks and came out hauling a quivering prisoner. His arms were lashed behind his back. The man was an Aquor with a military cut and lank black sideburns.

I blinked. So, the Yesmians hadn't killed all the marines. The man had bloodshot eyes, blackened around the rims, a bruised left cheek. His blue and mauve uniform was tattered and soiled and ripped in many places. His eyes were sunken pits. He looked as sullen and withdrawn as a half drowned rat.

Makala seemed to recognize the man and she started with a startled grunt.

"Our scouts found him skulking around the new front line of the fire," said Dalree. "East of the river. I saw him myself crouched on his knees with a fireproof bag, working his fingers, spreading liquid at the base of one of the giant mangalorns. His bag was an arsonist's kit if I ever saw one. Lighter fluid, combustibles, torch. Two of his henchmen got away. Fortunately this one didn't. Go on, tell them, scum," he sneered, kicking the man in the shins. "Did you light the fires?"

At first the prisoner was reluctant to speak, but then, seeing all the glowering hostile eyes around him, he spoke in a low, thick voice, "I lit them. True."

"Why?"

"You already know the answer, why ask?"

"When?"

"About eight days ago."

"Where are your henchmen?"

"Dunno. Disappeared." The man shrugged.

"To where?"

"Into the forest somewhere. We were supposed to go far away and show no evidence of our work."

Dalree gave an angry grunt. "We would have killed you, scum, but you were too valuable for our campaign of truth and as a proof of misinformation. Who hired you?"

The man hesitated. Dalree gave a terse nod at Iwan and the driver lumbered over and slapped the man hard across the face.

The Aquor licked his bleeding lip. Makala started forward again but a thicket of rifles trained on her torso. She stopped in midstep, like a deer in the headlights, unsure of what to do.

"Who commissioned you?" Dalree snapped.

The prisoner scowled and glared at all of us. "I don't know. No one! No one that we knew anyway. We were told by some anonymous source through our ear communicators. To slip away from the group, light the trees while our recon mission was in full swing. On pain of death we were told to do this without the notice of our team leaders, Savas and Makala."

"How could this 'source' get you to do all that?"

The prisoner scowled again.

"Answer the question, you twatwad!"

"The voice that spoke to us was garbled to avoid recognition—it told us our families would die horrible deaths—if we didn't do as we were told."

Dalree turned to Makala. "And you know this man?"

She gave a slow nod. "He's Axar. One of our marine corp. I

helped train him in the field."

"Did you know he was an infiltrator?"

She took a long time before answering. "No."

The gun muzzles dipped.

"There you have it." Dalree slumped back, looking drained.

There was no way this man Axar was lying. I could tell by the way his hunched body sagged, his frank face, his sullen, defeated look. I scrutinized him with a mixture of pity and loathing. I glimpsed the fuzzy finger's width patch of brown, thin cut gills under the ears and the lank brown hair. He faced death at the hands of these Yesmian vigilantes. The only thing keeping him alive was the fact that he was their leverage to convince others that their mission was just.

Skel chewed on his lip. His face was grim.

Makala showed a sullen defiance. She could not bear to look at the prisoner. Nor he, her.

I felt a surge of anger ripple through my body. "These people are bastards. If this is true, Dalree, they are the worst possible scum."

"You got that right," Dalree said. "I've hated these industrialists all my life. They've forced us away from our roots more and more. Cut down our trees. Zoned us out of our own forests."

Skel nodded agreement. "Yeah, sign of the times. I've seen it on other worlds. Just like the barbarians of old. The marauders used to torch the lands they'd conquered to stop the peasants from growing grain and feeding themselves or getting back on their feet. To 'quell' rebellion. You do any research on the dark truths of Old Earth, you'll see the old climate change religionists used the same technique with their billions of wealth to torch whole swathes of forests. They'd hire teams of agents to set fire to the great forests bordering the cities, called them 'wildfires' caused by 'global warming'. Tried to sell their zombie cartoon fantasy and sell their slavery and slave grids to all the people of Old Earth."

"Yeah, and what happened?"

"Most fell for it. They cheered and chanted for their own enslavement, confined to smart cities and climate lockdowns. But there were those who saw through the hoax. The lies of the globalists and the cultists. They resisted. They created 'dome' communities of their own and oral traditions to teach their kids the old ways and how to respect nature."

"Amen," said Areth. "But how did the people figure it out?"

Skel shrugged. "Some of the arsonists were caught. The people who were in the know tortured them to get the truth out of them. No different than your friend Axar here. All their tricks didn't work. In the long run the people figured it out and set the globalists back a century."

"But this fire thing," I said, "how do they keep it all together?"

"They control the weather, to pave the way and grease the wheels for their land, sea and air terror, Kip."

"Yeah, and how do they do that?" I said with rising skepticism.

"Weather stations. Power stations. They create artificial clouds, dump the sky with nanoparticles. Use their high frequency EMF waves on ground to move and manipulate the nano-rich clouds over certain areas to burst their loads or to induce floods. Or the opposite, create dry areas that get only sun."

I rubbed my chin, pondering over the concepts Skel'd shared that I'd never heard before.

"They use radar stations to stop rain and keep the winds blowing smoke over the cities."

Dalree nodded grimly. "There are weather radar stations north and east of here. The winds have been slack for the past three weeks even though the prevailing winds are always from the west. We've had more strong winds from the east than normal for this time of year."

"Rain?"

"None."

"Some things never change," Skel sighed. "Even in a few centuries."

"I find this all disgusting," I said.

"Get used to it, Kip, it's a big bad world out there."

"It's Rusco."

"I forget. Right."

"Can we put these fires out?" Areth asked in a tremulous voice.

Krake squinted up into the sun that struggled through the smoky haze. "Not unless we can rig a big ship to take boatloads of water and dump it over the trees."

Skel rubbed his chin. "The idea's maybe just crazy enough to work."

"How?" asked Dalree with sudden incredulity.

I shrugged. "We could maybe run a hose through that sealed vent in the XT6. Pump seawater into the hold, fill her to the brim."

"Why seawater? You can get it from the river," Razen said.

Dalree nodded. "The river widens about 10 miles north of here. Plenty big enough for your ship."

Whoever had started the fires had started them on the eastern strip of Yesma, a thin wedge between the Umena river valley and the eastern coast. Why? So that the scumbags could contain it? In their infinite forethought they'd forgotten about the ford at Dryback where the river narrowed to mere sandbanks and where treetops from the opposing giants on either shore almost touched.

"I'd guess them at about 20 feet apart," said Toemlin. "Sparks and cinders can fly in strong gusts, catch on the dry leaves to the west. If those flames cross the Umena—" his face turned ashen "—all of upper Yesma will be lost."

"We have to stop it," said Skel.

"Where do we start?"

"With the XT6. You up for it, Krake?"

"You betcha." He gave a crinkle-faced grin.

There was always the chance of Cyr's catching wind of our movements by spy satellite or getting suspicious of our lack of activity dealing with the Yesmians, but that was a risk we were prepared to take.

We flew to a place 10 miles downstream where the river widened to 100 feet and the channel was deep enough to draw sufficient water into the XT6. When we got to the Umena, I knew even before we started up the pumps, it would take too long to fill the hold, even reversing the bilge. I suggested something else.

"Try backing the craft up into the shallow water. Open the cargo doors full out and let the water gush in. We can use the door's hydraulics to shut her tight when we're full or almost full."

Krake rubbed his jaw. "It's a crazy idea. But I like it, Kip."

We tried. Though the rear thrusters at first balked at the soaking, we used the midships' impulse boosters to keep us afloat.

It worked like a charm.

We were able to load tons of water into the hold and get the ship into the sky in good time and over the Yesmian danger areas. 50 tons of water a pop! Fly low over the crackling branches, one man stays on bridge to control the cargo door. Open it ever a crack and let gushing water sheet down while the XT6 flies in a direct line across the hot spot. The classic water bomber. The same procedure repeated a 100 times: Drop the load over the danger area then back again for more water.

One ship over a hundred trips over a period of two days.

Cyr kept trying to contact us, demanding an update. But I convinced Makala to stay dark until we had dealt with the fire. To this she reluctantly agreed. Only because she'd felt complicit training Axar.

We worked in shifts. Skel, myself and Arcth on days. Krake, Lisse and the others on nights while Razen and Dalree pitched in on both teams. The night team used the ship's powerful search lamps to illuminate the water. The night winds had been favorable. Little to none. By the end of 48 hours we were all soot-covered, limp, exhausted, but we put out those destructive fires. Infiltrators, saboteurs be damned!

Dalree was overwhelmed that the fires at the choke point were quenched. He stroked his thinning hair with trembling excitement. "I'd not have thought it possible." He shook each of our hands in genuine gratitude and admiration. "This calls for a celebration."

We'd won over the hearts of the Yesmians, a grim tough crew. This last act of good will had cemented our friendship. It mended the feud that would have ended up in bloodshed on both sides, Cyr's and the Yesmians.

"How about some campfire chow and a friendly game of touchball?" one of the Yesmian drivers called out.

There were 'hear hear's'. The Yesmians set to frying up some fresh mondrian and cracking out crocks of bitter mangalorn ale.

We shrugged and tucked in, happy to be waited on.

A bonfire was soon crackling with healthy fervor alongside the half-tracks. Before long I caught the waft of roasted mondrian which I didn't care for. "Don't you think we've had enough smoke already?"

"We have to eat," said Dalree, spreading his palms.

"Knock yourself out." I firmed my lip and trudged off to grab some snack packs from the XT6 while the others ate.

CHAPTER 19

The road was an ideal place for a playing field of touchball, a game akin to the ancient sport of rugby and tackle football. Five or six to a side. No padding. Only the soft dirt and some skillful rolls a meager cushion for the harder take downs. I gleaned that the game tended toward the rough. Why wouldn't it, given the nature of these bushwhackers? But then again, we were in rough times.

The trucks had moved up to an out-of-the-way section of road where the shoulders were naturally cleared of brush, so we got another 20 or more yards of play.

It was Team XT6 against the Yesmians.

Dalree stood in the center field, tossing the ball from hand to hand. His face was carved in a mold of statuesque competitiveness. The ball, a lizard-hide special, green-brown, shaped like an olive, had hard pointy ends.

Makala opted to be on the Yesmian side which at first puzzled me. It became clearer why as the game progressed. Razen offered to join our team to counterbalance. So it was outlanders versus Yesmians. Aqua Rex versus the locals.

After a while Areth warmed to the idea of joining in the game. At first she was reluctant. Tackling didn't seem very lady-like play. The Yesmians played coed. It was all the same to them.

I played quarterback. I got our team in a scrum, with our heads tucked in, arms wrapped around shoulders and I directed my words at Areth.

"I'll fake out Fatso, the one to the left with the harelip—I think his name is Goble, for now let's call him Gobbler. You deke in to the side, Areth, and wait for my pass. They won't expect me to throw it to you being new to the game. Krake—the rest of you—stick to Skel like glue and make them think he's the one I'm going to pass to. Watch out for Makala. She's a terror, a sneaky, fast bitch who likes to pounce on anyone who has a ball."

"I know, Rusco. I saw the play," Areth said.

"Good. Just saying. Any questions?"

"When do I get to be quarterback?" Skel asked.

"When I say so."

Someone blew a whistle and bodies on the field started moving. I stepped back out of the way of any interference while I let Krake and Skel do the heavy lifting. They were not half bad at bulling their way through the shoulders of the others.

Areth was making for the far left under the low branches just as I told her. I laid my arm back and threw a long bomb improbably to left field. She caught it as the ball sneaked in between holes in the tree foliage and to her credit, she nipped up in the air and snagged it with both hands. She tucked it into her belly and ran like the wind toward the end line, but Makala, who was everywhere at once, reached out a monkey arm and tackled her roughly to the ground. She butterflied her body on top of Areth's and groped her nethers indiscriminately. It was not pretty. Makala was all over the slimmer woman, hands feeling her up, knees pincering her in a body lock for long moments with grunts and curses.

"Get off me, you stupid bitch!" Areth kneed her off and crabbed back finally to her feet.

Makala rose, smirking, her breath slightly labored and her face flushed. She sauntered away, play-kicked the ball to her teammates.

I had to laugh.

A mistake. Areth marched over to me and laid a good one on the side of my head. "How's that for funny?"

There were sniggers among the Yesmian team while Razen frowned. "You always have such rude people on your team?"

"Not ordinarily," I said dryly.

When it came time to scrum again, Areth shafted me a look of daggers. She refused to speak to me. In fact, she walked off in a huff. Razen said in a low voice, "Pass me that ball next time, Rusco. Let that freak of an Aquor try something fancy and she'll get what's coming to her."

"Okay, knock yourself out, Raz," I said with amusement. "It's all yours. Skel. You run some interference for the lady, will you?"

He saluted me with a '10-4' and a know-all grin which I didn't appreciate, because well, Skel, was Skel.

The opposing teams faced each other. Each in his half crouches on the rude playing field. Someone grunted, "Hup 1, 2, 3..." Something like that.

I looked into the faces of the Yesmians—cool, serious, mean: tow-headed Dalree, our resident bully-boy Belhed, and our all favorite groper, Makala-turned-Yesmian.

What a crew.

The opposing team was always tackling Skel, so I faked a pass to him early on. He deked in between their defensive lines, grinning to himself. It confused the opponents, so whatever he was doing, it was working. I threw the lizard-ball low and fast. Razen leaped up like a fish. She caught it while booting up the right sideline. Right on cue, Makala was there in her face, ready to get another freebie in with an attractive young female.

The way I figured it, whatever potions they pumped into her or operations they'd done to give her those gills and whatever else, seemed to incite the fire in her blood. It got her stoked up during full contact sports. It gave her a bad case of the gropy-feelies. Maybe it was the only way she could release her tension? Her sexual fantasies? Who knew? Engaging in roughhousing as prepubescent teens do was chiefly fun and games. Maybe not so much on a touchball field. It was a strange world. It could also explain why Makala was so turned on about doing marine maneuvers up the beach with the other Aquor.

Whatever it was, she was all over Razen. Worse than Areth, likely emboldened by her last bout of success.

But Razen was anything but willing or slow and not without tactics. She wriggled out of the tall Aquor's grip and made a beeline for the end line with the ball.

That's all of the drama I caught for the moment.

Belhed had got a bee in his bonnet. Maybe my long bombs had irritated him? More likely he was still raw from his earlier failed attempt at cutting me up with his favorite bowie knife so he decided to sack me even though the ball was in the air.

"Hey, what the hell are you doing, buddy?" I yelled. Either way, it was his mistake.

I backpedaled, taking some of the momentum out of his knuckles coming in at my face and his arm reaching around my head. When the first hand tried to curl around my neck, I grabbed his arm and twisted it at the elbow, prompting a grunt of pain. I snapped him over my shoulder before he could get me in a head lock. He landed with a thud. He came up winded, but bouncing on both feet. He came after me, all teeth-flashing, losing all sense of pretense. There ensued a vicious wrestling match which I don't want to waste many words on. Normally a guy like Belly-boy would get the upper hand on a lean guy like me in a wrassle. He was heavier, meatier and more brutal, but the events of the past had stoked my rage and I was sick and tired of being pushed around, chased in ships by murderous Skurgs, shot down by RPGs, by cocky rebels and now bullied. This was supposed to be a friendly game of touchball. The inner Jet Rusco showed its fangs, a very violent Hyde and don't-screw-with-me character.

Suffice it say that Belhed limped away from that field with several aches and bruises and a torn ear and an near-shut eye that would be blackened before the night was up.

I came out of the scuffle to rise to my full height and catch the last of the action with Razen and Makala.

Makala had caught up to her again and tackled Razen's legs. Now her long snaky arms were moving up toward Razen's crotch.

Razen was belly and face first in the red dirt and didn't look to be in a winner's position. I winced as Makala's fingers lay into her private areas, but Razen wormed a leg out of the grip and hoofed Makala in the chops. Makala gave a low yowl like a tomcat. She rolled over, dazed, licking her bloodied mouth.

With a last burst of effort, Razen scrambled to her feet, belted toward the zero yard line, ball tucked at her gut.

She slammed the ball on the ground and let out a wild cheer.

Dalree came gamboling over to mime a timeout signal. "Just a game, folks, just a game."

The score was seven zip and the game was called off before more violence could ensue. Belhed limped away and Makala tucked tail.

What a ride. It didn't bother me much to see this game end as I think I'd had enough excitement for the day.

Skel and I shared drinks with Dalree and as Skel became increasingly drunker, Areth and Razen sauntered off to engage in girl talk.

Dalree flashed me an intense look and tipped his glass of ale toward me. "There is still the issue of Cyr."

"Hold off your aggressions, Dalree. We'll confront Cyr about the fires, as soon as we can. If he's guilty of the fires, we'll get him to lay off his tree-torching and squeezing people into acceptance of the underwater city. I'm sure others, not just him, are behind this."

Dalree stared at me as if I were speaking the language of crows. "You think you're going to do all that?" He gave an indifferent shrug. "And if you don't communicate with us again, or you fail in your 'mission'?"

"Then you have every right to destroy Cyr or anyone who threatens your livelihood."

Dalree clapped me on the back. "Now we are on the same page, Jet Rusco! I like you. Let's shake on it."

And so we did.

After a time Areth returned glowing, her eyes bright, her face flushed. "Rusco, that woman is amazing. You wouldn't believe what these people are doing. Projects for water irrigation, creating holistic communities, nature education groups for kids, much, much more."

I was only half listening. I watched Razen drift over to sit by Makala. Curious, I drifted over to eavesdrop.

"Look, I'm sorry I hoofed you during the game," Razen said ruefully. "It wasn't a very lady-like or sportsman-thing to do."

Makala just shrugged.

"Friends?" Razen reached out a hand.

Makala took the hand with only a slight hesitation. Her gaze dropped. "Sometimes, I don't know what comes over me. I end up acting inappropriately."

"It's alright. We are what we are."

My ears perked. I liked end-well stories and it was the most words I'd heard Makala say.

Razen smiled and beamed. "The guys over here wish you were part of our outfit permanently. You'd make a hell of a touchball player."

Makala gave a quiet chuckle. "And that's a strong leg you have too, Razen. Some good squirming to get out from underneath me. Even the guys in my marine unit can't do it."

Razen grinned.

So, there was a real person under that ice queen veneer of Makala's and not just some NPC robot.

I thought to test the waters. "You happy you joined Cyr's outfit?"

Makala shrugged. "I could find worse places to be."

"You don't appear to have a girlfriend, but there seems to be ample pickings among the Aquor."

She stared at me with glassy-eyed intensity for some time. "I've always been a lanky girl with too much spunk and energy for her own good. In early years more feminine than I am now. Between you and me, Rusco, I was conned. I was continually told I was supposed to be a man—then encouraged to take a bunch of injections and drugs. Now I don't believe in that anymore. I don't know what I am. It's all confusing. I harbor a resentment at how I was manipulated, but then again, it was my own choice."

"You harbor any resentment against Cyr? For keeping you in his corps and rewarding you for being what you are, a GI Jane with gills?"

Her shoulders lifted in a resentful shrug. "I think of him as a father figure. He took me in, made me his favorite Aquor."

"Commissioned to fight his wars?"

She shrugged.

I couldn't see how in any way that could be good, but it was her trip. I was sorry I'd made fun of her all the same. Victims like her were in all of us. Somewhere shoved deep under the carpet. Forgotten like the dusty statistics in an institute's library or some computer database. Human beings at the core were wholesome, if at times judgmental. I had thought of her as a type of sterile robot, willing to go to any length of transgenderism. It was easy to lose sight of the bigger picture, to not see the forest for the trees. We're quick to target people who are different than us.

Skel sauntered over to tip me a nod and lay a comradely hand on Razen's shoulder. "If you ever want to upgrade, Razen, say up your mission goals, feel free to look me up. Maybe you'll start doing some more hardcore freedom fighting work, like standing up to Skurgs and sending them to hell. You're welcome to join our vigilante movement. We're a small outfit, but have lots of perks and could use a few more courageous hands like you."

"Thanks for the offer." She smiled. "I'll consider it. As you can see, Skel—the boys and I have our hands full over here fighting guys like Cyr. Our independence and way of life still hangs on a thread."

"I understand. True."

It was getting dark. Most of the Yesmians had wandered off back to their vehicles for private parties. The air mercifully was clearer of smoke. We could actually see the pinpricks of stars at times. Skel sighed and took me aside, "We should get going, bro, give old Cyr the benefit of a doubt. Sounds as if, according to the Aquor prisoner's testimony, that he had no knowledge of the arson or that he'd been infiltrated."

I gave it a thoughtful nod. "I feel the Aquor was telling the truth. We'll have to sit down with Cyr and confront him at one time or other. Not going to be easy, Skel."

"Not liking it, Kippie." He shook his head. "We're treading in dangerous waters."

"And what do you think this whole expedition's been? Flying into enemy RPGs? Taken prisoner? Coming from you, who wants to leap into a hornets' nest of Skurgs every five minutes?"

Skel laughed then pointed a pistol-like finger. "You make a good point, buddy. Let's pack up and get this over with. We'll face down Cyr soon as we get to Aquatown."

CHAPTER 20

Skel and I armed ourselves with R1's from Krake's arsenal. But first we doffed our shredded rags and bathed. The comforts and security of the XT6 were only too welcome. We shaved and grabbed fresh leathers out of Krake's lockers.

The hour was nearing dawn. In the indigo gloom turning pale orange with the rising of Oranthe's sun, we made the dreaded journey back to the seacoast.

The XT6 landed on the pad at the beachhead. With some leeriness, Skel, Areth, Makala and I traipsed out on the tarmac. Oddly Cyr was waiting for us. Remus too with his grim face and arms-crossed-on-chest attitude, conversing in low tones with Cyr. Cyr's eyes narrowed on us with murderous intent.

"It's about time. I was about to fly in there myself on Narwhal." He gave us his most intimidating frown. "What the hell have you been up to? Playing tiddlywinks? Where's your ship, Vargon?"

"Destroyed," Skel said.

"And you lived?" He noticed our beat up looks for the first time, also our cuts and bruises.

"We're here, aren't we?"

"What of the Yesmians?"

"Contained...For now."

"And my marines?"

Skel studied his fingernail. "Slaughtered, as you suspected."

153

Cyr bottled his anger. His fist balled. "And why didn't I hear back from you for two days? Not one return communication."

Skel looked away.

Cyr turned his inimical glare toward Makala. "And you too. Just as guilty."

Her lips pursed. I saw her eyes trained straight ahead, unfocused. It looked as if Makala warred with her allegiance to Cyr and the direct evidence she'd seen with her own eyes of his complicity in the fires and the dark truths behind Aqua Rex.

Cyr growled, "Are you a bunch of mutes then? Speak!"

"We put out the fires," Skel said sullenly.

"You what?"

Remus snarled, "I told you not to trust them, Cyr."

"Shut up, Remus. I'll hear the full story from the horses' mouths."

Skel's lips curled in an imp's grin. "We put out the fires, admiral. The worst of them. The locals tanked my ship, but they weren't as menacing as we were told and we made peace with them. Rusco and I stopped their advance north, softened the force of their anger which was all the time those stupid fires."

Cyr's fists clenched. His dull nails dug into meaty palms.

"Isn't that what you hired us to do, admiral?" I asked facetiously.

Cyr's bearish face creased in a ruddy frown. "Damn it. You are required to check in with me before truckling off and doing such things."

Skel bristled. "You hired us to do a job, admiral. We did it. What's this stuff about treating us like kiddies? You should be giving us a medal for what we did back there. Not quibbling over what we did and didn't do. We're not a bunch of two-year-olds to be held by Daddy's hand."

A dangerous flush colored Cyr's brawny features. He seemed on the brink of an explosive anger but he bridled it. I had to admire the man for his composure. He could squash Skel and me like a bug. But in his moment of power he chose not to. Why? Was he aiming for higher hanging fruits?

"Rusco, walk with me," he said curtly. With brisk strides he headed for the ion guns which stood protecting the gorge. I followed him. What else could I do?

He called back in a gruff voice, "Remus, fetch Fustas. Bring him to the Comb."

"Aye, aye." The captain's face crinkled in a grin of savage relish.

I did not like Remus's grin or the waves of heat emanating from 'admiral' Cyr. I did not want to be in the clutch of whatever he was radiating. But dammit, there was too much at stake here! Too much murkiness, too much skulduggery. I wanted answers.

"This fiasco," Cyr began, "is bordering on insubordination. I want the truth from you. But first I want to show you what happens to individuals who defy my orders and sneak around behind my back."

He shafted me a menacing glare and held up a hand before I opened my mouth to speak. "Before you say anything, Rusco, you have to see something. The only thing keeping you out of serious doggie-do is that no damage came to Aqua Rex. My surveillance sat shows no evidence of further aggressions by the Yesmians or trucks advancing into our sector. Had it been the opposite..." He let that thought dangle in the air.

He strode briskly up the gorge, his knee-boots kicking up sand as he walked. Not much activity at this hour. A few cloaked military figures, all Aquor, traipsing up the gorge on some errand, garbed and cloaked in trenchcoats to ward off the morning chill. The faint daylight streamed down desultorily. The sand was a mix of dark sediment and a coarse grain of broken shells.

We passed two warehouses where many heavy machines sat parked inside, doubtless used to haul building supplies stacked at the sides.

Cyr led me past these warehouses to an iron-riveted door carved into the face of the cliff. It was almost flush to the edge of the last warehouse.

With a heavy key he drew from his waist belt, he unlocked the door, screwing it in with an unusual relish, then yanking wide the door. A gush of musty vapors poured forth, causing my nose to wrinkle.

"Come. Don't be timid."

I licked my lips. Cyr flicked out a blaster when I hesitated. He motioned to somewhere behind me. Before I could lay hand on my own weapon, a noiseless figure crept up behind me and snatched the blaster out of my belt loop.

"My assistant, Fustas," Cyr said pleasantly. "A caretaker who manages this section for me."

Fustas motioned me inside with my blaster. "Move it." He took the lead, Cyr taking up the rear.

Fustas led me down a curious stone stair. A safe house? A dungeon of sorts? Each step took us to murkier depths. The stone was smooth, rounded, like the surrounding walls. The steps were wide and of varied lengths, as if molded by natural processes and the passing of many feet. Dim bulbs cast a dubious glow over the dank stone.

The place was extensive. I could feel in those gentle drafts coming from deeper within, an earthy odor of sea, brine and something else.

"What is this place?" I hissed with wonder.

"An ancient stronghold."

"Whose?"

"Creatures long before our time. I discovered these catacombs while looking for places to start building Aqua Rex."

I gave a troubled frown.

"Miles of these tunnels were dug beneath the bluffs. An archaeologist's wet dream. Centuries ago, the water rose higher. Seawater came right up this gorge. The beings who lived here used this as a hideaway. A repository, if you like. For their treasures, as they developed their technology. But that story is for another time. It is not why we are here."

"So why are we here then?" I chipped in gruffly.

"These beings...they were as mysterious, Jet Rusco, as they were incredible."

"I appreciate the history lesson, Cyr, but do I really need—"

He stopped me with a raised hand. "Inside." He was no more the fatherly documentarist or friendly narrator.

Fustas motioned me into a shell-shaped chamber. It was of unknown age and origin, similar to the other shadow-welled depressions scalloped along the way.

We were in a cubbyhole deep under the gorge's floor. Cyr's hand settled on an invisible switch. A ceiling lamp lit and bathed the small space in a murky glow. Off to the side hung an ancient circuitboard or power box from a wall. It had been long corroded and the casing was stripped to reveal spiral-helix components and other stuff that did not look like anything human-made. Hourglass-shaped vacuum tubes, inverted solenoids, crystalline relays, weird-ass inductors. Several tubes and wires ran to various areas in the ceiling and along the wall. The place was altogether creepy, with an otherworldly vibe, rendered creepier by the murky atmosphere and the molder, must and strange moaning cry that suddenly emanated from deeper within.

My head twisted around. Cyr prodded me on with the butt of the gun.

What remained of the Skurg renegade strapped to the chair bolted to the floor was not pleasant. A figure hardly deserving to be labeled a living creature, an emaciated wretch stripped to the waist amid the tubing in the center of the chamber. Ugly welts and lacerations covered his pale body. Only the feet and face were burned a dark brown, from exposure to the sun amid arid environments where he had been stationed. Skurgs, I had learned from experience, favored the desert, which allowed them anonymity and free rein to squat on land that no one cared about. They were also conditioned by their own caution to keep their limbs covered at all times. Only the face was exposed to the blistering sun, and their feet on odd occasions when they let down their guard and dunked them in small pools.

This prisoner's eyes were sunken, his cheeks hollow pits, cracked with rivulets like a parched mummy. A skull-like face gaped halloween-like out of the dimness at us, almost weaselish with a long, feral nose. But the mostly hairless head was white, like an albino. Budding horns protruded above each ear like comical knobs or tree knots.

Cyr stepped forward. "Well, Kogreu," he said with fatherly cheer, "I trust you've had a chance to reflect since our last interaction? No? I will ask you again, who commissioned you to attack my supply chain? Where is the shipment?"

Fustas quickly translated, voicing a series of short barks and grunts in a husky, barbaric language that held no meaning for me.

The alien's near hairless head jerked up, looked as if it would fall off. From the slobbering mouth came a cryptic and slurry moan.

Cyr smiled. "Fustas has spent five years in a Skurg camp on Olassa, the sand planet," he explained to me. "He escaped miraculously while the Skurgs were being attacked by Daulks. He picked up some of the Skurg gutturals. To my fortune. I find Fustas's skills useful now. He has a robotic arm and leg, a result of Skurg machinations, which you are familiar with, but do not let that handicap deceive you."

The wiry, rat-faced Fustas gave me an eerie grin. "The Skurg scum says it was Gy-ar who greased the pot and sweetened the deal, admiral Cyr."

Cyr smoothed out his beard in thoughtful meditation. "Gy-ar... I might have known. Who else?"

I knew instantly then the identity of the mysterious 'source' who had instructed Axar in Yesma to light the fires. The cretinous shit-weasel, Gy-ar.

Cyr's eyes narrowed cruelly. "So where is the shipment, Kogreu? The one you stole and hypered to some dim forsaken hole?"

The Skurg remained mute, defiant.

"No answer? Pity."

Cyr leaped over and wrapped one of the ancient wires around the Skurg's neck. He pulled it taut and the Skurg's tongue flicked out between his brown teeth. The corroded metal dug into the wretch's wattled neck. His eyes bulged. His bound wrists strained. Stubby, fat fingers clawed feebly at the air. Cyr released the wire and spat out a curse. "Where is it? I'll starship out to this pigshit world and decimate your entire maggoty species."

The Skurg shook his head, a lunatic's gleam of fear writ in the pasty whites of his eyes.

Cyr's brass-knuckled fist swung in a violent movement. A meaty *schtok* had the Skurg's jaw left half hanging. The creature gave a mournful bray, something of a cross between a donkey and bull ape. Blood poured from his gibbering mouth full of broken teeth and saliva.

Cyr licked his lips.

"Now you will die, scum, unable to feed yourself." His chest heaved. "Serve you right, as an example of what happens to those who choose to betray me." Cyr's burning blue eyes flicked my way. No sympathy, no mercy.

"Was that necessary?" I took a step backward, repulsed.

"To prove a point? Yes, Rusco. Very necessary. One day you will appreciate this, if you are ever in my position."

With a grimace, I hoped to never have that opportunity. I had no love for Skurgs. But torture like this made me sick to my stomach. I wondered why Cyr had brought me here, if only to guarantee my loyalty and bring me one step closer to the base animal nature of what he was himself.

The man made me feel guilty for things I'd never done, perhaps things I'd done but hadn't considered crimes. There was something in him that made me aware of the black-hearted evil that resides in each of us.

We left the prisoner in his death crypt and as the heavy door clanged shut, I knew it would not open again until the Skurg was a maggoty corpse. The sickness and anger I felt was at a breaking point. We got topside and I heaved my guts and gusted breaths of fresh air. Every cell grateful to have the warm light on my skin again.

"You okay, Rusco?" He studied me curiously. "I hope you do not find such methods off-putting?"

"Did you light those fires?"

"Definitely not."

"You knew of them though?"

He stared sightlessly to a point out at sea far away in the hazy sunlight. "Maybe Gy-ar released some agents into the woods, big deal. Set some trees afire to scare the locals. He just expedited the inevitable. If it brings people closer to my vision, then the ends justify the means."

"They do not," I said adamantly. "People die. Lands are poisoned. It is fraud."

"You're theatrical, Rusco. A thousand deaths and destruction occur on a daily basis on a hundred planets. We are not harping on them now, are we?"

"No, but this is different—"

He held up a hand.

The hypocrisy of Cyr's eco-preservation bandwagon while being on board with Gy-ar's burning whole swaths of forest made me feel empty and soiled. I saw too much of his ambition at that moment: the beachhead, the Aquor, the futuristic prison city.

Thunderbolts of unease and warning pulsed through me.

Cyr motioned. "Some distinguished guests will be coming this evening. Someone whom I would like you to meet."

I don't know why that caused me a shiver. "What of Skel, Krake and Areth?" A frog stuck in my throat.

"They're invited too, naturally. In the meantime, I wish you to familiarize yourself with our operation on the ground. I've reassigned you and Skel to beach patrol where I can keep my eye on you."

"Whatever."

He handed me back my blaster. "Take it, Jet Rusco. Use it wisely. Fustas will bring you up to speed on our operation. Also he will

160

escort you to the exchequer where you will be given cash mekhs for your three days of work."

I dipped my head in acknowledgment. Somehow I knew Skel would not go along with the new assignment. It felt like blood money. He'd be out of here before he could say 'Jack Spratt'.

I would too, for good reason.

CHRIS TURNER

CHAPTER 21

Sure enough, Skel was less than thrilled when he learned of our 're-assignment'. Back and forth he paced by the towering, black-armored flank of the XT6. "Bastard. Trying to sideline us. I'll take my 3k and skedaddle, Kip. You can join us."

I filled Skel in on my experience down in the Comb. It disturbed him, chipped away at some of his breeziness. We had Krake contact Dalree and tell the Yesmians that Gy-ar was the one who engineered the fires, not Cyr.

"Tell him we're still probing how complicit Cyr is in all this," I told Krake. "We're watching Cyr and will give Dalree an update as soon as possible."

"Roger. Anything else?" Krake asked.

"For now, no." I cut the channel and turned to Skel. "Cyr says it's okay for everyone to come to this little meet of his. I'm leery of it, though."

"Let's humor the old boy."

Areth was indifferent, but seemed more concerned about the status of her daughter's safety after this breaking with Cyr. "I say we should stay. If we jaunt off and leave Cyr in the lurch, he'll no longer honor his promise to protect Slevana."

"He'll go along," Skel said in a dry voice. "He dotes on you as his pet."

Areth gave a troubled scowl.

"You could always stay here," I suggested, trying to feel out as slyly as I could where she stood with me.

She gave a pained grin, bordering on a grimace. Something in the gray area between hopeful anticipation and trepidation.

The bad part of the mystery meet was that it was in Aqua Rex, of which I now felt leery.

Skel and I agreed to leave Krake and Lisse and the others aboard the XT6. We didn't trust Cyr and his motives after our recent drama. We needed a getaway vehicle if things went sour.

We were working with the Aquor that afternoon, observing their hand-to-hand combat. On the beach they kicked and swatted, then moved over to the main area by the ships where we joined in. Krake, Areth, Lisse and the others participated too. Makala was thick in the fray. I found the Aquor's movements somewhat programmed, so it was easy for me to predict their strikes and their blocks and anticipate the essence of their tactics, but a couple got past my guard and gave me a good whacking.

While we were deep into training, a space yacht dropped down on the landing pad. High glass belvedere on forepeak, big impulse boosters to the side, impressive quad-cannons mounted at bow and midships. A hint of familiarity set my instincts on alert. Cyr attended the landing reception but from a distance, I could not make out who the arrivals were. Evidently his mysterious 'guests' wished to remain incognito. Another faint trace of unease stirred my gut. But I didn't have time to pursue it as an Aquor moved in and hip-bunted me while another sucker-punched me in the ribs and sent me reeling.

After we'd accumulated more bruises and doled out several ourselves, we familiarized ourselves with the monster, twin ion guns flanked at the entrance to the gorge. Eight yards long, black hypertilized metal, piked on 360 swivel cement base.

Skel gave a low whistle. "These babies are some piece of fancy hardware, Kip. Wide Ion sweep. Holo scopes, full spectrum AI sighter. Look at it! Automated tracking of targets. The whole shebang. Our boy Cyr seems to value his gorge somewhat inordinately."

I wondered if Cyr's anti-air weaponry had anything to do with the presence of the alien tunnels in the bluffs. He seemed wantonly protective of that area no less. I gave Skel details of the captive Skurg and the gruesome fate he awaited. Also the network of tunnels, dank and mysterious, that stretched deep under the hill. Not to mention the weird-ass ancient circuitry I'd seen.

"Don't know about that stuff, but I should have guessed about Cyr," he murmured. "He's always been a little sinister and tending toward the shyster side."

"News of the century."

The meet at Aqua Rex was at sunset and Narwhal took all four of us down: Skel, me, Areth and Cyr. We entered into the main foyer where our richly-mannered host, Elengskar, greeted us. He bowed low in his golden-robes and after Skel, Areth and I got our bearings, we assembled in the great dining hall.

A man in voluminous brown robe, his back to us, stood staring through the massive oval viewport into the deep-green sea. He was contemplating the marine life in the same place I'd stood at myself on more than one occasion. When he turned, my eyes nearly popped out of their sockets.

The languid face and thin disarming grin...the same stoic poise of the Prime Ascendant Weasel of the Moon Temple!

"We meet again, Kip Rees," Gy-ar said in a sonorous, resonant voice, "or should I call you, Jet?"

"Call me whatever you want," I growled. I took in his milky blue-gray eyes, the man who was my nemesis. He was a person of no great stature, the tip of his nose coming level with my shoulder were he wearing high heels and a fancy dress. His low, easy voice held a melodic ring to it which had a way of inducing calm, even entrancement in the listener. His lips were thin, pale and emotionless. The robe, casual and without adornment, trailed to his ankles. The sleeves were rolled. The eyes, spread far apart in a bovine fashion did not lend confidence in the viewer.

"Back from the dead? You are a most curious creature. Full of surprises. And an irritant to boot, like a crawling ant. Difficult to kill."

Cyr squawked in pleased surprise. "What? You two have met before?"

"Of course we have. Does it surprise you, Cyr? It doesn't surprise me we've both had the pleasure of crossing paths with Jet Rusco." He made small precise steps over to me, reached up a hand to trail fingertips in my hair. "The purple is a bit gauche, I think. Yellow is more your style." He laid a hand on Cyr's shoulder and guided him over to the spread of iced wines and hors d'oeuvres on the table. "Mr. Rusco took our last meet very badly, I regret." He sighed. "He took pains to rebuff our association. It astounds me that he is so ticklish. This is a lavish table you've laid out, friend Cyr."

Cyr nodded and blinked, still recovering from his initial surprise. "Why would Jet Rusco sabotage a salubrious relationship?"

Gy-ar lifted his shoulders in a baffled shrug. "You will have to ask him yourself."

"Still up to your old tricks," I croaked at Gy-ar, "spreading bullshit wherever you go, creating chaos so you can bring in your Order? A nice racket. But not everybody falls for it."

"But enough do, Jet Rusco. That is the rub."

"Gentlemen, let us not get off to a contentious start," Cyr said soothingly. He held up both hands. "I have gathered us here so we can celebrate, and pool our resources."

Skel gave an amused smile. Areth, pale as a ghost, slipped into the background, as if she wished to disappear. I saw her fingers pass nervously over her throat.

"Quite an achievement you have here, Cyr," said Gy-ar in a casual manner. He extended an arm. "From that first blueprint four years ago you showed me on a rainy eve on Aldeberon, you have gained my utmost congratulations. You have birthed surely a wonder of the galaxy!"

Cyr bowed. "I thank you for your confidence, Gy-ar. I appreciate your feedback and good faith. I wish to create a consortium of futurists—of great beings like those gathered—of like mind and vision—to create a network of advanced cities under the seas across all the frontier worlds! With Aquor as the builders and serving as underwater marines, a militia of associates including Rusco, Remus and Skel, and wealthy investors and venture capitalists like you and your friends at the Moon Temple."

"A grand vision!" Gy-ar cheered. He raised both hands and clapped. "You shall have my full support. I applaud your verve and vision. The Temple shall install lodges on each Aqua Rex around the galaxy. We will host ceremonies and celebrations. In fact, our first celebration shall be right here on the morrow. It is the eve of Evensooth, an auspicious occasion."

Cyr blinked, slightly taken aback by the idea. "This is premature, Gy-ar. Such short notice, but I'm sure we can make arrangements."

"Then it's settled!" Gyr gave an ingratiating caw. "That's what I like about you, Cyr. Flexible to the last, especially when it comes to matters aligning in your favor."

Cyr gave an uneasy rub of chin. His eyes seemed slightly glassy, uneasy, watchful.

We ate and drank and talked of lighter things. We dined on dishes ever more sumptuous and richer than before: braised oysters, curried squid, swordfish, shark stew, sliced grouper in a tart red anemone sauce.

Only when Cyr brought up the matter of Lady Areth, did Gy-ar's jaunty mood dim.

"Lady Areth failed in an important mission," he said darkly. "According to the tenets of our creed and arrangement, she must atone for her transgressions. Either she or one of her loved ones must pay penance."

"The Lady Areth is under my protection," Cyr said coldly. "She shall not be harmed—or her family, including Slevana on Ares II—to whom you seem to have made gross allusions." Cyr shafted him a glance that would shatter glass.

Gy-ar paused in mid-bite. His smile was glib but his neck sweated and his complexion was pale. "Of course, Cyr. Let us drop the subject. Let us turn to other matters."

Cyr would not be mollified. Perhaps he was stirred by Gy-ar's smug airs and hints of violence. "Gy-ar, I fear you have become a bit regal in your extended stint as Ascendant. Perhaps it is time for a 'changing of the guard'? The nominations are coming up in the temple, come the new moon of Abrasus. I don't doubt you will be nominated, but perhaps you might be passed over, say superseded—" he lifted shoulders in quizzical amusement "—by a visionary—perhaps one even as myself."

Gy-ar set down his fork, mopping primly at the corners of his mouth with his napkin. "It is insulting that you'd suggest such a thing, Cyr. I think I have supped here enough for one evening."

Cyr tilted his head in a playful manner. "Some fish are not for everybody. Many find the seafood of Oranthe a trifle rich for their tastes—those who have weak stomachs or are of weak temperament. Another curious thing: I learned through my agent Jet Rusco here, that you have had quite the extracurricular dealings with my Aquor, inspiring them to become good firestarters for one and meddling in local politics."

Gy-ar fixed Cyr a bitter glare. "Is this some kind of joke, Cyr? Was it not a month ago that we sat here and discussed privately the very way to deal with the Yesmians whom you openly agreed—"

"I also learned through several bloody means of persuasion," Cyr interrupted, "that our so-called rogue Skurg captain Kogreu, was under your direction."

Gy-ar waved a casual hand. "A cretin will say anything under duress. Kings will do the same. It means nothing."

"Perhaps," said Cyr. "But in this case, it was his last breaths. I know of no man or hybrid man who can withstand my methods without telling me some semblance of truth."

Gy-ar gave a diminutive shrug. "There is always a first time." He cast both of us a chilling inspection then rose to his feet.

"Gentlemen, Lady Areth, I bid you good evening."

Our conversation had wound to a halt. Areth pleaded fatigue and asked to be excused.

CHRIS TURNER

CHAPTER 22

I was out in the walkways gazing into the cool shadows cast by the hanging lights when Cry came up on stealthy feet beside me. "Ah, Rusco, let's take a walk, shall we?"

I shrugged.

"What do you think of our little conversation with Gy-ar?"

"Not much. Nor your own feigned preempting of the conversation when he called you out on your secret 'arrangement' with the Yesmians."

Cyr waved it off with a grunt. "A bluff, Rusco. Subterfuge. Obfuscation. All the trappings of fencing and rhetoric."

He caught me staring out the porthole again at a school of manta rays, these ones phosphorescent with green and yellow bodies. The large, kite-shaped fish had come to dive bomb each other in some private war. Whether it was serious or play fun, I did not know. Mantas, or at least these big ocean dwellers, were not known to be vicious, rough-and-tumble marauders of the sea.

"They are a special breed. Mantacoats. Transferred from the sea world of Melanka, if I recall, a planet of unusual characteristics and a prospect for one of my cities."

I pointed at the bigger enemies that had swum near. "It appears the light attracts the dolphins which is not in their best interests."

Cyr tilted his head in a frown. "Disadvantageous and advantageous both, Jet Rusco. The mantacoats can lure predators more easily and away from their young ones. Like many phenomena in this universe, all is not what it seems."

"You think?"

He sighed. "I see you are distraught. I love the sea, as you know. But another thing that has been a passion of mine is anthropology. Come, I will dispel your gloom, show you what I have added to my miniature museum." The hand he laid on my shoulder was as gentle as a block of iron.

We passed through a topiary of exquisite configuration—sea brush, juniper coral amid statues of mermaids and sea lords. We ascended a set of wide marble steps that took us to a heavy double door carved of dark mangalorn. Cyr withdrew another strange key from his well-equipped belt which unlocked the portal. It swung inward without a creak. He flipped the lights and beckoned me inside.

We entered an oval-shaped room with glass-encased exhibits. Some were upright, roped off figures, protected by a low rail and a small moat fed by dwarfish fountains. The exhibits stood somewhere toward the center. My eyes were adjusting to the dim light and at first I didn't recognize what they were.

"In my exploration of the gorge where you met Kogreu, I discovered some interesting finds, deeper down in the Comb. Do you find them intriguing?"

My eyes warily followed where he gestured.

I gaped. Never before had I seen such an impressive collection of artifacts, bones, skeletons, marine specimens of species definitely non-human.

Insectoid skulls hunched on four-foot high chitinous bodies. Even through the display glass they brought a chill to my blood. A shadow of an experience I once had in my dreams surfaced. I had swallowed the I-TERA, the alien artifact had given me powers.

I remember all too vividly, mysterious and unknowable phenomena. Of alien races, like this. Like the ones whose bones Skel and I had dredged up in the ore pit on Skaldar.

"It seems there have been others that walked the soils, who ruled before us. Perhaps they are still out there, Jet Rusco." He lifted a hand. "Rather than just another of the many lost ancient races. Like this one." He made a casual motion to the insectile skull fully intact upright on its grasshopper-like body. It stood almost four feet high. The eyes on either side of the ebon-like gleaming skull were wide ovals, deep pits staring into nowhere. The hands could be used as useful pincers, to reach out and snip off a finger, possibly the wrist of a child. The upper body, compact, hardened without wings, was weirdly imbued with odd, triangular fins carved on a sloping back like a fish. Effectively, a walking half-mutant, or some quasi-marine locust.

"This appears to be an early form of the Mentera that came from the sea. See the budding fins and primitive dorsals? My guess is that these marinoids evolved and came to land, then founded the first colony in the caves abreast the beachhead—which I call The Comb."

It was a bold and chilling theory. One in whose plausibility I took no relish pondering. "That is a daring supposition."

"The boldest ones are usually the truest ones, Jet Rusco."

An inexplicable wave of atavistic fear swept over me, for I'd seen these skulls before. Why did it so unnerve me? There must be hundreds of similar skeletons scattered about the known worlds...and even stranger troves of mysterious palaeontological remains and fossils across the frontier worlds and their moons. But these particularly made me nauseous. It was most disturbing and perplexing.

"So many mysteries under the sea," mused Cyr. "We came from the sea, and we will return to it. I found these fossilized skeletons while excavating the first foundations at Aqua Rex. Just think of it, Rusco. Ancient extra terrestrials! Proof. They filled me with an uncomfortable excitement I'd never known, and a horror, humbled as I was, realizing just how insignificant we were in the overall scheme of things. The myriad races the universe has spawned! It made me painfully aware of my own mortality. How I will pass into dust. Maybe posing in a glass case of some ape-lord's space yacht museum a thousand years from now." He gave a bray of laughter. The concept seemed funny to him. "Think! Our lives pass in a blip. They are over before they have begun. We cannot fathom what has gone before, what is to come. So much we don't know, and will never know, and yet we persevere with our childhood fantasies and ask ourselves what is the meaning of it all? What is it all for?"

I gave a slow, solemn nod. "I have thought of these very things, Cyr. I have asked some very hard questions, but I abandoned them because my head hurt too much."

He chuckled at my remark and gave a low rumble. "You are too young, Rusco. Too young. Give it time, your head will hurt less."

I shrugged, somehow doubting that very much.

"Gy-ar and his brood of ritualists talk about the Masters," he said in a darker voice. "Of the supreme race that ruled the universe and seeded the races, including humans. What are your thoughts on the matter?"

"I've heard many mythologies. They are all a blur in my mind, and a batch of utter nonsense."

Yet I would never forget my visceral dream: the one about the encounter with the envoys of the Masters aboard Goliath while I lay beside the vivacious Trix in her steamy embrace. I was about to mention something of this to Cyr, but something stayed my tongue. Something in the way he looked at me, raised my guard, and his intense stare.

"Gy-ar claims to have irrefutable proof of the Masters' existence. In his reliquarium he boasts of things undreamed of." Cyr's brows rose in bright excitement, possibly wishing a glimpse of that reliquarium which he was denied.

"Gy-ar," I sneered, "is a man so caught up in his own dogma that he could make rainbows drop out of the sky. He'd have entire populations truckle to his whims and his transhumanist agenda. To rule side by side with his boyfriend, Xi-ar."

A cagey smile came to Cyr's lips. "And you disapprove of Cyr's proclivities?"

"I don't approve of him in any way, let's put it. He's a louse, a cruel and diabolical kingpin, as depraved as they come."

Cyr nodded. He rubbed at his chin in deep thought. "I can't say that I disagree with you."

"Then why do you do business with this perverted weasel? You two are as thick as thieves, despite your pretend argument with him. So what makes you any better?"

Cyr's eyes blazed for a moment but he spread his palms in a relaxed manner. "These are life's little ironies, Jet Rusco. You will come to know them in time. Inescapable as the ebb and flow of life."

I scoffed and turned away. "Pure rhetoric, Cyr. You rationalize your tyranny and your imperialism with pithy phrases."

"Perhaps, but money and power talk and bullshit walks! This is not all I have called you here for, Rusco. I need you as eyes and ears." He gave a low snarl. "To manage Gy-ar. To protect me from his wiles. You are right in what you say. We will thwart him together."

My brows arched. "Why dance around? My advice is to kill him."

Cyr clicked his tongue. "You cannot kill someone as high in rank as Gy-ar. There are repercussions. When word gets back who commissioned the hit, what then? A small army would be sent to my doorstep and destroy me and Aqua Rex and everything I hold dear. These people are vindictive and have that far enough reach, Jet Rusco. They are established."

I fidgeted with my hand. I tapped a fist against the glass that held the Mentera. "Somebody has to do something against him."

"Who?" he laughed. "You? Me? No. They are far too powerful, Rusco. I will say it again in plainer language—you need a thousand agents on every world to combat his network. I need you as an agent in the field to be my first line of defense and warning against Gy-ar and his cult to garner me an advantage."

I licked my lips. So, this was Cyr's plan from the very beginning. Every cell in my being balked at such a sordid task. But I couldn't be too hasty in denying Cyr. He was embroiled beyond repair in this fanatical underwater city enterprise and his relationship with Gy-ar. I chose my words with care. "I have no love for Gy-ar, so anything is possible. We can talk more of this later when I have had time to think."

Cyr nodded and beamed. He could appreciate words of his own I echoed back to him. "Gy-ar is here for two days hence while this celebration is on, so I'm sure we can work something out. It'll be enough time for you and your friends to initiate some espionage."

My eyes drifted to the blue green waters past the small porthole on the bay side where his divers finned with a competent ease. They were performing some maintenance tasks.

"The man is good for some things at least," Cyr muttered. "He has supplied us with tinctures—cutting edge serums that can change the chemistry of a man. I myself have self-injected his latest batch." He gave a proud inhalation. "I will become one of them." He gestured to the aquamen. "Able to breathe water and withstand high pressures."

My body shuddered. "Then you are a more trusting soul than I am, Cyr." I turned away and left him, feeling the small hairs on my neck prickle as I made my way back to the sleeping quarters.

CHAPTER 23

I didn't relish staying locked in our single berths so I decided to pull an all-nighter and just wander the paths, scout out more of Cyr's wonder dome. I caught up to Skel and Areth sitting in conversation on a flat rock in one of the garden paths near the guest chambers.

"What's happening, guys?" I hitched in beside Areth.

"Nothing much," Skel said, "unless you call Gy-ar's scheming 'everyday affairs'."

"What else would you call it?"

"I overheard friend Gy-ar talking with one of his associates, how they're proposing working on genetic modification and implants for all citizens of Aqua Rex so they can adjust to the high pressure and swim and breathe underwater."

"Right up Cyr's alley. Sounds marvy."

"But for what purpose?" Areth asked, appalled.

Skel gave his head an amused shake. "For the sheer excitement. These people are obsessed with playing God. They're imperialistic freaks. Transhumanism is ever on their minds. Never has it been so pervasive in today's age."

"It seems inconceivable," she murmured.

"Expand your mind, Lady Areth. If you follow the money, you'll see—the more you study galactic history—that all paths converge on Rome."

"Meaning what?" I demanded.

"Meaning that this is all part of a cosmic plan. Cyr and Gy-ar are just the instruments bringing it about. If it weren't them, it'd be others."

"It is all too scary." Areth shivered. "There must be more layers to the onion we're not seeing."

I inhaled a sharp breath. Maybe she was thinking of the role she'd played in putting her daughter at risk by working for Gy-ar and his minions and helping bring about their dystopian vision.

Skel shook his head. "It is simpler than that. Our boy Cyr is a control freak. Anyone goes up against him, he gets hunted down and crushed. You can see it in the man's eyes. Pure instinct. He'll come at you a hundred times harder than you came at him."

"No different than Gy-ar," I grunted. "They're two peas in pod...But get this. Cyr's getting cold feet. He wants us to run interference on Gy-ar. Spy on him."

"Does he now? He's not going to get much action there. We have to be on our toes though. Easy to get our throats cut with a single wrong move."

Areth whimpered. We exchanged uneasy glances. Skel had an uncanny knack for saying it as it was and reading people and situations in a way that struck hard to the truth.

I filled them in on more of Cyr's plan, omitting the part about his taking the therapy serums to turn himself into an aquaman. I didn't think either were ready for that. Besides, if Skel was going to be taking off and flying into the blue yonder anyway...what difference did it make?

Skel just seemed to shrug with sleepy amusement. Who knew what was going on in his head? Of anybody, he was the hardest to read.

The next day we returned to the beachhead and we practiced more maneuvers with the Aquor. We continued our reconnaissance of the gorge. All the time my mind was brooding, wandering over the disparate events in motion. I could not feel at ease, knowing that our snake Gy-ar was so close: creeping, wiggling, like the lizard he was. Probably right this moment he was in Aqua Rex plotting and wheedling with Cyr. Come to think of it, I hadn't seen Cyr all day, an unusual circumstance. I was not getting a good feeling about this 'celebration'.

The night of the celebration was upon us and I was secretly dreading and curiously looking forward to it in some sick, twisted way. Call me a nutcase. It was as if everything in my psychic body knew that strange, devilish things were in the works. Not like the visions the I-TERA, that diamond-shaped artifact no larger than a dice, would give me, or the level of detail, but a tingling anticipation mixed with a borderline queasiness.

Seventy five of us thronged the main hall. Some of Gy-ar's crew added to the count, but mostly they were Cyr's Aquor. We mingled with the attendees, drinks in hand. I counted about sixty Aquor, dressed in some form of weird or old-style costumes.

Gy-ar had insisted on a masquerade and I recalled our own costuming. We were required to wear outfits like everyone else as we celebrated the ancient ritual of *All Hallows Eve*. A fete from time immemorial back on Earth, when spirits wandered the night, ghouls haunted the graveyards and witches flew on broomsticks across the full moon. There'd not be much of that tonight. Solas was waning gibbous. Nothing more than a dusky red oblong in the night sky...or so Krake had informed us by communicator.

Some of the costumes were easily revealed their wearers. Cyr was clad in his big bear's outfit with a false animal snout and furred gown of black fur. Gy-ar in his bull's gown with curved ebon horns looping over his ears and face much like what Areth had described in the masquerade she'd attended. Makala in her tall huntress's outfit, wearing a black visor over her eyes, loose green and brown leather pants with a faux-quiver on her back.

Skel, Areth and I had raked through Cyr's extensive wardrobe earlier that evening and found garb we fancied. Areth had initially selected a troubadour's outfit with bright blue vest and tasseled hat, but Cyr had stopped her, shook his head and placed his hand on hers. He pulled out a white, skin-tight gown more suited to a forest nymph or town strumpet. "This will look much better on you, Lady Areth. Enhance your magnificent figure."

No doubt that was true, but I surely had not approved of Cyr's ogling. I stood silently, jaw jutted. On seeing my irate, jealous look, Areth had opted in delight for the courtesan-whore's gown. Damn her hide. Maybe a reckless echo from the last stint at Gy-ar's pseudo-orgy? Who knew what went on in the female mind?

I selected a Robin Hood-like outfit, in mild annoyance, with a rakish green cap and gray goose feather stuck on a jaunty angle. I strutted around with some pride in brown-green tights and black ankle boots. Areth, the nymph, stood smirking at my side, dressed in her skimpy outfit and white bandit's visor showing only her hazel eyes while Skel stood smugly in his pirate's garb: loose dungarees bagged at the knees. He wore a black skull-cap and bandanna, looking like a cross between a drunken Sinbad and mean-ass Captain Bligh.

Now, here we were, hours later with Cyr standing back to admire us, a drink in hand.

"Skel and Rusco, you look like a pair of rakehelly rogues." He touched the ornamental cutlass looped at Skel's waist, which matched my own fake, three-foot scabbarded sword.

"Hi ho, shiver me timbers!" Skel mimed. He did a little jig while he crouched in a bent-kneed stance in the midst of all gathered. He jabbed the pointy end of his curved blade at my midriff.

I pulled out my imitation sword and blocked his jab and took up the challenge.

We faked a mock sword-fight in the middle of the hall which caused some stirrings of laughter even among the dour Aquor.

There were drinks and food aplenty. Couches and divans had been pulled out, arranged to the sides amid the shrubbery where guests could lounge and chat. Cyr had arranged quite a spread per usual—an all-you-can-eat buffet on tables to the sides to the tune of twenty seafood dishes. Attendants ran about pouring drinks and refilling glasses. I chose not to drink the punches and wines but sampled the entrees and found them excellent. Areth ate frugally and only drank water. Beyond the giant oval porthole facing bayside, an astonished array of fish had come to gaze upon the weird mix of humans who'd come to celebrate this age-old festival in their bubble under the sea.

A sedate music piped through speakers hidden in foliage around the hall. A quasi-classical mix, fit only for the likes of dancers who preferred the old style balls and operas from Old Earth. Some of Cyr's crew took to the floor and moved about in graceful sweeps and dips, which could only be performed by the Aquor.

"An amazing display, Cyr!" Gy-ar gushed in admiration. "I knew I could count on you."

Cyr bowed low in his bearish costume. "Thank you, Gy-ar. It was your creation after all."

The Prime Ascendant sighed and dipped his horns. "It was, wasn't it? Let us raise a toast to this inestimable occasion...and the blessed fortune of Aqua Rex!"

"To Aqua Rex!" Cyr boomed.

The two moguls tipped their glasses while I stood sullenly to the side and watched them drink wine from goblets adorned with precious jewels like kings and ancient princes.

One might wonder what I did to amuse myself during that ceremonious time in that big crowd. Not much. Watched and listened. Danced with Areth a few times. Her face was flushed, her movements were animated. She was like a seraphim who truly came alive in environments such as this and I saw more of her than I cared to see. And more than one set of gleaming white eyes admiring her lean body, trim waist and healthy sexuality. Makala—it did not surprise me—being one of those admirers. There was also much drinking, and I noticed a distinct change in the energy of the group after the two hour mark. The Aquor became less staid, more vocal, freer, almost aggressive in their overbearing and exaggerated movements. Maybe the excess of alcohol had combined with their altered body chemistry? An altercation broke out between two hooded figures over who was to be the official 'escort' of a female dressed as a fairy princess. Because of their androgynous cast I could not tell if the ones arguing were male or female. Almost as if the punch too, or whatever it was, had been spiked. And why shouldn't it have been? Gy-ar and Cyr were devious people.

It was about mid evening when Skel angled in toward me and thrust a glass of sherry in my hand. "Well, what do you think of Cyr's little party?"

"Much as I would have expected," I intoned. I dumped the drink in the bushes while Skel was not looking.

"Don't know about you, bro, but I'm kind of fancying the skinny Aquor dressed in the mink costume over there. What do you think?" He nudged me in the ribs.

I cast him a lukewarm grin. "Go for it, chief. You only live once. You can give her a hickey too while you stroke her gills."

He made a sour noise, followed up with a laugh. "Why'd you have to spoil it?" Just as he was about to saunter over and try his luck at a dance, a fork tinged on a glass.

"Your attention, please!"

All heads turned.

Cyr stood on a small podium in between towering dendrons. "Welcome, friends!" Through the nearby porthole more exotic fish had come to gather. Even a billhead shark with a mouth full of saw-edged teeth.

"I am pleased to announce the inaugural opening of Aqua Rex! You are the first to experience her charms at this formal occasion. Next week at this time, citizens from all over Oranthe will populate these very halls. So shall begin the migration from Oranthe's overtasked soils to Aqua Rex's endless fastness under the sea. I call on Gy-ar, my associate, Prime Ascendant of the Moon Temple, to share his thoughts on the occasion."

Gy-ar stepped up beside Cyr and spread his arms to encircle his bull horns...a trick to maximize the drama of his entrance. "Drink up, friends! The hour is now midnight on your world, Oranthe. Let us commemorate the ancient rite of *All Hallows Eve*. We shall initiate ourselves into the Ecstasy of the Ancients. The Star Of Tomorrow!"

There came a thundering applause from the wine-soaked Aquor.

Elengskar, Cyr's maître-d', approached with twin goblets in hand. Cyr clutched the first and upended it in a single gulp. Gy-ar took his more frugally and only sipped it.

Cyr's bear-like eyes seen through his mask seemed to glint in ruddy fervor. The chandelier light shimmered in the citizens' hall. Attendants drifted among the guests, bearing trays of similar ceremonial goblets decorated with red jewels. Gy-ar and Cyr had spared no expense or showiness in this formal ceremonial ritual.

And ritual it was. For the music had altered—and not subtly. There was no more classical. From airy motifs of the arias to now a rich, drum-like melody from the gallows of ancient earth.

The Aquor, completely submissive, drank as one.

Areth flashed me a warning glance. Skel was about to take his goblet, but I caught his arm before he could swallow more than a mouthful.

Skel bunted me in the ribs. "Go grab your own drink, bro," he snapped at me. "There's plenty to go around."

"Maybe you should grab a brain, bro," I hissed. "You can't trust these devils. I didn't tell you about Areth's experience at one of Gy ar's 'celebrations', did I? When she was rising up the ladder as one of his 'agents'?"

"No, you didn't." His arm lowered. Gingerly he set down the goblet at the nearest table.

Almost immediately a change came over the gathering. The Aquor began moving in synchrony, pairing up, some forming threesomes, as if guided by a single primitive impulse. I stared, spellbound.

Makala had glided over to kitty-corner Areth between the tables and the shrubbery. She was breathing sultry words in her ear which I could not discern. Areth snarled and shook off her arm, indicating she'd have nothing to do with whatever Makala was proposing.

One of the aquamen tried to get frisky with me and curl an arm about my shoulder. That resulted in three broken fingers and a rib for Mr. Suave. "Save your paws for your bed buddies," I growled. He looked at his twisted fingers with a confused grin, then gave a high-pitched yammer, totally intoxicated by whatever gunk they'd slipped in the drinks. That any of them had been naive enough to quaff such a brew was beyond me. Skel, no exception. Whatever little he had drunk seemed to have addled his brain.

Cyr strode over and thrust Makala belligerently away from Areth. Makala reeled back, seething. An intense hurt look lingered in her eye. I hurried over and Cyr bunted me aside too, as if I were nothing more than a straw man. He made to corner Areth as she tried to scurry away.

"Lady Areth, I now choose thee for my hallowed partner for the evening!"

She wrinkled her nose. "Lord Bear, I think you're a trifle drunk," she said facetiously. "What makes you think I am to be chosen?"

"My decree is final!" Cyr said with a jocular sway to his bear-like body. "Drink brings out the best in a man." He pounded a fist on his barrel chest. "A real man."

"Oh? Does it?"

She flung off her visor. "What if I tell you I have no interest in participating in your rituals, or your 'contact sports'?"

"Then I will tell you, Lady Areth, that you have no choice." His grin was evil, the last words sweet but ladled with venom.

He reached out a hand and clutched her around the waist. "Do not slink away from me, Lady Areth! We can make beautiful music together. We must dance. Dance! Dance with me, fair damsel!"

"Not tonight—Ow, get away from me, you brute. You're hurting me."

"You heard her!" I came in and chopped at Cyr's wrist, breaking the contact. Areth had time to edge away.

Cyr made daggerish eye contact with me then beckoned significantly to Makala.

The Aquor did this impossible series of cartwheels in the air over a distance of about twenty feet, smacking people out of the way. Her heels and elbows bloodied some noses and took out a few teeth before they came whirling at me. I tried to dodge, took a blundering step backward but her legs got somehow hooked around me in an improbable way. She got me in this scissor lock that I couldn't break out of it.

Holy shit! What was it with this stupid bitch?

While I was grunting and gasping, trying to break free of her snake grip, she began to tear off my shirt, pulling me closer, a lascivious grin carved on her androgynous face. I pounded on her legs with my fists. To no avail. She was impervious to blows. Meanwhile Cyr had stripped Areth to the waist. He too was butt naked. She screamed a high-pitched plea and batted him with her fists. She clocked him a good one in the throat, but again to no avail. He was too strong and impervious to hurts like the others. She tried to kick him in the nuts, but he blocked. This was getting insane!

Skel was laughing his ass off, lolling back on a padded couch with three aquawomen caressing his chest, arms, groin. One was straddled over his loins, making sultry faces at him. Cold, purple, botoxed lips sucked on his cheeks. The others were licking at his throat on either side like a couple of she-lions, all yoked up on the secret punch that Cyr or Gy-ar or both'd given them. Was I in some secret hell? What was going on? Skel was useless, a zombie.

All the time this bizarre, hypno-drone came humming through the loudspeakers. While locked in Makala's python grip, I figured out what it was. An overdub, spliced tracks, one subliminal, the other forefront, switched now to an underwater techno beat put through a lot of reverb. It was dark, plodding, sinister. The subliminal was laced with some classical opera—my ear could pick it up as I'd studied the classics when Shorty and I were cranking out rock opera at

Carnivale—'Ride of the Valkyries', if I knew my music history. With just enough dissonance to raise the hackles on any sane person's neck or who was not completely sloshed or stoned.

Fights arose: blood and teeth spilled. The uneven mix of pairing was just enough to ignite a firestorm of jealousy.

Gy-ar threw back his head. He bull-roared. Despite my constricted breath, I gaped. The man was getting off on the chaos! He was ready to cream his robes. With his curved ox horns and goatish costume and hoofed shoes, he looked more like a devil than a man.

Like the orgy that Areth had described, this was of the same order of debauchery, even more insidious, considering the dosing of Gy-ar's serum in the mix or whatever it was.

The sounds of vague echoes bounced along the tiled floors, echoing high in the looming dome. Laughs, shattered glass, rude slaps. Women's cries. Moans. A nightmare. Glimpses of Gy-ar's horned head drawn back in maniacal laughter. Males ripping off masks and sucking each others faces. A clown world gone mad. Where was Areth? Skel? My head felt like it was reeling under the enormous pressure of Makala's suffocating grip.

I processed all this in a few moments. Terrified, energized, I came out of my trance and swung hard at her mouth.

She'd managed to fend off my fists thus far but the last punch had the she-bitch's eyes rolling. They went wet and glassy and I felt her leg muscles slacken. I scrambled out of her noxious grip and staggered to where I'd last seen Areth, but five figures were on my tail before I could as much as throw a punch. Sick-drunk on the brew, they looked murderous, given the violence I'd inflicted on their beloved captain, Makala.

I made a mad dash for the garden paths, scrambling for the exit. A cold sinking dread stabbed at my guts, leaving Skel and Areth back there. Was I a coward?

No. I was lucky to have escaped with my hide and my wits about me.

Make the most of it, you stupid duncehead. Before those ghouls plug you back into that zombie hell...

CHRIS TURNER

CHAPTER 24

The echoes dimmed and I could hear only the sinister music rising above the background hum of garbled and intoxicated human voices. My body gave a brief shiver. No one in sight. Everyone was back in that demented masquerade area.

My sixth sense knew they wouldn't be for long.

Dark figures came gliding out at last. The Aquor, heads bobbing, spreading out looking for me.

Bare-chested, I scrambled deeper into the garden along the half-shadowed walkways, caching myself in some shrubbery. It was going to be a long haul.

Makala burned my ass. What the hell was with her? The drink had made her gonzo like the others. All semblance of our early camaraderie had gone out the window. Maybe she was not all dike, or the cursed drink had pushed her into bi territory. What did it matter? I pushed the useless pondering out of my head.

Low voices. Brisk footfalls. I tucked myself deeper behind one the bushes. Through a web of jade-colored leaves I saw a gnarled hand gesturing—of Rolph, the helmsman. "It's that shitbag, Rusco, Cyr. I saw him dip his ass down that path. He can't be far. We should have wasted him back when Spiff brought him aboard the bridge."

Cyr growled at him, "And if you had, you and Vipra'd be blown to atoms. Think about it. Jet Rusco's an asset. I want him alive."

The helmsman gave a derisive snort. "He's nowhere to go. What are we even doing out here? I mean, I thought you were more interested in boffing that luscious girl? If you're not, I'll—"

"Shut up. Do you hear me, you idiot? I want Rusco alive. Now! ASAP!"

"Yes, sir." Rolph saluted. The two trod off, moving deeper down the garden path.

I went the opposite way, my mind made up. I was grateful that somehow Areth had been given some reprieve, maybe managed to escape. But Skel? Who knows? He could take care of himself. I made hasty strides in the direction of the docking station.

The way was clear. I managed to get to the main sublevel dock. Cyr's ship loomed out of the nearby waters, a hulking goliath. Farther down, I discerned a small submersible berthed in the underwater gloom. To my left loomed diver's chambers that the Aquor used for their construction forays and patrol launches. The chambers had heavy steel doors and pressure wheels to open them. If I could get in one, slip in and get to the surface...I might have a chance. A longish swim maybe to the beachhead to Krake's ship. But no one would suspect that I'd go this route.

Like a weasel, I crept past the first hatch, peered through the glass: a ten foot square plain yellow chamber with air tanks clustered on the floor by the far wall. Scuba gear and wet suits were hanging up. I managed to crank the wheel and creep in before sealing the door behind me. It made a small pop of pressurized air as it closed.

So far I'd made it inside undetected...

Yet a flutter of movement came up the dim-lit pathway. I stared through the thick glass, a tingle in my chest—at Gy-ar and one of his stooges. Damn the rogue! I ducked under the porthole, but he'd seen me.

I snatched a wetsuit off the wall. All the time my mind was thinking the worst case scenario: to try to swim out of here and hope for the best. Unlike what I'd heard about neoprene wetsuits, these were fairly easy to put on. I dragged over a tank, turned the valve, tested the nozzle in my mouth. I was getting enough air so I hurried over to the decompression switch.

As I passed the porthole I saw to my dismay Gy-ar's bull shape move in with unhurried steps. He peered at me through the glass. He took off his bull mask and his pasty face showed round and bland and stared grotesquely into my own. Our faces were inches apart. His lips moved soundlessly. His eerie opaline eyes dipped hungrily down at my bare chest through the half-zipped suit. There could be no doubt as to the man's sexual preferences. I flipped the intercom switch so I could hear what the louse had to say before I made an exit.

"Jet," he tsked his tongue. "Come out of that dreary box and we can talk. How long can you keep up this charade? You've devolved into a woman basher who cowers in a cubicle with no friends. Revelers are having the time of their life back at the masquerade! Come and join us, accompany me!"

"Bug off, you slimy creepshit. Crawl back to your slimy hole. I'm sick of your idiotic rhetoric, your lies and toxic schemes."

"Ah, you marvel at my skills. Genius perhaps?" He shook his head in a slow, sad way. "You could be part of all this, Jet, and yet you choose to—insist on this—" he lifted a hand, widening his eyes in bafflement. "It is most puzzling."

"This aquaman brigade, the fires and the underwater cities, all part of your underground pilot projects?"

"The more projects we have going, the less likely the common man is to tie them together."

"Sure. Create a bunch of deviant, sterile muppets who wish to live undersea and believe in your fairy tales about natural wildfires, allow their lands to be stolen by thieves and psychopaths."

"You like it?"

"Sign me up." I gave an exhalation of pure disgust. "Cyr will not allow the takeover of his cities."

"Cyr has no choice. The underwater cities are not his. They never were. You still do not understand the fundamentals about power structure, Rusco. We take what we want. Anything anyone builds or makes great, we take. We absorb it into our own infrastructure, use it for our purposes."

"Meaning you're an evil motherf—"

"Come now, no ad hominems, Mr. Rusco. We're just practical. If we do not do it, another will."

I shook my head. "Cyr is not going to—"

"Cyr is so caught up in his mania for the sea, he will sew his head on backwards to see his vision materialize. He has no idea what the aquaman serum does, or its far reaching effects. My associates are working on other concoctions that will allow us to modify the entire human race."

"Why does that not surprise me?"

"You have no idea how far our plans run, Jet Rusco. How vast our network is. We've been thinking this out for centuries, before the ancient Egyptians built their mighty pyramids on Earth as beacons for travelers from the stars. We have perfected our methods, operated in the background where no one is looking, made sure no one can identify us. You cannot conceive how profound our control is over all humans across the galaxy."

I wanted to strangle the man. He stared so blithely at me through the glass. "These serums...the recipient becomes androgynous being the side effect?"

"Yes."

"Friend Cyr hasn't figured this all out?"

Gy-ar gave a sarcastic laugh. "Even if he does, he will stay in denial. He's obsessed, to the point of no return."

So these...transhuman aquamen, it struck me, were none other than the same neutered breed of creepy Mentera, crawling from the sea and slimes onto dry land. The only difference was the former were a product of natural evolution, while the willing aquamen were a chemically-induced aberration orchestrated by diseased minds.

"Your potions and orgy masquerades will backfire on you, Gy-ar. They can't fool everybody. Others will see through them like I did."

"Whether you like them or not, Jet Rusco, they will be part of the

Moon Temple's vision to be unfurled on all the frontier worlds."

"But why?" I frowned.

"Because—" he hesitated before answering, as if gauging how much he wanted to divulge. "I'm putting myself out on a limb as I speak, but the long and short of it is, people who are drugged and living in a bubble world, cannot rebel. We keep them in constant containment, regulate their orgy time and their contact rituals and narcotics. While they remain incurably addicted, they remain enslaved. It's that simple."

"A very evil scheme."

"The world is evil, Jet Rusco. One has to be selfish to amass wealth and maintain control over the multitudes. It is not logical to let another group sweep the rug out from under you and steal your ideas."

"You aim to control the planets then by sequestering humans in a drugged up world?"

"No, Jet Rusco, to control the gene pool. The genetics, the reproduction cycles and social norms of humans. Ultimately the future direction of human evolution. Even the Aquor's sexual deviancy is living on borrowed time. The serums they take will make them sexless and sterile, desireless and completely androgynous. Neither identifying as male or female. Don't you see it? Whoever controls the biological direction of a people, controls destiny. It is the ultimate goal. Call it a divine service."

"How're you going to fool that many people into taking your brews?"

Gy-ar shook his head in tolerant amusement. "How do you get a favored pet to take an ill-tasting medicine? You sprinkle it over his food. You casually watch Fido gobble down his meat without a second thought."

I gave a graceless laugh.

"When you erase the sexual desire from an organism, it becomes docile. It becomes obedient like a neutered pup. Sexless beings are useful drones which can be employed for a variety of purposes. Why have slave compounds and camps, like our doltish friends, the Skurgs, when a population is willing and able?"

"You're a sick and twisted man."

Gy-ar's lips quirked in a diabolical smile. "I'll take that as a compliment." For a second my attention fixed upon his left eye, which was pure opaline. He looked like one of those many gaping predators I'd seen out of Cyr's portholes. Like the eye that never blinks, just stares at his hapless victim.

"The Masters had some of this embedded in their Screeds eons ago. They gave their creations—monsters and aberrations like the Zikri and Mentera—free will to go about and build their empires, to overthrow their creators and their overlords. A mistake. We have simplified the Masters' protocols to effect a more direct result in line with our agenda."

"Where should I pin the medal?"

"Sarcasm is fine, Jet Rusco. Show contempt and anger, but there is something you do not understand.

"Yeah, what's that?"

"Humankind are like errant children. They need to be guided and punished for making the wrong moves. Mischievous, foolish, impulsive. They are short-sighted creatures who, like teens, will turn everything topsy-turvy, if left to their own devices. They have to be tricked, sometimes strong-armed, into doing what is right for the common good. They have to believe in the rules and to follow them unquestioningly."

"Like mindless robots while you play God?" I shook my head. "It doesn't work like that, Gy-ar. People will get wise. They don't like to be manipulated. They don't like treachery and lies. They'll rise up against you and come after you, and God help you then."

"No they won't, Jet Rusco, and here's why. If they can't figure out what's happening to them, what war will they wage? What is there for them to do? If they don't know who to come after, who can they kill?" He gave a boyish laugh. "It is ingenious. Even your employer, Cyr, for all his creative brilliance, look how easily he takes our potions, to become this plastic, iconic sea god he craves. How pathetically easy it is to control the masses, Jet Rusco! Dangle a carrot in front of their noses and they come running like lemmings by the thousands. If they don't bite right away, just make it sweeter. Ultimately they'll come arching their necks to lick at it and stomp each other out of the way." He gave a contemptuous laugh that jangled my spine and had my stomach churning. I loathed the man more than ever in that moment. He was a non-human that needed to be put down. They all did, he and his brood of psychopaths that ran that twisted religion at the Moon Temple.

"Once again, Jet Rusco, or Kip Rees, whatever you go by, I offer you a last chance to join us. We can use your talents, as a man of influence and persuasion. Like your friend, Skel. We will arrange it so that both of you can never betray us or divulge our secrets or break away from our Order. In return, you get everything you ever wanted: ships, land, women, glory, feasts, anything you desire."

I gave him a contemptuous sneer.

"A reminder and a warning. Once you go down this path—there is no turning back."

The man's voice was hypnotic, a melodic pulse to lull the deepest thinker. The offer, tempting as it sounded, was complete trash. The same, I'm betting, friend Cyr had accepted and was well on his way to becoming a sexless aquaman.

Unlimited wealth.... Positions of power.... Prestige.... Every desire glutted.... And yet, the price: to be a slave forever to the Moon People and carry out unquestioningly their orders.

"No Gy-ar, my answer is the same as it was moons ago on your fancy space yacht. Go screw yourself."

The Prime Ascendant stared hard at me through the glass. I saw movement down the hallway. A black-haired shape dressed in a bear's costume: Cyr.

The bear-shape beckoned Rolph and two of his minions. Aquamen.

My marrow froze. Cyr'd rip open this chamber like a can opener and come after me like a bear on honey.

"Give it up, Jet Rusco," Gy-ar murmured sadly. "Here comes Brother Cyr. I can smooth this out with him. I can make it all go away. You will become one of our captains, a chosen one, on par with Cyr."

"You expect me to join somebody who slung me into a Skurg camp a few months ago?"

Gy-ar grimaced and his lips lifted in a soft snarl. "That was a mistake. I admit, an impulsive error. I was distraught from the loss of the I-TERA. I am still suffering from that loss. I fear my—my punishment is only beginning."

A look of real fear came over the man's bland features and it surprised me, for it was the only time I'd seen such emotion on his patronizing face.

He saw me sucking on the air intake valve, donning goggles and headlamp and made a stilted movement.

"You throw it all away...fool!" He sucked in a sharp breath. "Think, Jet Rusco, before you act. You were chosen. The bearer of the I-TERA! The universe does not make mistakes. It's not a random engine. You cannot run. Nor can you hide from being the influencer you were put on these worlds to become."

I'd closed my ears to his dogma. His words were drivel, filth, empty rhetoric.

I made my move. Something they wouldn't expect.

"Don't be stupid," he cried one last time. "The pressure will kill you. You are not a practiced diver."

My ears weren't listening. I slammed the decompression button. The small port opened and a flood of water jetted into the chamber. My heart beat a mile a minute. Every fiber of my being vibrated with a sinking feeling, but out of desperation I hoped for the best.

The chamber was filling fast. Past knees, waist, now neck, until at last Gy-ar's face was lost in a flurry of bubbles. With great nervy kicks, I pushed myself out through the hatch-hole, my heart thudding in my chest.

CHAPTER 25

Past the masquerade ball entrance about fifty feet, Areth took stealthy steps down a narrow garden path. Skel blundered behind her in drug-induced stupor.

"Hurry up, you dumb jerkoff," she growled back at him. "You're slower than a pile of dogshit."

"Cut me some slack, Areth. Everything's a bit blurry around the edges."

"Yeah, I wonder why. It'll be more than blurry, if you don't hurry up," she hissed at him. "If I hadn't pulled you away from those she-ghouls, you'd be—"

"I was having this beautiful dream. Nymphs all over me from heaven. Petting, massaging—then you had to spoil it."

"It only took a couple of punches to wake you up to a better dream."

Skel felt the growing lump behind his ear. "That's why my skull is pounding."

"Quit your grumbling and keep moving. Cyr's probably posted watchdogs around this place to make sure people aren't where they're not supposed to be. Our only chance is to make it to the submersibles."

Even before she'd rasped out the words, the two came to their first roadblock—a dark-khakied figure stepping out from behind a dendron in a mini garden. An outspread arm moved to stop them.

"This zone is out-of-bounds, people. You'll have to go back to the masquerade."

Skel came in bobbing his head, grinning. "Really, chief? Why?"

"Yeah, tell us?" Areth gave a sardonic challenge.

"Cyr's orders," he snapped.

"Bro, you've gotta lighten up," Skel wheedled. "This is a party, right?"

Areth cast the Aquor a suggestive smile, turning seductive eyes over his lean line of leg and waist. "Perhaps you'd like to join us in a little threesome? Room for three." She fluttered her lashes and curled a finger.

The guard's eyes rounded. "It's not protocol but—"

"Want to show you something, friend." She undid the laces in her top, showed some more cleavage. "No fun for you out here all alone while all the action is happening back there." As soon as he leaned in, she smashed him hard on the nape of his neck.

Skel kneed him in the face for good measure. "Now what? McGoo here looks like he's not coming up anytime soon."

"To the south bayside wing," Areth muttered. "My sense of direction isn't the greatest here, but I think it's that way past these stupid nymph statues and noisy generator."

"Hope we find some more of those fishmen aquapoofs," Skel said, rubbing his hands. "Just like hide and seek. Reminds me of the times me and Smally used to play hide and seek on the old man when we were kids. Woohee! Like playing tiptoe through the tulips."

"Shut up. You're drunk."

"Really, maybe it's you need to loosen that cunny of yours, Lady Areth. Should have let Cyr work you while he had the chance."

She slapped him in the face. "I said, shut the hell up!"

He wiped his split lip. "Okay, take it easy. No use getting sore. Just trying to lighten the atmosphere."

"Like hell you are."

He made a monkey face.

She shook her head, muttering curses under her breath.

"Wow, someone's in a sour mood."

"Kinda happens when you've got a bear-like lug trying to take you by force."

"How'd you get away from him anyway? It's all a blur. Last I remember he was roughhousing you pretty good."

"Kneed him in the nuts. Didn't seem to faze him much—he was so jacked up on whatever juice Gy-ar'd given him. Lot of good you were."

Skel made a noisy show of protesting.

She flapped a hand. "Quiet down. Sounds echo in these garden paths."

With luck and a bit of maneuvering they managed to get to the port dock where as expected, a guard was posted. To their ill timing, he was just arriving at his post.

"Over here," she hissed as they ducked behind some aromatic juniper, "pretend like you lost your way, that you're hustling me to some dim cubbyhole for some slaps and giggles."

Skel feigned a look of horror. "What would Jet say?"

"Can it, would you? Good for nothing 'Jet' abandoned us, remember?"

"Okay. I'll work my magic."

Skel sauntered over toward the guard while Areth trailed.

"Push over, chief," he said. "Got a lady here. This place is too small for two dudes."

Areth winced.

"You can't—" the guard began.

Smash. Skel's fist laid into the guard's gut, another to his skull. He fell with a thud and Skel kicked him in the ribs for good measure. "There. Now who'd you say is drunk?"

Through the port glass, the imposing form of the Narwhal sat docked, a dark blot of brawn, fins and cannonry. Her sloping hull was bathed in the blue-gray shadow of underwater lights. To her side sat a smaller submersible docked. Likely the vessel that had transported Gy-ar and his crew to the underwater city. Farther down, in increasing blue-gray shadow, loomed another ship like Vipra.

Skel rubbed his chin in thought. "There's our ticket out of here." He was not as impaired as he'd made out to be.

Areth peered. "We don't even know how to operate that ship."

Skel's smiley grin annoyed her. "How hard can it be?"

"No time for backup plans," she murmured.

Movement and sounds of footfall came behind them. "Let's go." She grabbed his arm and pulled him along.

Skel pulled out his ear bud and snapped it in his ear. "Krake," he rasped. "Krake! Code red. Things have gone to shit down here. Meet us on the surface, above Aqua Rex in say, seven minutes. We're coming up. Look for a gray submersible with fins." There was a muted acknowledgment and Skel cut out.

He and Areth bolted along the covered passage into the air lock.

CHAPTER 26

The dome loomed to my right. My eyes opened wide and I flipped the headlamp to its highest setting, straining to see in the vast gloom. Up was where it was lighter, a faint ruddy glow of a gibbous moon. My muscles tensed, my long legs drove me far away from the nightmare of Aqua Rex. Upward on an angle toward a place of freedom.

The pressure gauge on my mouth nozzle showed 25 minutes of air. Time enough to get up 150 feet. Or was it more? My heart thudded like a drum. If the Aquor could handle the pressure, so could I, couldn't I?

I willed myself upward. Time seemed to crawl to a stop. I could feel the pulse in my veins. The blood pounded in my ears.

A high-pitched ringing roared there too. It was as if my suit were too tight and my limbs felt sluggish while my lungs labored for air.

This deep diving thing was not my shtick.

Snap out of it, Rusco. You're just a short jaunt up into the world of air and light. Away from the glass and steel and jackboot of dystopia.

Along the underwater shelf of coral and age-old sediments the blue lights illuminated the ghost forms of the dendron under the nearest dome. Farther along, the smaller dome with its unique renaissance architecture loomed.

I finned along the shadowy mass of Cyr's ship. Its smooth,

submarine stern seemed less menacing in the underwater gloom.

There was something I'd heard about getting the bends. It alarmed me—trapped gases in the diver's blood expanding under higher pressure that blow out blood vessels when said diver ascends to lower pressures too quickly. For the life of me, I couldn't remember the stats or how deep the domes were. A hundred feet, two hundred, three? I wish I'd paid more attention to Cyr's monologue when he'd spouted figures to us so easily during that first voyage undersea.

So what makes a man what he is? Is he worth something more when he steps up, risks his neck, even when frightened out of his skull? To do what he believes in? If the challenge stares him in the face and he accepts it, does it count?

All these questions flipped through my mind as I finned up through that gloom, through the schools of tropical fish, past the sloping surface of the fabulous dome, hoping to break surface before Cyr's agents took pursuit and sighted me.

Yet no such luck.

My eyes caught the sudden movement emerging from the divers' port: a half dozen figures not far from where I had emerged. I turned my attention back to the dome and flippered my way up faster. I killed my headlamp, caught a glint of a few dozen green-and yellow triangular masses drifting toward me in a lazy, undulating movement. They were high up and to my left. What now? Were they more enemies?

Then I recognized them. The school of mantas I'd seen earlier beyond the portholes. The ones that gave off the firefly glow. Large ones, like great eerie kites. *Mantacoats.* Long gill slits marking their ventral surface.

I fled without care on an upward angle toward the phosphorescent school.

I saw they looked quite deadly on closer inspection. Large, swift-moving beaks painted a phantasmagorical yellow—some genus of the Mobula, or the devil ray family, relatives of the stingrays. Their sleek bodies were covered with small, green-glowing scales, like plate armor.

When I came closer they didn't bunt me away, as I expected.

Instead they glided over my black suit and under me without fear or concern. Then kited toward the approaching divers.

It could do no harm being in their midst, I figured. Perhaps it would even the odds and give me an edge while I was outnumbered by a stronger, more versatile enemy.

Yet my relief was shortlived.

I heard the swoosh of a weapon, a low thrumming sound of a projectile swifter than an arrow, as it swept within an inch of my right arm.

I jerked back. The noise surprised me, but then I remembered that water was a better conductor of sound than air. Noises carry four times as fast under the waves.

Another Aquor's dart gun lifted. A four-inch metal bolt flew through the water and nailed one of the mantacoat's fin-wings. A dark liquid poured out of its fleshy underbody as it thrashed about wildly. Through narrowed slits, the whole school eyed the Aquor intruders with distrust, perceiving them now as a threat. I wondered if these sea creatures associated the neoprene mutants with the enemies come to build the man-made monstrosities that blocked their habitat and their way of life.

Another projectile grazed my shoulder. And yet another came whizzing past my ear.

Almost at once, the water churned in a frenzy of phosphorescent kite shapes. They blurred with the divers. One of the black-clad Aquor jerked at the touch of a mild electric shock the instant one of the mantacoats bumped into him.

Not just phosphorescent creatures but electric eels.

I recognized the tall, sinewy form of Makala slithering out of the gloom and finning in to hip bump me as I kicked away out of her reach. Like the others, she wore a skin-tight wetsuit with open flaps at the neck that allowed her gills to breath in water. Her long, grasping arms came hooking at me. I fist-clubbed her back. More of her companions came angling in closer, aiming their underwater darts at me, despite the anger of the mantacoats. More silver-hued arrows spun by me with disturbing velocity. Barely finger-widths to spare. Makala's long arm grabbed at my back leg. I kicked off the grip. When would this relentless bitch give up?

The mantacoats went crazy, frenzied by the death of their comrade and the disturbance the divers were creating.

I saw movement above me to the left. Two long, sleek billhead shapes of menace. Sharks! They were veering in. My blood turned to ice. The predators were attracted by the brisk movement of the divers and the trail of blood.

The first billhead grabbed a ray close to me and ripped it in two with its awful maw of serrated teeth. It devoured the first chunk in a single gulp. The other snatched one of the divers by the arm. The creature thrashed its head to and fro like a pit bull. The sea churned with red. A dusky, murky color with fish and human blood. The armless Aquor sank to the bottom. His limp body jerked occasionally, blood spurting from his stump at the elbow as he sank. The other three Aquor including Makala, panicked and fled.

I wanted nothing more to do with this. I finned the hell out of there as fast as I could. Too panicked to think, I thrashed upward. Maybe not the wisest thing to do against bloody-hungry sharks, but there was no bucking survival instinct in these dark perilous waters. These monsters had enough eye candy to keep them occupied. The two billheads finned after the hapless divers with cold, ruthless intensity. One got distracted, veered off, and turned its toothy attention to the mantacoats.

But now a new mystery came floating my way—a dark buoyant shape rising from the dome. I could not outrun it. Its rounded hull rose far below me like a great balloon with back fin up-pointed and churning propeller at stern—the small submersible once docked beside Narwhal.

It came floating up with no great finesse. Which was odd. It gave me cause to pause.

Through the pilothouse glass I saw two familiar faces. For a moment I could barely breathe. Could it be Skel and Areth? I must be hallucinating. They both motioned me toward the vessel's hatch to port. I snapped out of my torpor and gave a startled cry of understanding.

I edged along the starboard, grabbing at handholds. Skel must have activated the decompression switch for the panel slid back and the decompression chamber flooded with water. I fumbled my way inside through an oval hatch and hit the release switch. The steel door slid shut. I breathed a gasp of relief. Through the thick glass I saw a five-yard long shape drift by with glaring eyes. There was a red switch on the wall so I hit it and allowed the water to drain and the decompression process to begin.

After a minute and a half, the green light blinked on the wall above the interior hatch. All the water had been pumped out. I swung open the inner hatch door and stumbled gamely into a small hallway. It appeared to lead to the pilothouse. I pulled off my mask and goggles and let out a wheezing breath.

There, a slim figure emerged from the pilothouse and stood in the short hallway, blinking. She was beautiful. Her dark hair was a fountain of curls all mussed up, a long scratch on her left cheek. Sexy as hell, clad still in her white gown, snug and tattered, narrowing at the waist that showed to advantage ripe, luxurious hips. Her brow was streaked with sweat, her eyes bright with concern.

She gave me a puzzled frown, then came tripping over to clasp me in a strong, breathy hug. She was mindless of the water that soaked her skimpy gown from my wetsuit.

"I couldn't do anything back at the masquerade, Areth," I babbled. "They were all over me. That Makala bitch, she—"

"I know. I get it. "

"How the hell did you commandeer this rig?"

"Let's just say we got tired of the skanky vibe down there."

"Cyr?"

"The man's brain's messed up. He's vulnerable. Jesus, what are you doing finning around with sharks?"

I gave a gruff laugh. "Like you, I preferred the party out of doors than in that crummy hall." My voice cracked. "You guys seriously saved my ass."

"Dude," came a low voice from the pilothouse. "You'd have been toasted if you'd tried to make it to the surface. It's way too deep in one go, like over 200 feet. Strokes, hemorrhages. What were you thinking?" Skel swiveled in his navigator's chair to frown at me, his lips hitched in a crooked grin.

I shook my head. "So how do those mutants do it then?"

"Do we care? They're mutants."

A cold feeling washed over me as I realized I'd literally signed my own death warrant. *How do you feel about that, Jet Rusco? You have nine lives? Used up eight of them?*

"What's the current plan?" I croaked in a hollow voice.

"We're meeting Krake topside. We ditch this love bug. If I can get it moving fast enough, that is."

Areth pushed past me and hunched quivering beside Skel. Both stared with mounting dismay at the approaching mass through the glass. "Shit, that looks like Cyr."

I clambered in beside them. I saw the goliath shape of Narwhal slowly lifting her curved bulk away from her berth and coming toward us like a hungry predator.

"Right on cue," Skel stated grimly. "We just have to figure out how to get this tub up as quick as possible. Haven't totally figured out how to work the thrust. We're doing okay so far on short bursts—"

A dull thunk echoed on our underbelly.

The submersible did a faint lurch. I grabbed for support as I bumped into Areth. Skel cursed.

"A pressure blast. Shit." He worked the nav stick-lever direction control jerkily.

To no avail. The submersible continued to slew sideways. "This bug's gyros are screwed. It's not going to get us far, even if we make it topside."

"So what do we do now?" I rasped.

"Pray?"

"No way to get it topside? I mean, can we swim the rest of the way?"

"No. Narwhal's faster. She'll shoot us down."

With a grim sigh, I teetered back on my heels. Skel angled the damaged craft up toward the top of the dome as best as he could. His brow was ridged in deep furrows. We traced a wobbly path. I looked at the instrument panel. The depth gauge showed us at 76 feet. Now 62.

62 feet to the surface of the bay and the moonlit waves above us.

"Why're you going there?" I protested.

"Cyr won't fire on us so close to his precious dome."

"For fear of damaging Aqua Rex."

"Right. It's the only leverage we have. Which gives me another idea."

We hovered beetle-like above the flattened curve of the dome and all of us tensed, each waiting for death or capture either way. Were miracles possible? My memory flashed back to the first time Cyr'd taken us down to Aqua Rex. At that time we were hired defense against saboteurs. Now we were targets.

Cyr's voice snapped over the com. "You shitbag thieves are going to get your asses handed to you. Guide the submersible down to its berth. Move slowly away from the dome."

Skel cut the channel. "Already enough noise for one evening."

A hopeless feeling washed over me. How could we escape that madman? I smacked a fist on the control panel. "I wish to hell Aqua Rex was nothing more than a pile of rubble buried under the sea along with all of his schemes."

Skel blinked and his face broke into a ruddy grin. "Brilliant. Why don't we do just that, Kippie?"

I didn't like that devious look.

"It's staring us in the face. Don't you see? We use this ship as a battering ram."

"A what?"

"A bomb. We let the sub's dead weight drop down on that eggshell dome. Humpty Dumpty. Game over."

"It's crazy."

"Hurry, Narwhal's moving on us," Areth cried. "They're going to try something. Maybe implode us."

"Make for the decompression bay," Skel ordered. "Get geared up. This baby's going down."

"Whenever I'm around you, Skel, my world goes batshit."

"Your world's already quite gone batshit, Kip."

"Amen, fine. Can we stop the bickering and just do something?" crowed Areth.

"Get to the hatch!" Skel cried.

I grabbed her arm. For once, I followed Skel's advice.

My stomach felt a tug as he guided the submersible down toward the closest edge of the dome. Narwhal hovered over us like a black bug. As if unsure of what to do, the ship jerked forward. Another pulse blast struck us topside, rocking our submersible. It knocked me off my feet. I clutched for a handhold and Areth in the same motion. I felt the floor of the dive chamber rock underneath me. I heard a curse from Skel as he jammed the thrust—or whatever was left of it—to max. He raced down the hall and piled into the decompression chamber with us. He squirmed into the last available suit while Areth and I, already suited, hit the fill-load activator.

The water gushed in. As soon as the green light flashed, I hit the release. We finned out the hatch like minnows from a fisherman's trap. Skel's fins had just cleared the upper rim of the hatch when the nose of the submersible slammed hard into the dome's surface. It caught one of the porthole glass ovals above the level of the guest suites. Skel had timed it nicely. Even with the ship's nav out of whack, it was a clean hit. Whatever could be said of the man, he was an ace when it came to navigating ships.

There came a crack as the submersible bounced off the surface and went skidding down, grinding, shearing metal and glass. The starboard dorsal sheared and smacked the glass again.

I couldn't be sure, but when I looked down, I saw the porthole glass flower in cracks then the submersible careen on its path of doom to sink somewhere into the bottom weeds and coral far below.

We finned upward with our best efforts. The blue-gloomed water lightened to the ruddy shine of Solas which filtered down from the night sky.

My body buckled as a massive blast pulsed up from below. It sent me skidding sideways. I caught blurred snatches of Skel and Areth doing somersaults in the murky water. My ears were ringing. I shook the daze from my skull, almost rendered half deaf from the blast, but regained some of my sense of direction.

I was tilted upside down, looking above, which was down below. I saw a massive cone of flame erupt in a bright flare as one of the dome's generators must have blown. How the hell could that have happened?

A structural flaw? Maybe the submersible had hit some sensitive wiring or cable or power box? In Cyr's reluctance to blast us out of the water, he had unwittingly contributed to the doom of his brainchild.

The main dome imploded. A massive air bubble ballooned up under our bellies, swept us like toys to the surface. Almost as fast as it had come, I felt the strong tug of currents drawing me downward as the sea raced to fill that enormous gap.

I thrashed, clawing at the water. Scrabbling my way upward, with all my strength, I resisted the downward flow of currents that would inevitably send us all into that roil of oblivion. The explosion had caused a chain reaction. The three nearby domes were compromised. Glass and metal caved inward. Thousands of cubic yards of water flooded into the interior, crushing everyone and everything within. Brief bursts of flame engulfed exploding circuitry and short-circuited power boxes...and yet, the fires were quenched instantly.

Millions and billions of mekhs of damage in the space of a few seconds. One of the wonders of the universe destroyed. A singular achievement among humankind. Did I care?

No. The place was destined to be an infamous outlet for Gy-ar's Moon Temple dystopia and I was not sad to see it go. If anything I was happy to be alive.

Narwhal had halted and rocked in the roil. Across that murky water I could only imagine the raw emotion flooding through Cyr's brain. Possibly torn between hunting us down and racing to assess the damage done, he must be wanting to torture us over slow fires.

I remembered his deadly promise—to hunt down and bring fire and brimstone to anyone who dared inflict damage on Aqua Rex, his poster child. A cold shaft of dread stabbed me in the gut. In Cyr's eyes, we were fish fodder.

CHAPTER 27

My head broke the surface first, then Areth's, finally Skel's. The moon stared down on us, a giant red gibbous shape to the east, resembling some drunken eye, its wash leaving a dusky reddish stain over the waters. From what I'd heard from Dalree, about half of Solas was red sands, the other graced with oceans like the Dead Sea on Old Earth.

Stars twinkled overhead. I could make out the near shore, a darker blot against a lighter indigo sky where the great Yesmian bluffs rose like a wide-browed taurus-like beast.

We blinked at each other as we bobbed in the gentle swells like frogs in a big pond. Within moments a rumble of engines came overhead, and with it a squat, oblong shape of immense size with a pair of rescue lights raining down on us.

Skel gave a joyous cry. Never before was I so happy to see a friendly ship. Such a welcome sight for sore eyes!

The XT6's rear thrusters whipped and churned the water to chop as the cargo door jerked open. With grateful dog paddles, we hitched our way nearer.

But another shape came hurtling from the direction of the beachhead across the dark surface of the bay. A ship with dorsal fins and a spine fin from the contours lit by her pilot lights. She was yet a quarter the size of Narwhal. *Vipra*. It could only be Vipra.

Bright yellow fire ripped by our arms and legs, sizzling the water around us, sparking off the XT6's plate armor.

I ducked underwater as soon as the dolphin-like snout of Vipra came bearing down on us like a scourge. Six foot swells tossed us like corks.

Skel signaled madly underwater. Damn Vipra! She'd come like a dog at heel.

We gasped into our masks and resurfaced when Vipra had banked and in the moments before she could turn our way again. We scrambled up the half-submerged ramp like rats. Krake'd held his ground, waiting for us to board. He'd let the XT6 absorb the damage instead of taking evasive action.

Remus's ship came screaming in for another assault. We clawed our way up the ramp, but cannon fire blew the cargo door to shreds. The shrapnel zinged off the hold's walls, spraying all around. Skel caught some small bits that shredded through his wetsuit. He cried out, swatting at the hot metal speckling his thigh. I steadied him and we managed to get through the double door at the back of the hold. Jesus, were the XT6's shields that low? Wind whistled around the jagged edges of the open hold before we sealed the hatch and the XT6 finally lifted off from the churning waves. Into the sky she roared, leaving Vipra in close pursuit of us.

We staggered up the main gangway and into the half light before the midships companionway where we shed our wetsuits and tanks, plomped on our asses and kicked off our flippers. We hustled up the stairs to the bridge, Skel hobbling after us.

Baskra met us halfway. He gave us high fives, a short, barrel-chested man with oily skin and a hound-like face. We all helped Skel along.

On the bridge, Krake, Lisse, Jerome, Comby and Quassa were at their posts. Krake and Comby manned the nav, Lisse and Quassa the sensors while Jerome, the weapons' grid.

Krake turned and scratched his sweaty brow in appreciation. "Nice to see you boys and girls." His face broke out in a grin. "You three look goofier than hell in those costumes."

"For a goofus occasion," Skel growled.

"And a clown world," I put in. "Just be happy you gave it a miss, Krake. Unless you like being gang-banged by Aquor and chased by sharks and dart-wielding divers."

Krake turned back to the controls. "No, can't say as I do, Kip. All I know is that shitbox Vipra is on borrowed time. Jerome!" He jerked a fist at his gunner, a youngblood with curly dirty blond hair and a pugnacious face. "Sight on that crapbox and kill. No mercy."

"Aye, aye."

Skel laid a hand on Krake's wrist. "No, buddy. Set aside your revenge. Don't waste time on the peanut gallery. Our priority is to get the hell out of here. When our friend Cyr mobilizes his forces, it isn't going to be pretty. We'll need every bit of distance between us and them."

Krake gave a grudging nod. He aimed the XT6 skyward. Wincing, Skel picked out some fragments from his left thigh while Lisse got the first aid kit down and soaked the wound with antiseptic while she wrapped gauze around it. Skel waved off the cut as superficial.

The sea fell below us, like a midnight-indigo blanket. Through the forward viewport we could see lights wink from the beachhead.

The XT6 raced along the line of the bluffs, trying to escape Vipra's fire. Our shields were dipping lower with each hit. The ion guns along the beachhead lifted in unison. Long muzzles trained our way and belched fire at us, unleashed full fury, raking our stern. Krake gave a colorful curse. The AI sighted with disturbing accuracy. Red streaks skidded our stern plates, knocking and sapping our shields even more. Krake grimaced. I saw the needles dip another notch.

We saw Narwhal at last emerge from the depths as Skel had predicted. She turned her whale snout toward the beachhead. Oddly, the ship did not join in Vipra's attack, instead she flew to the landing pad, disgorged some passengers then came rocketing back to intercept us.

"Stand down, XT6," came Cyr's cold voice over the com. "There are many words that need to be spoken. Reparations are in order. Land that shitbox or the worst will come of you."

Skel grabbed the com from Krake. "Words, Cyr? More like death sentences. We can outrun you and play cat and mouse all day. Call off your rottweiler, Remus. We can light drive out at the 6000k zone any time."

There came a tense pause as the man behind the wire pondered Skel's ultimatum. "Perhaps. But there is also something else to consider. Look to your starboard. At 35 degrees."

Skel's head tilted in that direction with a frown. My neck craned too. Through the viewport I saw a hundred, puke-yellow lights appear in the sky above. What the hell? They were bearing down on us, getting brighter.

"Shit!" Krake licked his lips.

"Skurg ships," I murmured. My heart sank to a new low.

Skel had to eat his words because we couldn't get to hyperdrive until we were clear of Oranthe's gravity.

My jaw sagged. How could we reach the safe zone through that enemy net?

"A whole fleet of them?" Krake winced. "Why? Where'd they come from?"

I asked the same questions. Gy-ar's backup? A contingency plan should his capers in Aqua Rex go sour?

Vipra and Narwhal seemed to hound us ever closer.

Movement came to starboard. A new ship entered the fray, Gy-ar's cursed space yacht. Her fancy hull rose like a cocky imperial cruiser from the beachhead. Unmolested, she flew up toward the intimidating mass of approaching Skurgs as if she were their commanding flagship.

An uneasy standoff. Birds of prey lit the sky from all sides and we grit our teeth, sped at full impulse across the dwindling line of bluffs to the eastern sea. Anyone could turn on anyone. Anything could happen.

Heavy Skurg fire rained down on us as fighters pursued in

random formations. Firefly-like.

"Shit, it's going to be hard to dodge them," Krake muttered.

The ships were friends of Cyr's. For now. But could we make them foes? I pondered the idea as the ship rocked.

An open three-way channel crackled as Lisse or Quassa managed to hack into the local air chatter. Cyr's angry voice broke over the com like a shotgun blast.

"What gives, Gy-ar? You bring Skurgs into my backyard?"

"You are distraught after the recent events, I understand. I urge you to calm down, Cyr."

"Don't tell me to calm down, you traitor. I set you down by your space yacht in good faith, I treat you with hospitality in my home. Then you do this? What are you playing at?"

The Prime Ascendant paused before answering, "I had a feeling you wouldn't be able to contain the situation, Cyr. So I brought in reinforcements. It seemed the best thing to do and it looks as if I my hunch was correct. I had the Skurgs waiting on the dark side of Oranthe's moon."

"This is an act of war."

"Life is war, Cyr. Of all people, you should know that."

"Traitors everywhere!" Cyr bellowed. "You will pay. You will all die: Rusco, Skel, you Gy-ar and all these Skurgs. Death to traitors!"

"That is a tall ticket, Cyr. Perhaps you're drinking too much, like you did at the party?"

Krake muted the channel. "With a flotilla of Skurgs overtop us, we can't get to hyperdrive."

"We go back down to the planet then," Skel declared.

"Are you out of your mind?" I croaked. "We've got to get to light drive!"

"That's exactly what they expect, Kip. Even if we could get by them, we'd never make it to light speed before they blasted our asses. We don't have the impulse power to outrun them."

I bit my lip. "So what then?" I clenched my fists.

Skel's lips curled.

How could the fool smile at a time like this? The man was crazy...and yes, he was still probably drunk.

"It's called a merry-go-round," he said.

"What the hell are you talking about?"

"I think what friend Skel is getting at is the old twaddle game." Krake banked the XT6 toward the Yesmian forest. Our stomachs lurched as bright Skurg fire clipped our starboard wings and I watched our shields dip even more.

"Back on Tildara," Skel said, "we went hedgehog hunting." He moved over to crouch by Jerome at the tactical post. "The hedgehogs dug holes in the fields. They lamed the horses whenever they stepped into them and my uncle'd get my brother Smally and me to shoot them. Problem was the critters were smart enough that when we went out with our pop rifles, they hid underground and we had to draw them out—with snacks, smells, bright objects, water hoses."

Areth nodded slowly. "I think I get it, draw them out."

"Yes. This is much the same, but sneakier. Get them out of their comfort zone. Split them up. Get them making mistakes. Last thing they want to do is to go flying planetside over unfamiliar territory."

"I'm getting it," I conceded.

The XT6 came screaming down low over the trees. I guessed we were about 40 miles southeast of the beachhead.

We took the XT6 lower, buzzing the trees. We banked over the Umena river and hurtled down its dugout of a natural canyon. Skurgs were tailing us like flies, trying to lock onto our rear thrusters. Krake weaved in unpredictable patterns. Jerome sprayed fire at the half dozen kite-like craft that dogged our heels like mayflies. But I saw that he was too slow on the draw and was giving the Skurgs far too much leeway.

A missile clipped our port bow. Jerome fell back, his arms singed to the elbow. He gave a sharp cry then slumped half hanging from his seat.

"Damn." I leapt over and felt his pulse. His eyes stared blankly. His bloodless lips remained parted in an astonished 'O'. I shook my head. I hopped into the chair beside him and took over the auxiliary controls. Every cell dreaded a similar fate of electrocution by power surge. But I dreaded a worse fate at the hands of the cannibalistic Skurgs.

I sighted on the bastard ships that stuck to us like glue. They hugged our behind as if they wanted to make love to us.

I worked the controls to the best of my ability. I sighted on our closest targets and unleashed unholy hell on them. It split the immediate bogeys. They went skidding close to the trees that crowded the shore. Four more came screaming up to take their places, cocky sons of bitches. I lay into them with every bit of vehemence I could muster. Three long-nosed craft burst into flames then went plummeting to the trees, balls of crimson fire.

"Hot damn!" Krake beamed at me with pleasure. Nice shot, Kip. You been taking lessons from Skel here?"

"Hell no. Skel takes lessons from me."

"In your dreams, pal," Skel growled.

Areth hunched in the spare seat beside us. Her light tattered gown was wet and it was not warm on the bridge. Baskra unstrapped himself and draped a blue-and-gray service coat around her shivering shoulders.

Three Skurgs decided to play daredevil. They hyper impulsed ahead to cut us off.

Shit, they were coming straight at us, playing chicken. A death-defying game of nerves. Who would crack first? Bright fire traces whipped across our hull, dimming our shields. Smoke drifted from the panels above onto the bridge. The XT6 was coming apart.

Krake chewed his lip, but he remained calm.

At the last instant he got the XT6 jogging up fifty feet and I laid fire at those bitches as they passed, sending them converging to the sides. One smashed into the shoreward mangalorn erupting into flame. The other two went hurtling on a zigzag course to crash head on into the swarm of gnats on our heels.

Multiple explosions lit the air. The Yesmian forests were

illuminated for brief seconds as a half a dozen ships went up in flames. Twenty more got ensnared in the inferno and were either wrecked completely or came smashing into the dense brush and tangle of trees below.

Skel, Krake and I whooped.

I grinned with a warrior's enthusiasm. I smacked palms with Skel. I could get into this gunner gig.

But red alert signals flashed on the console above Krake. A familiar whale-like shape came veering down at us out of the blackness.

Narwhal. Almost on top of us.

Heedless of the Skurgs, she beat a reckless path.

Cyr's bear-like voice boomed once again over the com as we continued our hellish plunge south to who knows where.

"Give yourself up, XT6! Your pitiful attempts at escape are useless. Enemies surround you eighty to one. Your shields are at near zero. The end is near, traitors. I promise you a quick, clean end. Only if you land that pile of junk right now back at the landing pad. This is a generous offer. Consider it a warrior's due."

Skel grunted explosively. "It means our deaths, both slow and torturous! You can't fool us, Cyr."

An angry silence ensued over the com. "As you like. You act well under pressure for one so young. Perhaps I overestimated the strength of my fortress under the sea. My mistake. There will be new policies in the future. Half of my Aquor are dead. Four domes destroyed. Incalculable damages to others. The setback is beyond description. My priceless collection of Mentera fossils lost forever." Here Cyr's voice turned a dangerous crackle of murderous. "For this sabotage, death can not be considered worthy."

"We're sorry for your loss," Skel said.

There came a flurry of invective from the com. It burned our ears and Krake was obliged to cut the channel.

"A boor." Skel sighed. "So there you have it."

"What now?" I croaked.

"Just keep out of their sights, Kip. If one of those ships get their tractor beams—"

No sooner had he said it when a strange, blue-yellow light formation came starfishing at us from one of the larger ships behind us. An evil net ready to clamp on our hull.

"Krake, bank left!" Skel cried.

Too late.

The weave caught us midships even as Krake tried to dodge out of the river valley. I clamped sights and fired on the guard ship protecting the spin-weaver, but didn't get to the spin-weaver fast enough. Damn! Now she had us in her death hold as the guard ship erupted in a ball of flame.

Our power dropped by half. Suddenly there were Skurg fighters all around us.

Gy-ar's space yacht came gliding in to witness our final defeat.

We were caught in the Skurg's weave. Our heavy bulk could barely move. Impulse thrust was struggling at a third power.

Krake gave a mournful croak.

"Time to die, bitch." A wave of fury coursed over me. I amped up the electro-fission, channeled everything the ship's shields had into assault mode. We'd blast him with everything we could!

Krake came stumbling over to grab my arm. "No! You'll kill us all with shields down."

I shoved him aside. I laid everything into the cannon fire and a bright streak arrowed out from the XT6's starboard bow.

Gy-ar's ship caught the composite pulse-and-ion blast. Her stern turned an unreal, fantasy orange. Her bow dipped. The ship sloughed on a shallow angle toward the thick black forest, ironically close to where he and his bastards had lit the fires. Smoke trailed from the space yacht's rear fins.

The XT6 had ground to a near dead halt, caught at last in the Skurg's accursed weave.

"You nailed him, Kip," Krake wheezed, "but now, we're screwed."

"We were always screwed, Krake," I said softly. "From the moment we set foot on this cursed planet, in Aqua Rex, and that damn masquerade. Damn Cyr and damn Gy-ar and his machinations."

"Was it worth our lives?"

I turned away. Paused in mid-swivel as my mind passed over the images of how many would suffer at the hands of Gy-ar, how easily he would take control of the underwater cities and roll out the Temple's protocol. How much evil that lizard would unleash on the millions around the frontier worlds was immeasurable, and at last I nodded my head. "Yes. It's worth it."

Areth shook her head wildly and trembled. "What the hell are you guys talking about? Why are we just sitting here?"

"They locked us in a spider-weave," I said simply.

"I heard, but what does that mean?" she shrieked.

"That you'd better say your final prayers if you have any god," said Krake.

Through the viewport I saw an odd image. Narwhal and Vipra hung wrapped in the same creepy, inescapable weave around their hulls. Why them too? Eighty Skurg ships swarmed around all three of us now, hovering like scavenging vultures. My eyes flicked off the pale, dead face of Jerome and searched for some meaning in it all, some retribution.

There was none.

Gy-ar had turned traitor on us all.

I turned to Skel and saw the same defeated look in his face.

What did I feel? Nothing.

Only a cold, stark emptiness at the fate that awaited us.

CHAPTER 28

A clunk came to the hull and that characteristic lurch as we entered the limbo of hyperspace. The gigantic hulk of the XT6 merged into the light stream and fled to God knows where. Time seemed to slow. All was deathly silent aboard the XT6 but for the thud of our own hearts.

For hours we flew in deep hyperdrive in the clutch of the Skurg tug. Skel, Areth and I raided Krake's locker and traded our foppish costumes for standard spacer leathers. We armed ourselves with blasters and defensive armor from the weapons' stores and fueled up on frozen chicken snack packs, knowing this would be the last chance we would have to eat such stuff. We held conference and debated how we were going to prepare for the Skurgs when we landed, though we knew the chance of winning past them or surviving a full-on assault was slim to nil.

So we were not surprised when the final jolt came and the XT6 bumped down somewhere in the universe.

We had sealed the bridge. And we waited, crouched behind the weapons' grid seats and whatever else we could, which was scanty at best. We clutched our blasters in white-knuckled fists.

A metallic clank came at the bridge door as the Skurgs set explosives. The double doors were blown open and a dozen figures came scudding in past the wreckage and into the smoke. We aimed fire, killed six of the rushing figures and sent two more rolling to the cold steel floor, inert black-armored shapes.

Skel fought like a madman and was rewarded for his efforts with bruises and a bloody jaw before the rest of the Skurgs stormed us in numbers. I clocked a leather-armored brute that smelled of musk-ox with the butt of my blaster, breaking his teeth before the weapon was snatched from my grip. They dragged me by the arms out onto the tarmac into the wan sunlight.

I expected an arid waste but it was a cool, dry plain.

A sharp wind that rustled our hair was peppery and dry, the smell and taste heavy in our mouths. Low-scudding clouds moved across a grayish-yellow sky. There was a howl in the air as the winds carved their way over the reddish soil and around the few stunted trees and cacti and odd boulder that we saw in their midst. The Skurgs had toeholds in many parts of the galaxy and this was one of them. But a far different setup than the last hellhole on Skaldar.

I crawled painfully to my feet, gazing left and right. I was surrounded by over a dozen seven-foot monster Skurgs.

Their black-brown leathers were worn and scuffed. In places smeared with dried blood. Leggings, arm pads, torso—reinforced with tougher leather and steel beneath. Open-faced helmets rounded at the back, square at the front, fingers outfitted in big black-leather mitts. They walked with a slight stoop, backs curved high at their wide shoulders. Some had gimlet eyes, glassy and cold, with weaselish snouts. Others had eyes wide and staring and noses snubbed like hogs, as if maimed during battle. No brows. The bottom lip fatty and swollen, underslung like a sullen animal's.

Ugly sons of bitches.

The only way to get at them was by face and neck, and the skull, if you could ever get the helmet off.

It was a very strange setting. The purl of trickling water echoed over my left shoulder past the landing area. To my surprise, the Skurg outpost was flanked by a waterfall which fell down a sheer cliff about 40-50 feet tall into a brackish, greenish pool. All around us ranged cactus-like woods that had been mostly stripped. Remnants of the battered hulls of about a dozen or so starships lay scattered throughout. Gaping holes showed in their sides, blackened husks with weeds growing out of their fuselages. An ancient battle had been fought here. These antique ships looked to be about 200 years old. Cylindrical hulls with basic single cannon mounts and small, cramped pilothouses hiked up on the bow. About 4 miles distant I saw the vestiges of a ruined city. Crumbled towers and skyscrapers, the top halves chopped off as if in an air battle. A snapshot out of a grim, frightening dystopia. The Skurgs had used a place that nobody of sound mind would ever want to return to—now a base and work camp and one of their ritual outposts.

The Skurgs herded us to the bank of the shallow river about 1000 yards away where a somber huddle of about 40 wretches crouched in the shallows, panning for crystals or gems or something that looked like gold. Really? We were beckoned forward with cryptic grunts and motions of arms. Circular pans were thrust in our hands.

I looked back to the scrubby airfield. More ships were arriving. Two tugs, bright with spider weave shining a ghostly hue under their midnight black hulls. Suddenly the weave disintegrated and dropped their loads. The two captured ships were released from their death grips and clanked down loudly on the asphalt.

Narwhal stayed upright. But Vipra lay on her side, crippled. She had a gaping hole in her midships flank and I wondered if Remus had survived.

The pack of Skurgs grunted at us like the swine they were. We were pushed toward the shallow water on the sandy reddish bank where we were to crouch with our pans amid the other hollow-faced workers, to sift the waters and sediments for flakes and nuggets, of gold.

I mean, come on?

In today's age of starships and varwol and futuristic cities, we were to go back to the stone age and gold rush days to pan for gold?

Skel laughed when he saw their setup. "You a Klondike gold rush man, Kip? I could be. This is too funny." He wiped the blood off his chin and hawked out a great wad of spit. He looked relatively unscathed, given what he had been through. No broken bones that I could see and his limp mostly gone.

So demoralized was I that I could only grumble.

It was to my astonishment that this Skurg camp was by this waterfall and a river where gold was sieved and mined. Why so old school? Why the lack of dredging machines and modern tech?

But then my brain kicked in. The Skurgs were a quasi nomadic people who made these remote outposts the places of their traditional blood rituals. The mining was secondary. More important were the blood games and cannibalism, giving them an identity, a purpose, a culture of violence.

I shuddered at the simple truth of my revelation.

The cactus-like trees were thick, squat, rising up to ten feet high with prickly branches forking out on 45 degree angles. The waterfall fell from half way up the bluffs—out of an arched hole fed by some mysterious spring. Into the deep green pool it spilled, making white froth on the surface.

A massive fire pit ranged by the waterfall between the river and the nearest downed ship. This was a 40-foot circular pit marked with white chalk on reddish sand. The same dimensions and same configuration as the one on Skaldar.

My hackles rose. I recalled those blood games and barbaric rituals with a shudder.

Something else caused the hair to rise on the back of my neck: a low, squat, cube-like outbuilding with one thick window a stone's throw away. It loomed between the place where we worked and the airstrip. The meat shop...where they amputated limbs of the losers at the games and fed them to the ravenous Skurgs.

Use your brain, Rusco, get your creative juices flowing. Think of a way out of this hellhole.

Across the river only more desolate plain. Even if we could make a beeline to the far bank, we'd be sitting ducks to a barrage of ship fire.

I estimated we were just over 3 miles out from the city, a possible place of refuge. But how to get there? The riverbank we pan-sifted was the center of the camp. No fences. No artillery guns. Strangely, no barracks.

This lack of security was a good thing. Nothing was stopping us from just walking out unless they'd planted land mines. But so what? There was nowhere to run. The Skurgs would goad us down in an instant and sling us into the meat shop.

Areth hunched dourly to my left. Skel squinted into the sun, whistling an out-of-tune melody. Krake and the others dug tin pans into the river and worked further downstream. When I lifted my head from my work, I counted about 70 downed ships littering the cactus-strewn plain that stretched between us and the city. Those ships could be used as cover if we could get there, or as places to lay booby traps, deadfalls or snares to outwit and slay the cursed Skurgs.

A pipe dream. There were too many of them. They were like ghouls wandering the desolate stretch of river with glowing goads on the ready.

I estimated about thirty of them roving the area. We were shy of fifty slaves, in various states of health and morale. The newly arrived were fresh and full of piss and vinegar, ready to fight their way out, but the others looked exhausted, emaciated and defeated long ago. Wrinkled age lines marked their faces, wraith-like with their sunken eyes, cheeks and spirits. A mixture of men and women, mostly men, but no children.

Areth's eyes darted about wildly. "What the hell is this place? Where are we?"

"A work camp," I muttered. "Could be anyplace, on any frontier world."

Skel peered up from his pan-sifter. "We traveled for a day? Could put us anywhere between Perseus and Maerikor."

"That narrows it down," I said cynically.

"Look on the bright side, Kip, we're alive."

"For what?" Areth cried. "A lifetime of slavery, panning gold dust on an alien world? I'll never see my daughter again." Her voice cracked. She looked ready to burst into tears.

"No, it means we can escape," Skel rasped. "We can outwit these stupid Skurgs. Kip and I escaped once, we can do it again."

I gave a grudging nod. Skel's carrot-red hair was askew, his face and arms bruised from the battle on the ships. The man was a wildcard. I learned never to underestimate him. His resourcefulness was legend. If anyone could do it, it would be Skel.

Areth's head hung low. Her face was grimed with dirt, streaked with tears.

Skel softened, laid a hand on her shoulder. "Don't give up, girl. We can escape. You'll see her yet."

A Skurg with glaring eyes came over and jabbed him on the shoulder with his goad.

Skel howled, jumped back two feet in the water. "Back off, you piece of shit!"

The Skurg lifted back his goad to strike again. Skel arched his arm to block. Two more figures lumbered over to assist should Skel decide to be unruly.

Wisely he kept his cool.

The Skurg drifted off, voicing gutturals, to chastise others who dared to slack off.

"Bastards," Skel muttered under his breath. He nursed another bruise on his left shoulder.

The sounds of cargo bay ramps clanking on asphalt came from the airfield as the two Skurg tugs whined down to a drone. A huddle of miserable figures were goaded from the holds by a squad of six Skurgs—Remus, Rolph, Cyr and three crewmen. Cyr flung vile curses and murderous looks as he passed nearby to spit at us. The six prisoners were herded downstream with the bulk of the other slaves.

I exhaled a sigh of relief. I was in no mood to tango with that bastard.

We conversed in low whispers, halfheartedly doing our work, keeping our lip movements to a bare minimum.

"Old Cyr isn't looking too happy," Skel said.

"Neither are we."

"When the time is ripe, we can make a break for those ships," Skel hissed. "But the time's not now."

The wrecks got more numerous as they spread toward the city, implying that an epic battle had been fought here to take or defend the city. A graveyard of ships. I noted two kinds of vessels—the cylindrical ones with silver hulls, then the smaller, black-armored starfish-shaped ones. Probably in a 10:1 ratio so I guessed the starfish ships had prevailed.

I asked Skel about it and he frowned. He was only able to recall such ships as belonging to early Mentera warships, prior to their adoption of the newer insectile lightfighter hulls and the much later mammoth ring stations.

Another ancient war of lost races whose tale would never be told...

Were we the only humans on this planet? If not, where were the others? What planet were we on?

I'd give my teeth to know the answers.

A vague dirt road ran alongside the stream, zigzagging as it followed the water toward the mysterious city.

To my right the covered metal hangar loomed at the edge of the airfield where about twenty vessels sat, including Vipra, the XT6 and fifteen Skurg lightfighters.

Areth slapped her pan with resignation. "I never imagined I'd be here in this dismal predicament with a couple of grungers and carrot-haired daredevils."

Skel beamed. "Is that a compliment, Lady Areth? The universe is a strange place." He wiped his grimy face with a cat-like grin.

"How'd you escape this camp you were in before?" she demanded.

"You want the short version or the long version?"

She shrugged. "Does it matter? Looks like we're here for a while, so why not the long version?"

"We grew up on a farm on Tildara. Smally, me, my Uncle Dodkin and Aunt Mallie. Dad put us at Dodkin's place when we were five and—"

"Not that long," she said with a toss of her head.

"Bear with me." Skel resumed. "We were destined to be ranch hands when we got older. Smally got bucked off a horse when he was riding rough, half drunk. He got crippled at age 15. I took over his spot on the farm, but the interest was not there. Earned the disappointment of my uncle. Not my old man, because he knew I'd never be a rancher anyway. He just wanted someplace for me and Smally to grow up and toughen up. Dodkin had me slated as the next manager of Everbright Ranches. I was more into seeing the planets, traveling the worlds, finding out about exotic places. More what my old man was all about, but he was a history buff, an archaeologist. He took part in digs on various worlds. I joined him on one and we ended up getting nabbed by Skurgs along the way." He paused as a haunted look passed over his face. "I reckon I spent upwards of 5 years in that god-forsaken camp."

Areth paled. "You still haven't said how you escaped yet. This is the place where you and Rusco met?"

"Yepper."

"How's it compare to this one?"

He dug his pan into the sandy bottom. "Same idea, different setup and stuff they were mining. Same shit-for-brains Skurg slavers. All you need to know, Areth, is stay out of their way, keep your head down and follow my and Rusco's lead." He gazed curiously at me. "What about you, Kippie? Any childhood tales to share?"

I let out a tired breath. "I used to do runs for a con boss named Tyger on Yiba. Mean son of a bitch. He knew the streets like the back of his hand, was lord of the streets. A tough burlward-thug as they called them. Ever since, I've had a dislike for crime lords."

"Nice tale," Skel said wryly. He edged in beside me. "Sorry to rain on your parade, bro, but here comes our guard again."

We stayed glum and silent for the next two hours as the guard whom we named Walleye, kept the evil eye on us, all twirling goad in a black-mitted fist. The water purled on down across the cactus-strewn plain between the hulks of ruined ships and on toward the broken city. We sifted sand on our hands and knees with the primitive pan-like sieves dipping in the shallow riverbed while the Skurgs watched over us like a flock of hawks. Five-foot goads were clutched on the ready to strike us, if we lagged.

More than once we heard the sharp zing of arcing electricity, then the wailing cry of a figure falling in water caught zoning out and zapped by a merciless slaver.

It was a humiliating experience being slave to these monsters. On our hands and knees all day doing menial, mindless labor.

The gold fragments and chunks we collected were put in rocker-box-like sieves at the shore and shaken to separate the gold from the pebbles and silt. They were hauled away by four-wheeled quads to the landing field from where they would be shipped by small cargo vessel to open markets somewhere in the galaxy to up the Skurgs' profit.

There seemed an endless supply of such gold spread across the stream which slowed and fattened at an area about sixty feet wide and one and a half feet deep where we toiled. Fed by a spring somewhere under the catclaw-like woods atop the bluffs, the spring which sourced the waterfall.

I screwed up my eyes and squinted into the sun. I'd never seen such a thing. But who knows what miracles and mysteries the universe hid on these alien worlds?

CHRIS TURNER

CHAPTER 29

When the sun set and the work day was over, the Skurgs fed us a coarse gruel warmed over the bonfire in the fire pit. If I were generous, the slop might have been potatoes and onions mixed with dry seeds that had an aromatic taste. Also in the mix were leathery gray chunks of meat whose origin I shuddered to guess. The vegetables must have been shipped in, as I didn't see anything growing here. If it weren't for the river, there'd be no life here at all. The stash of vegetables was kept in a cookhouse, ironically next to the meat house and I suspected this fare might have been served to stave off parasites from our guts and keep our gut flora alive. A dead or sick slave was of no use to them, except for extra limbs to roast over their fires.

The flames licked high and we were forced to watch them crackle. They'd herded us toward the 40-foot ring by the fire with our arms loaded with dry cactus logs to feed the fire. The flames blazed on the other side of the combat circle directly opposite us.

We were contained in a kind of stockade: a semicircle of sharp stakes at our backs, shoulder high. Skurg spectators hemmed us in to either side, crowding close to the combat circle and armed with goads and mallets. The only way to bolt was forward into the circle. A quick ticket to either a fiery death or zapped by goads and shipped off to the meat shop.

The Skurgs forced us to be part of their blood rituals. Such that they could pick any one of us at any time to be the objects of their sport...their sacrificial goats.

A lean man was selected first from our huddle of miserable souls. A tough wiry fellow with long straggles of golden hair and gaunt cheeks. He had a gleaming brow, sun-browned arms. A man with quick steps and unsmiling face. He wore a soiled T-shirt, cutoff at the shoulders. Obviously he'd been through this torture many times because his movements were precise, his nerves taut. He was prodded with goads into the 40-foot circle. His Skurg opponent tossed him a wooden stave, 4 feet long, whittled from one of the few scraggly catclaw-like trees scattered around the compound. The Skurg came at him, his electrified green-glowing goad whirling.

I watched how he moved. His strategy was simple. Keep the opponent busy. He took quick steps, not long strides or fancy evasive maneuvers.

He had this trick where, after the Skurg had struck and committed to his blow, quick as a viper he could deke around the flank and lay a decisive smack on the back of his head. All this to the jeers of his Skurg fellows. The Skurg was flustered. After the fourth clubbing, the Skurg overstepped. The man turned on his heel and smashed the stave end hard into the ugly face, ringing his helm and laying him low.

The man raised high his stave in the sign of victory while the Skurg lolled in the dirt. The Skurgs hooted and jeered. While they picked new adversaries, the victor was allowed to return to our group. It seemed they even had a grudging respect for him. I'd never seen such skill in the slaves on Skaldar, outside of what Skel and I brought to the table, fighting for our lives. I earmarked his strategy in case it was me in that circle with a stave.

Next up were two ugly-faced Skurgs. They strode into center ring with an arrogant ceremony. They stood before each other in bent-kneed stances. One clutched a mallet, the other a green-glowing goad. Both were dressed in ceremonial leathers with red bands. This was new. They faced off with gutturals, fist pumps then came at each other like lions. The shorter, stockier one moved in fast. He pummeled the other with sharp whips of mallet. He snapped the enemy's goad in half. The other ducked to defend, but mallet-slinger came in and kicked the helmet off his rival, laying bare the albino skull. It was gross, like a wet snail or night worm gleaming in the firelight. The wooden mallet came down with a boneless thwack on the exposed skull. It was all over. As a final act, the victor bent low, twisted off the weaselish snout of his adversary with a grim crunch and tucked the bloody member in his belt as a trophy.

The loser was dragged off to the spits where the Skurgs rejoiced in more fresh meat for the evening. The sloppy, guttural smacks of pleasure as they butchered and ate their meat with fingers and teeth made us sick to our stomachs. We had to turn our heads at the wet sucking sounds.

What did they care? They'd truck more Skurgs in from Timbuktu to be carved up and more slaves from other worlds to satisfy their blood lusts.

But we couldn't dwell on this now, for it seemed the Skurgs wished to make sport of us new arrivals. Remus and Comby were pulled next out of our pack to do battle in the center.

Brown haired and grubby faced, Comby stared with apprehension at the grim figure of Remus. Remus made a show of rolling his sleeves and cracking his knuckles. He peered at him with disarming insidiousness.

It was clear Comby was no match for the bigger man and he managed to get in two hits before Remus struck hard with a growling curse and grabbed our crewman in a crushing bear hug. He paraded him around the circle to the animated jeers and goad-piking antics of the Skurgs.

I sidled left and right, trying to get to Comby but the Skurgs thrust goads at us and zapped any of us who got too close. I nursed the burn on my shoulder where the tip of a stave had zapped me.

Comby had nothing to lose. He thrashed and flailed. His face was red with humiliation at all the glaring eyes around him. The Skurgs tired of the spectacle. A goad came teetering in at Remus's shins. He bellowed in rage and dropped his trophy. Comby had time to scramble to safety, panting, his eyes white, to the opposite end of the circle.

There ensued a cat-and-mouse game as Remus charged after him. The chase dragged on a trifle too long. Skurg goads came whickering in at both of them. Comby got the worst of it. He lay still, groaning, unable to move, curled in a fetal position. Remus came stumping over, prodding him with his foot. There was no movement. Walleye, the red-eyed Skurg, stepped in and pushed Remus aside, tested Comby with his goad then brought a foot down on this arm, cracking the bone. Still no stir.

I stared in horror. Walleye brought a boot down decisively on Comby's throat.

Three Skurgs strode in to drag him to the fire. There ensued a horrible clacking of knives and cleavers as Comby's slack body was worked over, his limbs carved up and skewered on spits.

Remus was allowed back to our miserable huddle, much to the dissatisfaction of Cyr who peered at him in disgust.

"Why didn't you kill him when you had the chance? What do I pay you for?"

"He's dead, isn't he?" Remus snapped. He fixed Cyr a glare of contempt.

The Skurgs devoured their fresh meat. Green of face, we all stared blankly, waiting to see who would be next, but they'd had enough of feasting for the evening.

They surrounded us in a tight circle, herded us downriver into the darkness.

I was alarmed. Walleye was at the head of the pack, his wicked goad swinging. At first I had the horrible thought they were going to mass murder us all; instead they split us up into two groups and pushed us further ahead, torches in hand, to two of the derelict, cigar-shaped ships farther downstream. Areth, Lisse, Quassa, Cyr and I were in one of those groups. Krake, Skel and the others were in the second one. With mounting relief, I realized that these dead ships were our 'sleeping quarters', devised such that we would live to wake up and start the nightmare all over again.

They had gutted and reworked the ships' interiors to use as prison cells. The Skurgs prodded us inside, through the blackened hatch holes. They marched us down the hallway to the makeshift dormers. A set of dim overhead lights illumined twenty or so steel doors to either side.

Like cattle we were prodded into our slave quarters. Two to a cell. At first I was worried about Areth being paired with one of the slaves, or worse yet, Cyr, but then I glimpsed Quassa, maybe Lisse being shuttled into a cell with her. I could not be sure, as we were moving too fast and it was all a blur. Roughly I was shoved into a cell at the end with the lean man who'd fought valiantly at the games. No unsupervised open-concept coed dorms here. They ran this place like a military barracks. Much differently than on Skaldar. I caught a glimpse of our coffin-like quarters before the door slammed shut and we were plunged into near darkness. A crude commode, small rusted sink, two cots bolted to either wall.

The last of the doors clanked shut, and we sat blinking in the murk on our beds. I could just barely make out the man's silhouette under the small rim of light that leaked under the door. The smell of stale sweat hung heavy in the air.

"Name's Somalon," he said, reaching out a hand.

"Rusco." I gave the hand a firm shake. "Well, here we are in the dark, alive and smelling worse than dog shit."

"You got that right," he laughed.

"Some good maneuvering back there in the pit. Where'd you learn to fight? Held your head and your nerve."

His voice was low and gravelly. It had a tinge of the gloomy. "It's the only way to survive against these swine. If they detect any weakness they'll make mincemeat out of you. Something to do with their mongrel breeding. They're not that fast, or quick of brain, but they can be brutal when they have to." He peered at me. "You look as if you're up to give them a run for their money when it comes your turn."

"How'd you learn how to fight them?"

"Of the five guys I came with, only one was left. Whittled down to robot legs and arms, more cyborg than human. They were all killed in the games."

"You escaped getting robotized?"

"The only one I know of," he said proudly.

"How long you been in for?"

"Couldn't say. Seen a lot of folk come and go. All deader than doornails."

"I was once in a Skurg camp myself—on Skaldar."

I could hear his weight shift incredulously on his cot. "Yeah? What was that like?"

"Hellish."

"How'd you escape?"

"Me and Skel—the guy with the carrot-red hair—took out a couple of guards and hoofed it to the hills. He was the mastermind. Through sheer luck and brawn, we took our opportunity when it came and got out of Dodge."

"Impressive." He shook his head. "That fellow seems cunning. Always something going on in his head. I can tell by the way his tawny eyes dart about. Looks like he's sleepy and slow, but he's always listening and watching everything."

I gave a wry laugh. "That's Skel."

"I came from Balsar. We were working a supply convoy of three ships. Sent to deliver military electronics to an outpost base on Duine. We come out of light drive and there they were, a whole battalion of Skurgs waiting for us, the bitching scavengers. They wrapped us in their spider weave and sent us to our separate hellholes around the galaxy. Don't know where the other two ships got to, but ours landed here."

"Sounds familiar."

"Don't know how they knew we were there," he said with a

venomous edge. "Everything smells of setup."

"It was a setup," I assured him. I told him how Vipra and our convoy had been waylaid by Skurgs before Oranthe. "Any idea where we are?"

"Not a clue. How'd you get aboard a convoy in the first place? You seem a little young to be in this trade, if you don't mind my saying."

My smile was mirthless. "It's a long story. Let's just say I got mixed up with the wrong people. Cyr, that bear of a man, for starters."

"Him? What's his deal? Seems like he's got a lot of piss and vinegar in his blood. I tried to show him a better way of sifting, save him some time and some clubbing from the Skurgs, but he nearly took my head off. Bastard. Mind you, if I'd got what had been done to him and his crew, I might be a little pissed myself."

"He tried to build underwater cities. He hired Skel, me and the others who came in today to be his mercenary guards. His elite little field grunts. It was an adventure, but it was doomed from the start. He was allied with Gy-ar, that king shit of the Moon Temple. It went downhill from there."

Somalon gave a low growl. "Heard some stories about that cult. Don't know how much more of the story I want to hear, Rusco. They're everywhere. Lodges and temples set up in all the cities on the frontier. They've infiltrated all political circles and trade centers over the settled worlds."

"Preaching to the choir, friend. Skel and I will be making our move soon. Watch for it any day. We'll give you word, if we can. Has to be on the fly. Soon as you see something going down, like a fight, a distraction or disturbance, be ready to make for the ships."

He gave a terse grunt. "I'll be the first one behind you. The happiest damn man alive if I can break out of this crib." He clenched a fist. In the murky light I could make out his flexing fingers.

I lay awake listening to the soft regular rhythm of Somalon's breathing. I guess he'd come to terms with his lot and could sleep at night. He'd learned how to cope with these days of horror. Something I should be doing as well, but couldn't.

I got up and paced.

In the dimness, I could detect, probing with my fingers, that the fixtures had been added after the fact by the Skurgs. Crude pipes ran from wash basin to floor through a rudely-cut out hole. A hack job. And yet, they were still bolted firmly enough to prevent an industrious soul from yanking it out and somehow engineering an escape through the floor to a lower level. The refurbished ships would imply that the cylindrical vessels were much older than what we'd assumed, possibly before the peak of the pioneer era of human expansion to the frontier worlds. The city was another mystery. Who made it? When was it built? Answers to these mysteries we'd probably never know. The broken, sawed-off skyscrapers looked vaguely human-engineered, but also had a quasi alien vibe to them. The town's layout was too sparse and odd. The octagonal, monolithic superstructures too peculiar to the eye even from a distance. The cylindrical ships could be any race—Daulk, human, alien.

I tried pushing my full weight against the steel door. Useless. Somalon would have tried this anyway and everything else in his months here. Always a slim chance there was something he hadn't thought of. I probed every square inch of that miserable rabbit hutch with fingers and toes but found no weakness, no loose screw or wobbly panel.

With a dismal sigh, I gave up and lay on my back on the musty mattress. At some time in the long night I fell into a troubled sleep.

CHAPTER 30

I awoke to a glare of lights and the sting of a goad arcing me off my bed. I rolled to my feet in groggy incomprehension. Braced myself to join Somalon and the bleak line of figures trudging down the hallway, sleep-deprived with bed heads, greasy skin and unsmiling faces.

Bright sunlight greeted me as the ship hatch was flung open. We were marched down to the stream. The sunlight stung my eyes. The air was cooler. The orb of the sun was a burning yellow blot somewhere across the trickling waters. They herded us to the fire where we saw Baskra, to our horror, a fish-white corpse, dragged there by Skurg hands. Apparently our friend'd been paired with Cyr in the other slave ship and that had not fared well. He lay there face up, saved for the evening feast.

I couldn't eat the gruel they warmed over the fire that morning. I'd rather have my belly crawling with hunger than puke it up a moment later. The Skurgs could care less if we ate or starved. They prodded us back to the stream where we resumed our mindless pan-sifting.

I couldn't get Baskra's face out of my mind. His matted black curls, his round, happy-go-lucky face and gap-toothed grin. They all worked together to give him a somewhat boyish look. He had a blank stare bordering on astonishment, one that seemed to say, 'why me?'.

I shuddered to think of me or Skel paired with that brute, Cyr, but I knew that day would come soon. Despite our not so shabby street skills, I doubted either of us could take him. We'd be pulverized to meat, or strangled in our sleep.

The day dragged on. Very few times could I see any window of opportunity. We were under constant surveillance, and even those fleeting moments had a 20:80 chance of success.

The yellow sun inched slowly across the sky. Each notch marking the long 14-hour workday. I gave a frustrated sigh as I pan-scraped the riverbed for the bizillionth time. I squinted into the sun and across the cactus-strewn plains. There was no life that I could see. No buzzards, no coyotes, no field mice, hedgehogs, snakes or wandering animals. No nomads. No humans or Skurg. No movement from the city. One of the giant moons of the planet hung over the colossal skyscraper tops, not purple but more mauve in the harsh daylight with progress no faster than the boiling sun. The Skurgs had effectively picked a dead dry world for their enterprise. No one would come looking for them out here. If they remained untracked, the Skurgs could exist here indefinitely.

It was no clever deduction to see that every night we spent in this hellhole lessened our chance of survival. We'd have to do something quick or perish.

The cacti trembled at small gusts of wind that kicked up dust devils and made mournful howls as they carved their way around the scraggly trunks of what looked like acacias. Occasionally the *thug-thug* of a quad came bumping up behind us to haul the bins of sediment we'd labored to collect, to the airfield.

Skurg ships dropped twice out of the sky. One landed to disgorge five new Skurg guards, another bearing a spider weave tightly coiled around some unfortunate cargo vessel with twin cannons. Three more laborers were added to our miserable numbers.

A larger Skurg transport vehicle departed later in the afternoon to carry off the gold sediments we'd painstakingly pan-sifted.

Skel contrived to move closer to where Areth and I worked in the shallows glumly. "How'd you enjoy your slumber?" he muttered.

"Not much. You?"

"I was paired with Krake. We searched high and low for any means of escape. Nothing. Half the night gone. Not a crevice. Locked tight as a drum, Kip."

"My cell was a bust too. Traded some talks with our friend Somalon there." I inclined my head toward his lean frame where he worked 50 yards distant. "He's managed to survive for months on courage alone. Keen observation and never showing fear." I cast a baleful look at Cyr who bent in the water another ten yards distant. "That fiend has to be dealt with."

Skel's eyes flicked contemptuously on Cyr. "He's out to murder us one by one. We've got to move fast."

"How?"

"I don't know. We'll think of something. If they pair any of us with him in the games, or the dorms, it isn't going to end well."

Areth gave a soft dismal moan. She fumbled for her pan. She quickly snatched it up from the water as I saw a whisper of movement several yards away—the 7-foot fiend with the red eye beetling our way.

The days were about 35 hours, possibly 40, which explained my sense of time dilation and utter exhaustion. The night was semi-illumined by the planet's twin purplish moons. I could only guess the moons' soil was a crystalline composition, maybe amethyst or another mineral. The universe was a strange place.

Areth dropped face first in exhaustion later that hot afternoon. I sloshed over to pull up her head before she choked to death. Walleye came lurching in toward us and I could not stop him from jabbing her with his goad.

The shock got her out of her stupor. She howled at the electric sting and clutched her side as if jolted out of a savage dream.

I flailed into the leathery bully-coward. The goad rose and fell. I winced with every hit of its electric sting.

Skel stepped in. He was at my side, his fists cocked. Both of us dared the monster to try something else. He took a sniveling step back, his warty face pocked and seamed. His red eye glinted with malevolence.

He raised his goad for another strike but something in our gaze and murderous fists warned him against further violence. He grunted a monosyllable then turned away, but he had his eye trained on us for the rest of that day. The brute we called Walleye now got the moniker 'Red-Eye', because his ugly red orb and the pale crimson scar that started at the eye's outer edge and ran along to the lip of his helm, had turned a darker shade of red. Whether it was congenital or the remnants of a past fight or injury, we did not know. Probably the former. His nose was snubbed as if it had been cut.

After the brute had trotted off, Skel growled a curse. "It's now or never, Kip. We make a rush tomorrow. While they're scattered around the yard at break-siesta, all of us, as a team. Spread the word. A couple of guys, maybe Krake and your friend Somalon. They create a stir, get in a fake squabble while the others beetle it toward the ships. The Daulk lightfighter and the XT6 are our only prospects. Vipra looks toast. We can't count on her or navigating the Skurg ships."

"Agreed," I said stonily. "What of Krake and Somalon? How are they going to make it out?"

He frowned. "They can loop around and meet as at the airfield. If they get snagged, they'll have to rely on us piling in a ship and shooting at everything we see."

"Sounds desperate."

"What isn't?"

"What about Cyr?"

"What about that bastard?"

"How do we deal with him? I mean, we'll need every available hand. Should we bring him in?"

Skel nearly choked on his tongue. "Are you loco? He's insane. As much as I hate the Skurgs taking another human life, old Cyr signed his death warrant when he turned on us. He's allied with Gy-ar and his Aquor mutants. They set the fires and screwed Dalree and the Yesmians. Cyr's a murderous scum. If anything, we kill him."

I could only bob my head in agreement.

As could be expected, the universe had something else planned.

CHAPTER 31

Dusk came with a cool, dry wind and already my guts were crawling with trepidation. I could barely eat two mouthfuls of that tasteless mash, even though I was genuinely hungry and felt lightheaded from all the long hours in the sun.

We stood like cattle in our corral. I heard grunts and laughter: Skurgs relishing the festivities to come. I smelled their animal sweat, their meaty, disgusting hides. When I blinked and stared across the well-worked sand of the pit, the red flames of the bonfire seemed to blur at the edges. I rubbed my eyes. The blur did not go away. Walleye ranged up and down the wall of faces of our huddle of bedraggled souls and his cruel red eye landed on me before I could sidle out of the way. He had his leatherbound, iron-helmed lackeys drag me by both arms into the center. Areth tried to cling to me but she was goaded back. It seemed the Skurgs wished to make more examples of us. Rolph was the next lucky contestant. They prodded him in with no less menace to center ring beside me where he stared empty-eyed, lip curled, his chest heaving.

He traded glances with Remus and Cyr and snorted at me. "You're the cause of us stuck in this shitpen, Rusco. I ought to gut you right here."

"Try it. Keep on believing that, Rolphie," I sneered. "Maybe point the finger back at your scum master and his ass-kissing policies. Truckling to every one of Gy-ar's whims. It took real guts to fire on

Gy-ar's ship, something you didn't have the balls to do yourself."

Rolph's face paled for an instant, then he gave a savage roar. I had struck too hard to the mark. His sun-addled brain couldn't handle his own hypocrisy. I sidestepped his rush and boxed his ears and tripped him as he came barreling through. He lay face first in the sand.

I shook my head. "That all you got, Rolphie? Come on. You can do better than that."

I put on my best smile, trying to goad our helmsman into a better fight and putting on a good show. It was the only way to keep both of our skins alive. As much as I knew Rolph was deluded and tainted by Cyr, I did not want to see him in the belly of the Skurgs. We were all allies here and the acts of even one able-bodied man could mean the difference between death and escape from this alien planet. The Skurgs whooped and grunted at the nose dirtying and piked goads into the air.

I pretended to be enjoying the spectacle but deep inside, my heart was thudding with malaise, for I knew one false move and it would be dismemberment for both of us.

Rolph got up, spitting sand. He wiped his mouth. Whipping back the lank black hair out of his eyes, he cursed and glared, eyes pinpricks of fury, lungs pumping hard.

He tried to smack me again and ended up worse, rolling on the ground and groaning as I blocked his kidney punch and struck him one myself mercilessly in the ribs. The Skurgs were not cheering as loudly this time. There were raucous grunts and low, cow-like sounds of booing. Rolph rose with his cheeks blazing. He sucked in a labored breath and a fearful look came into his eye. Something had snapped in him and I knew I'd pushed it too far. Was I caught in an evil dream? Was this man the same helmsman I'd fought side by side with against the Skurgs on Vipra?

He kind of danced around mouthing insults and I slugged him a few more times when he cursed and growled and tried hedging his way to the sidelines.

"Don't try it, Rolphie," I hissed at him. "You have to follow the rules. Pace this shit out like that other guy did. Give them a show, otherwise they'll cut you into rib—"

"Shut it, Ruskie. I'll take my chances."

"Don't be an idiot," I rasped. "We can fake this out together. Come at me, and I'll hit you a few more times and let you hit me. Better a broken nose or a few bruises than getting a robot—"

"Shut your mouth, you bastard," he said. "We're all dead anyways, what does it matter? I'm going to run you around this ring till you drop, then I'll slug you in the face and run for the hills before they—"

But it was too late. A couple of Skurgs bobbed in as Rolph dodged and did his circus act of trotting around the perimeter of the circle with a foolish grin on his face. He was doing a good job of staying out of their reach and the swipe of my fists and he laughed louder as they poked their goads at him, managing to evade their sting. I shook my head and after a while just stood there in the center of the circle, arms akimbo. Walleye snuck up behind Rolph and lifted him by the scruff of the neck. He tried to drag him off to the meat shop but I'd had enough.

I already hated that dickwad for jabbing Areth for not pan-sifting fast enough and I charged him. I lay fists into his flanks and somehow managed to get the goad off him hooked at his belt. I smacked him hard across the head and shoulders as many times as I could. He finally released Rolph and turned to me with a murderous look in his eyes.

We circled each other warily. The Skurgs went wild, whooping and jumping up like apes from their places. Two snatched Rolph around the torso before he could scamper away.

Walleye was not an easy foe to defeat. He came bulling in, helm down and such was his speed and violence that he had me staggering back, wind knocked out of my lungs. I still clutched the goad, but I was off balance and he struck at my hip this time and I went down, falling to my knees.

While I struggled for air, Walleye just circled me with an indifferent look in his eye. He was a coward and he motioned for a meaty monster-ass Skurg to take over for him. It seemed it was beneath him to personally battle me in the circle.

The seven-and-a-half foot giant came striding in and kneed me in the chest, sending me flying a quarter of the way across the ring before I could get up and defend. My goad was gone. The brute'd snatched it up and threw it into the audience as if it were a toy not worth his time.

In my ringing ears I heard a shriek like Areth's. Boots came down on my ribs. I gave a croaking groan. A sharp stinging pain twanged in my left side.

I shook my head. I rose in a half crouch trying to roll out of the way.

I was getting my ass kicked. Death was staring me in the face. Some Skurg chucked in a mallet which the giant agilely caught in a mitted fist. The weapon came whistling down on a deadly arc straight for my brains. I put up both arms to block. I heard a finger snap as the wood penetrated my defense and side-swiped me hard in the cheek, bouncing off my shoulder inches from my left ear.

I loosed a roar of agony, still scrabbling out of the way. With head hurting, heart pounding, I felt time slow as I waited for the final mallet strike to the skull.

A lumbering shape came into my periphery.

Cyr?

He came hupping in like a touchball player. A bear-like roar was on his lips. He tackled the Skurg round the middle and they both went rolling away in a blur of bodies. A cloud of dust arose. Cyr smashed the Skurg in the face then kicked him in the gut and got up huffing for breath.

The Skurg captain staggered to his feet. Gutturals spewed from his blackish lips. Blood dribbled from his horse-shaped mouth. His eyes were glazed. He seemed not to hear his fellow Skurgs as they hooted and hollered at him to fight.

I crawled painfully off to the side, nursing my cracked rib.

Cyr gave a snort of disgust. He flicked a contemptuous curse my way. "Get out of the ring, Rusco. You're a disgrace. The only reason I lowered myself to come in here and save your sorry ass was because I want to be the one to see the last glimmers of light fade from your eyes." I heard his echoey words as out of an underwater dream; the monster Skurg opened his mouth to spew, swaying where he stood.

I limped to my feet and licking blood off my own face, came stumbling toward Cyr. It was exactly what the murderer wanted. He stood there impassively, fists bunched, waiting for me to come at him so he could deliver the final blow.

Skel managed to bust past his goad-jabber and sprint to my side. He hauled me back with a hollow sneer. "Are you a damn fool, Kip? Don't try it. He'll kill you."

He pulled me away, even as I resisted, humiliated at my defeat, my cracked rib and broken finger. I looked on at Areth in shame who stared back white-faced at me.

The Skurgs went wild. Those who were spectators hopped from foot to foot. They smacked hands together. They loved chaos. They loved twists in fortune, new forms of torture and gore. These ghouls lived for it and the bloodsport ritual was their only chance at entertainment in their dull day—some new, gory twist and unpredictable hackfest to tickle their dicks and inflame their half-alien blood.

Cyr blew snot out of his nose and flicked a wad out way. "You little bastards. Tucking tail. So smug and confident. You know nothing about what you've done. You've destroyed something far more valuable than anything you're worth. It could have changed the course of civilization forever."

"What twisted world are you living in?" I shouted back at him. "Ladled with Gy-ar's evil? Do you like how we rid the world of the Prime Asshole's evil secret plan when he took over your slave cities?"

"You stupid gnat. I would have dealt with him."

"You sure? He's dead now."

"Dead?" Cyr snorted. "Mice die. Cockroaches like Gy-ar don't. They crawl out of the slimes and live on forever."

The look of dead earnest on the man's face caught me by surprise. No way Gy-ar could have survived that crash, could he? Suddenly, even in spite of all my hurts and throbbing body, I felt not so sure that we'd 'rid' ourselves of the master cockroach of the universe. The throbbing between my ears and the sour taste in the back of my throat was worse than ever. My good fist clenched. I ran knuckles over my aching ribs. When would this hell ever end? Would I ever be free?

In death you'll be free, Rusco. So suck it up and live.

I struggled halfheartedly in Skel's grip, but I knew he was right. He'd saved my ass. Cyr would have beaten me into the ground, snapped my neck. I could still not meet Areth's eyes who looked at me listlessly.

As the Skurgs continued to howl, pleased to no end at the unexpected shift in fortune, Cyr crouched and circled the wheezing Skurg. His arms were outstretched, hung to the sides like an ape. With a laughing jeer, he threw the Skurg's mallet back at him, straight at his chest. It was a taunt, delivering the ultimate insult: *Take your stupid weapon, worm. I can beat you anyway. Take your best shot.*

The Skurg came hobbling in, all gutturals and fury, his grunts low on his black lips. This was Cyr's intention. Bait and bash. The same as he'd played on me. I was glad it was the Skurg facing him in that ring, not me.

Cyr leaped aside with effortless ease at the last minute and smacked hammer fists on the monster's back. The Skurg stumbled, went staggering forward. Cyr kneed him in the face. There came a vicious smack and grab scrabble which lasted nearly a minute. Even my jaw dropped at the fury and violence of it all and I'd seen a lot of fights in my day. I marveled at Cyr's strength. His fighting skill was unpredictable, raw, brutal. There came an instant when the Skurg's left guard was exposed and it was all Cyr needed to wheel and strike. A loud crack came as the Skurg's middle ribs snapped. When the monster went down, a black boot rose and snapped the creature's neck. The Skurg lay dead, his neck twisted on an unnatural angle.

A deadly silence passed over the Skurg company.

No howls, no groans or yowls. They all came at once, stormed the circle, teeth flashing in menace in the firelight. They hauled Cyr away, kicking and screaming toward the meat house. He kicked and thrashed and bellowed like a bear as some of them dragged their dead comrade away by the heels to the crackling fires where his body was dismembered and slow-cooked over the flames.

Rolph cowered in the Skurgs' grip, awaiting his turn.

I heard grunts of rage, angry slaps, kicks, frustrated wails from that open window of the meat house and finally a dissolute howl of sheer, utter despair.

My guts twisted at the timbre of the wail. I'd heard such before on Skaldar when thug Braz had been operated on, his leg amputated not so long ago.

Cyr's fresh leg was brought out on a bloody pallet like a hallowed thing. Over the fire it was skewered on a spit and rosy flames licked up to sizzle meat and fat while Skurgs gathered in numbers with hungry, beady eyes to sample the warrior's flesh.

As for Cyr, I knew from experience that what was once a whole man would emerge from the butcher's den a fledgling cyborg, hobbling on an artificial limb.

So went the twisted rituals of the Skurgs and their primitive feasts and bloodthirsty rites.

They escorted Cyr after a time out of the meat shop, an arm around a shoulder each. Cyr winced, hobbling on his new robotic leg. They plonked him in the sand with us.

I watched him listen to the chewing on his limb with an expression of murderous calm.

What was going on in his mind, I could not guess. It gave me the shivers just to think of it.

Rolph followed, dragged to the meat shop by one of their stronger members. Two Skurg guards walked a few paces behind with goads crossed on their chests. Both were oblivious to the prisoner's shouts for mercy and his foul curses.

He was pushed through the door even as he starfished his legs out to catch on the trim. The metal door clanked shut.

There came a busy period of gruesome sawing and petrified wails and I recalled how Skel'd told me how easy it was for these brutes to slap new robot limbs on a victim for the ones they had cut off.

No anesthetic. No fancy surgicals. A couple of quick cuts. Cauterize the incision with torches. Interface nerve endings with a magducer. Slap on a prosthetic, add a power pack. Job done, everything good.

After a while Rolph's cries ceased and there came the clank of sharp instruments on metal trays.

A tray of meat soon came out, carried by lip-licking guards. They hadn't bothered to outfit Rolph with new limbs. They just carved off all his limbs. Maybe he'd put up such a fight that they hadn't thought him worthy of saving. Maybe he'd died on the operating table bleeding out.

We all peered with loathing and horror.

"They won't be getting this," Skel muttered. He lifted his left arm in a morbid show. "They already got this from elbow down."

Areth turned away, her mouth quivering. "Why'd you have to tell us that?"

"What should I tell you, Lady Areth? That we should just sit back and enjoy the Skurg picnic while we sift for gold in the sun? It's going to get very ugly very quickly. We have to figure out a way out of this mess asap."

"And how?" Quassa croaked.

Krake motioned to the airfield. "Those ships are the only way out of here. We have to get to them."

"Good luck getting past the Skurgs," I grumbled.

"1000 yards is not that far. There's a way," murmured Skel.

His words gave me confidence. 1000 yards was not that far.

Our favorite tyrant, Walleye, broke us up. He rallied the Skurgs to attention. Party time was over. The Skurgs'd had their sacrifices, eaten their meat and it was time to put the lambs to bed. Per usual, they split us up into our familiar groups and it was off to the dorm ships.

CHRIS TURNER

CHAPTER 32

After the horrible bloodsports, I'd made a point of being near Areth come wrap-up time. We stayed glued to each other like a swarm of bees. I realized it all depended on how we were clustered before we were paired and hustled to bed. The ones who cared for each other, tried hard to herd themselves close to each other when the ritual feasts were over. Likewise Baskra or Quassa stuck close to Lisse.

Despite his prosthetic leg, Cyr tried to muscle his way close to Areth and me. Damn the man! They must have given him some heavy Myscol or similar drug to dull the pain and spike his adrenals. Fortunately Skel and I inserted ourselves between him and Areth. Vicious blows were traded and the Skurgs dragged Skel, Krake and Cyr to the end of the line with the other slaves and they were shuttled off to the alternate group.

The Skurgs could care less. They just pushed us randomly into our slave cribs. What did they care if we maimed, killed or screwed each other? Deaths or injuries were all the same. They just meant more meat for their barbarous feasts, their amputations and their violent rituals.

Even after the horrors of the day, Areth and I made mad passionate love that night. We did it while we were still alive and had the chance. Who knew if we would be alive and kicking tomorrow? It was pretty hard making love with a busted finger and a fractured rib, but by God, nobody was going to deny me that pleasure in the face of our private hell.

They were the only moments of joy I truly felt in this grim prison hell. To lose myself in Areth's loins, to drink deep of her raw sexuality. Likewise, she felt the heat of my passion and was capable of a delicious sensuality in spite of our sordid confines and the precariousness of our existence.

My fingers traced practiced circles over the familiar spots of her body, the delicate peaks and valleys, the gentle sway of our interlocked hips, her sweat-misted skin. I enjoyed the poetic lift of her streamlined limbs, her sculpted shoulders while my other hand swept the hollow of her back, my own muscular thighs pressed intimately against her own softer limbs.

In these moments, we learned the secret language of each other's rhythms. Many murmured sweet nothings fell in each other's ears after our coupling: we traded stories in the cramped dark. I learned a lot about her.

"You never did tell me how you got hooked up with Gy-ar." My left arm was draped around her exposed shoulder; the cool tip of her nose was nestled in the crook of my neck.

She gave a languid sigh and lifted her head to the left away from me. "Are you sure you want to know?"

"I'd like to know, yes."

"A long while back, there was a guy I liked. He was the father of my daughter Slevana. We were young and we were in love. Or so I thought. At least in the classic honeymoon phase. We'd go on these long trips to exotic worlds: to the moon gardens of Ios, the grand canyons on Pharden, the White Palace on Xem, make love under the moonlight on the banks of the Ghost River on Tarak."

"Sounds romantic."

"No need to get jealous. Not nearly as romantic as with you in this dingy setting. Are you happy?"

"Touché. Point taken."

"Seriously, it wasn't until things degraded to a very low point that it was too late. It all kind of slipped away. He grew distant from me, almost as if he were a different species. Cold and aloof. I couldn't figure it out. It was as if he were under some external pressure. He was on assignment, working for people I did not know, undercover. He never told me much about what he did. I guess that was part of his profession. We got to visit all those exotic worlds because his employers paid him well, but I should have seen it—" She bit her lip. I felt her head nudge my shoulder restlessly in the dark. "Every trip some more new stress lines on his forehead, worse chain-smoking habits and binge-drinking.

"One day he dumped me. Cleaned out our bank account and disappeared. Left me nothing. No note, no anything.

"I was devastated. I called him every name in the book. I stamped my feet, beat my fists on the wall."

"Sounds rough."

"A week later, I got this call from a recruiting agency. Some guy says they'd received a good reference and wanted to hire me. At first I was skeptical. I was pretty young, and pregnant with Slevana. I was flattered, I needed work. They offered me a position as 'Information Consultant'. My hubby must have put in a good word for me down the line. He'd also worked for the agency sometime in the past. Good word?" She snorted. "What did I know about spying? I was charged up on getting answers and regaining some of the self-esteem that he'd taken from me. Rusco, it was almost as if they'd groomed me from the start, Gy-ar and his crew. They played me. They had all this information on me because of Charlie. They promised me that if I worked for them, they'd be able to find out what happened to him and get restitution for his leaving me high and dry with a child to raise."

"So it was Gy-ar and his outfit operating under a front?"

"Yeah, which I didn't know until later. Gy-ar took me under his wing. Seems he'd taken a fancy to good old Areth. Must have had a whole batch of covert videos on me from my perfidious husband. I shudder to think of the voyeurism of that man, Gy-ar." She shifted on her side. "I rose up the ranks. When I wanted to bail, Gy-ar told me I'd signed papers that guaranteed I couldn't back out for at least 5 years. What could I do? I never found out what happened to Charlie. I figured later they must have killed him then set this trap, or the hinges of a trap, to pull me in. Gy-ar would have me for his own once Charlie was out of the picture.

"Turns out Gy-ar's instinct was right. I was not just a pretty face. I had the skill to be a good agent: an information gatherer, infiltrator, sometimes backbiter, and even accomplice in murder the odd time. At first some of the stuff appalled me, but I got immune to the evil. To the point that what seemed like sordid missions of yesterday became just normal everyday business. That stuff with Katra I told you about back on Vipra, was a wake-up call. I started to see Gy-ar for what he was, a demon of intrigue. But by then it was too late, and I was in denial."

"You still in denial?"

"No. If that bastard were here in this room right now, I'd claw his eyes out. He's dead, thank the universe." She rolled in closer to me and I felt her breasts touch lightly against my chest. "Enough about me, what about you?"

"I've had my tribulations. I used to run with gangs as I mentioned, rough thug-types, not-nice people."

"So how young? You're what, only 19 now?"

"Young, like 13, maybe younger."

"You kidding me?"

"I wish I were. I was a go-between. A kind of informer, errand boy and 'information gatherer' like yourself. These guys did everything from drug deals to Myscol trade, to production and mafia muscle. The kingpin boss man ended up getting killed. Met with an 'accident', crushed in between a grinder and a forklift at one of the labs, if you can believe such a fairy tale."

"Not really."

"I was on the run with no protection and a bunch of guys out to kill me when they knew I had no dependable support."

"So what did you do?"

"I ran."

"Even as a kid?"

"They'd kill their own grandmother if they could profit. I escaped one life and ran to another. On Belruus. Hoag. A runaway, always the runaway. A refugee." I gave a humorless laugh. "Nothing really funny about it, though... I left that hellhole of a life behind and I think it was the music that saved me, Areth. Otherwise I'd have gone right back into vice and old habits. I put all my energy into playing music. *Carnivale* and the band gave me an outlet, a purpose, something creative. Building rather than destroying. I was good at it. A natural influencer, a lead singer, able to bring people to a place they didn't have access to. Offer them some passion and add some value to their lives, rather than taking away from them, like what Gy-ar does."

"You picked up music fast."

"Within a year and a half—I was playing guitar in sizable gigs. I already played banjo when I was a kid at seven. Had a natural talent. My mom taught me how to pick and do the fingerings."

"You play well. You're a natural."

"Thanks." I shrugged. "Like you and your secret agenting."

She sneaked a hand down past my ribs. "Look where it's gotten us, Rusco. Kind of ironic we crossed paths under the circumstances."

"And we still have another opportunity to make love." I tickled her shoulder and pulled her in closer.

"What are you going to do about that finger?"

"No worries. I'll survive."

"So what made you change?"

"Back then it was just a game. Running with the big boys. Even though I was just a tall teen with rabbit-quick legs, I was still a glaze-eyed errand boy. I didn't realize how bad some of the stuff was I was doing and'd gotten mixed into. A kid that young's easily influenced."

"Amazing that you survived."

"I was running on fumes, living an adventure. Reveling in the big thrill of hanging out in the wolf's den and not getting killed."

"You've still got that, Rusco. You're still a daredevil. Like that red-headed friend of yours. Remember *The Rocks*? The Skurgs? Escaping the slave ship, how we got away in the airnaut?"

"I do."

"Let's make the best of it. Here's to more of the good days." She squeezed me tight as her warm lips touched mine.

CHAPTER 33

Days passed.

I'd ripped off a strip from my spacer's leathers and managed to splint-wrap my finger with a sliver of rock I'd snagged from the river. The splint spared me some agony. I wrapped the jacket tighter around my chest to minimize movement of my ribs.

At first Cyr was barely functional. He'd come down off his Myscol and was struggling to learn how to use his new limb. On work detail, he stooped awkwardly in the shallows. He would wince, sometimes wobble on his feet, only to fall back in the water. He'd get up and curse, shake a fist at the sky. I was secretly glad he was impaired, as it meant less damage he could do to us. Truthfully, I would not wish that torture on my worst enemy, with the possible exception of Gy-ar.

Cyr quickly got used to his new legs. Every day his limp lessened, his stride became more brisk and determined. His eyes glowered with that brooding hatred of a man wronged. It was almost painful to watch. His burning loathing for us never ceased, if anything it only grew. Perhaps it was the only thing keeping him motivated to stay alive so he could inflict maximum damage on those who'd shattered his world.

The gills on his neck had grown too. They were about three inches long, now stretching from the bottom of his ears toward the collar bones. His face was increasingly fish-shaped, his nose distended, eyes rounder. It gave him a mutant's look.

It gave me the shivers. I hadn't seen such pronounced growth on Makala. But then, maybe she hadn't od'd on Gy-ar's serums. I could only liken the phenomenon to an athlete od'ing on steroids.

My lefty pinky ached like a bitch, but I'd get used to it. As too the rib, only a couple of hairline fractures high on the left side, but enough to keep me grimacing, aware of my physical vulnerability.

Three days later, as the sun was dipping closer to ritual time, Remus decided he'd had enough of combat circle and tried to make a break for it. For some strange reason, he aimed for Vipra. Illogical, but who knew what was going on his mind? He probably thought it was a stepping stone to get to the other ships.

It was a mistake either way.

Foolishly Quassa tagged at Remus's heels. I saw them both boot it in a madcap rush past stubby, scattered cacti. Both were run down and goaded. Dragged back to the compound, to the meat house to face the same grisly fate as Rolph and undergo the inevitable amputations. I had to turn my head at the sawing crunch and the cries of agony that drifted from the window. It set our teeth on edge. The smacks of lips and clacking of teeth as the Skurgs feasted on the spoils that night around the fire were nearly impossible to bear. The twin moons of this strange world rode high, grinning down on us like skewed eyes from a demented face. We remained locked in our own cocoons, dulled to the pain.

Cyr seemed immune to the Skurg cannibalism. Perhaps he'd seen enough of the universe's horrors to be hardened as knots on an aged mangalorn. The destruction of Aqua Rex was the only thing that had somewhat broken his world. Even superseding his capture here and the brutality of having a limb roboticized.

There was no opportunity for a breakout even after Skel's initial ambitious plans. Another day was coming to an end and the blazing sun setting low on the horizon. The Skurgs gathered us before the fire. Dried cactus was piled on. The crackling flames rose high once again.

I was dismayed that he had not come up with some alternate plan. Skel was usually the magician who could pull rabbits out of a hat. But now he shifted from foot to foot, scowling, cursing. I'd never seen him so agitated.

"Kip, plan B," he hissed in my ear as we were herded to the corral. "Spread the word. If any one of us goes in the ring, we all rush in. No questions asked. One last stand."

I swallowed hard and licked my lips. The sun was slipping below the horizon, a molten ball far past the airfield. He meant it and I knew many of us would not survive the night.

"It's not ideal, Skel," I rasped back at him. "We're better off trying to run in daylight when the Skurgs are scattered and we can see where we're going."

"I know, Kip. But we don't have that luxury. I feel it's now or never."

I exhaled a sick breath. "We better hope and pray this works."

He slapped me on the back. "It will, buddy. Have some faith. Have I ever let you down?"

He hadn't, but I was getting very cold feet about this desperado plan. Areth's face was pale and drawn. She looked frightened out of her mind. All her secret agenting skill and training had not prepared her for this.

Cyr glowered on the sidelines. Only one of his crew members was still alive. He'd gotten wind of our vague plot, was edging closer.

"Kip, if this goes south," Skel murmured, "you pick up the torch, where I leave off. You kill the Skurgs—as many as possible. Do you hear?"

I gave a terse signal and agitated nod. "You'll make it."

"You swear on it?"

"I swear, now let's drop it and focus on getting through the night."

He flashed me his catlike grin. Once more the Skel I knew, the die-hard freedom fighter risking his soul for a bit of justice, anything that'd make the universe a freer place.

A flash of movement came at the edge of my vision. Bodies were shoved out of the way. I tensed, knuckled my fists.

Perhaps Cyr had a death wish. Perhaps he plotted to take us all down with him. Who was to understand his diseased thinking? Who knew what it was like to have your leg cut off and chewed before your very eyes?

With a bear-like roar, he plowed into Skel. Skel bashed me and we both went flying. We arched our arms, blocked his bone-cracking fists. Cyr would have already killed me had not Somalon been quick enough to block a hammer blow and elbow him in the teeth.

Skel was up on his feet, shielding me from Cyr. The Skurgs rushed in and subdued the madman before he could inflict any more damage. Ten of them hauled us into the combat circle. They formed a dark ring around our bruised bodies while the other slaves stood mouthing curses, lungs pumping.

Skel smiled a grim smile. He wiped the blood off his lip.

"You scums planning on breaking out of here?" Cyr rasped. "Go right ahead. But you'll have to get by me first." I could see his gills working, gulping for air, as if they hungered for seawater, like the mutant aqua creature he'd become.

"You stupid cretin," Skel cursed. "You could have helped us escape. Instead you choose to die."

He gave a croak of harsh laughter. "You think so? You're a fool. I gave you what you wanted—your little distraction. But neither of you escape, carrot-head. Both of you die. By my hands. I could give a rat's ass about the rest of these walking corpses. They can all rot here for all I care."

Skel nodded somberly. It made sense to him. "Knock yourself out, merman."

The Skurgs began to chant, an awful, low-pitched mantra, *"Korgure Eus Sornid! Korgure Eus Sornid!"* I translated the cringeworthy words as 'Kill! Fight to the death. Kill!'.

On and on the chant rose while the crackling flames licked higher and the murmurs of the slaves grew.

The ten Skurg guards retreated to the sidelines. It was the signal that it was our turn to fight.

Skel made a significant gesture to the slaves as Cyr circled us. "You're going burn in hell, flyboy." The man had a look of death on his face. "First you though, Rusco. For destroying Aqua Rex."

"They would have used it for nefarious ends, Cyr. You know it, but you won't admit it."

He gave a cry of rage, his gills opening and closing like valves of a heart. Were they taking in oxygen? Hankering for some liquid base? "You know nothing!" he roared. "It was a mistake to bring in that temple ghoul, Gy-ar. The bastard double-crossed me. Maybe you did some good by crashing his yacht."

One of the Skurgs threw a wooden mallet into the ring. We all went clawing for it. Skel got to it first but Cyr ripped the weapon from his grasp and sent him staggering sideways. Then he came in swinging. A vindictive, murderous look lay etched on his face. "Events take a final shift, you scum. Prepare to die!"

With a hoarse yell I ran around his back while Skel assaulted him from the front.

Cyr whacked me in the arm. I slid a foot lower, moaning. Skel head-barreled him in the hip, knocking him sideways. He lay hands on the handle of the mallet, trying to wrest it out of his grip.

Without success.

A vicious free-for-all ensued. Two on one. Even though Cyr was outnumbered, it was by no means an even fight, even if he had a robotic leg. Skel and I dogged in and out, taking more damage our due. Cyr ducked low, swinging his murderous mallet. He hit us again and again. My shins and shoulders, forearms and ribs were raw with aches and bruises. My head was reeling from trying to stay ahead of his flashing weapon and his hammer fists, and I gasped in misery as time and again he managed to graze my cracked ribs. I heard another finger snap. Skel was panting, hobbling on a fractured ankle. A sick twisted grin lay carved on his face. The Skurgs bellowed more challenges then leaped up and down into the first feet of the ring, cheering like crazed apes. I heard through the roaring in my ears the slaves shouting, trying to break into the circle. Areth's shrieks rose above the din. The Skurgs pushed them back, hacked and jabbed viciously at their limbs with their goads.

Cyr's grimace turned to glee as he saw Skel's injury. He turned and fixed his full attention on me. He lunged up behind, wrapped brawny arms round my throat. He near lifted me off the ground. I could feel my legs dangling above the sand.

I kicked and thrashed but I could not break free from his python grip.

There came an infernal roaring in my ears. I was about to black out. Above the roar I heard Skel curse. "It was me who drove the sub into the dome, you stupid idiot! Not Rusco! You got the wrong guy."

Cyr turned to him, eyes shafting daggers. "You?"

"If I had to do it over again, I'd do exactly the same! You're a stupid imbecile, Cyr!"

A volcanic rage coursed over his fishy face. His gills opened and closed with inhuman menace. I knew Skel was mouthing words and insults to save my life but he might as well have waved a red flag in front of bull.

Cyr went apeshit.

He came at Skel first, roaring and swinging. He hammered him down. I lost track of the blows he rained as I crawled painfully to my knees.

I stared in horror. I scrambled over to Skel, my friend, my heart racing with sick apprehension.

He was a battered mess. One eye stared up at me, through a bloody veil of what was once a human face. Nose and the other eye were mashed.

"Sk-kurgs...kill them, Kip, do...the right thing." His last words ended in a choking gurgle. He lay on his back, eye staring up.

I beat my fists on his chest. "Get up! Get up, Skel! We can't survive this without you!" But he would not be getting up. My world reeled. In the kaleidoscope of my mind came that prophetic vision of him dying in space at the hands of the Skurgs far away from home. The last chilling gift given me by the cursed I-TERA.

Cyr stared down at us without sympathy. The Skurgs came trotting in to drag Skel away.

Something in me snapped. Like a man possessed, I leapt to my feet and tore the mallet from Cyr's momentarily slack grip. Two-handed, pain be damned in my broken fingers, I hammered those leather-bound, mummy-faced pieces of shit to death that came for Skel. Blood and brains flew everywhere. Nothing could stop me. Then I came at Cyr.

I don't remember what happened next or that murderous, awful flash of adrenaline. But Cyr was a dead man. I saw red everywhere. I didn't care. I would take as many of these shitwad worms down with me before I died.

Cyr was caught flat-footed. He was unprepared for my lightning attack. My first mallet blow fell hard on his shoulder, smashing the bone in two. He couldn't get away from my strikes fast enough. He whirled with a bellow of pain and rage. He pulled back his right fist, but I swung an instant faster and smashed that arm too. Then I kicked his feet out from under him before his fist could land a direct blow. I rose from my gasping, bent-kneed crouch and loomed overtop him, like a ghoul of his worst nightmare. I raised the blood-streaked mallet in a two-handed grip, ready to lay open the bastard's skull with a final blow.

But something in his swimming eyes made me pause.

"Kill me, you fool!" he rasped.

He had a Halloween pumpkin face, purplish, bruised, teeth missing.

My mallet angled down.

He held up a hand in front of his face. "Wait! Take this," he croaked. With his good hand he reached into his pocket and held up what looked like a silver coin. But it wasn't a coin. It was something deadly.

"Arm the thing, use it to kill these roaches."

I reached down to snatch up the spinner before he could pull some new trick on me.

He hacked and coughed out blood. "Bravo." A hairy arm snaked out, grabbed my wrist and pulled me toward him. His claw-like grip was like iron and such was his strength that I could not break free.

In a gasping breath, he wheezed, "I was saving it for you, Rusco. To blow your nuts off. You should use that fighting instinct more often. You would be a better man."

The Skurgs flooded in and with tears of sorrow and rage, I swung the mallet down and cracked his head open like a melon.

The dam broke.

I thumbed the engage switch on the spinner and hurled it in the midst of those cretinous leather-armored scum that came clawing for me. I had just enough time to leap to the side when a massive explosion ripped through their numbers and flesh sizzled and chunks flew. Blood-drenched limbs and fresh gore went hurtling every which way. The slaves were checkered in rich red splatter. A quarter of the Skurgs had been shredded to bits, the explosive ripping through their front line like a time bomb.

"Run!" I cred. "To the ships!" The bewildered slaves moved in one savage rush to the combat circle then plowed their way through the charred chunks on a beeline to the airfield. The last of the Skurgs staggered after them. The slowest slaves were caught, dragged back to the corral.

I hustled Areth around the back of the stockade. To a five-foot smoking section that had been destroyed by the blast. We hotfooted it toward the airfield. Krake, Somalon and Lisse on our heels. I was operating on adrenaline, heedless of my wounds. Krake was moving slower because of his prosthetic leg.

Areth caught up to me, huffing and puffing. She stared with new awe as if I were an alien. "Jesus, Rusco! You clubbed down three of those monsters and Cyr in a matter of seconds. It was unbelievable."

"It was either them or me. They killed Skel, damn it!"

I thrust the massacre out of my mind. They say that a person has three times his strength under the influence of adrenaline. An altered state of consciousness. Superhuman power. Auto hypnosis. Some shit like that. I say it is all bullshit and when your life is at stake you do what you need to do.

A pack of Skurgs came winging in from the side. They hedged us off with snarls of rage on their blood-flushed lips. Areth and I got separated from Krake.

I escaped the clutch of the first crimson mitt that grabbed for me, but another came looping around my waist. Areth skittered back, leaped on his back with a cursing cry. She struck the Skurg over and over with her fists, giving me time to shrug off the brute and land a crushing blow in his face with my mallet. Dazed and death-crazed we were off running to the ships.

How Cyr'd managed to hide that explosive on him I'd never know. Maybe he'd hid it up his ass? But a man like that who'd gone from the gang gutters of Parinossus to becoming the most visionary magnate this side of Perseus, would not have left himself unprepared.

CHRIS TURNER

CHAPTER 34

A night breeze brought the smell of tar to our noses. I knew we were close. We couldn't get to the Daulk lightfighter though. There came the sound of thudding feet thirty feet off to our right in the darkness. Skurgs. Too many of them.

I snuck a tense glance toward the airfield. A dim glow from the hangar illuminated twenty ships. So near but so far. The ships were on the crumbly tarmac, mostly Skurg lightfighters.

With sick dismay I realized we had to abandon our plan: reaching the faint, crescent shape of the Daulk craft that sat taunting us in the purple-stained moonlight. My eyes made out a ruined Mentera craft to our left. It was about fifty yards away: an eerie starfish shape, tilted on its side, both hatches riddled with ion fire.

I ran toward it without thinking.

Areth scuttled after me, breath hissing, "What the hell are you doing, Rusco? Where are you going?"

I didn't answer. I kicked open the rusted hatch, caught her arm and shoved her in before they saw us.

The hallways were low and gloomy. I clutched my mallet in my good right fist, breathing hard, thinking fast. We had to make this detour last. At worst, it would be a last stand in this shadowy crypt. A faint reek of decay came to my nose. The guttural cries of Skurg voices sounded behind us and I knew the bastards'd already spotted us.

Damn it!

We pushed deeper into the murky interior. Toward the bridge, our boots clacked on the old, corroded metal slats as we stumbled over skeletal humps, chitinous shapes that looked much like those specimens that Cyr had shown me in his cryptic museum on Aqua Rex, minus the fins. It confirmed Skel's theory that these starfish ships were early Mentera warships.

The pain was starting to kick in badly. A sharp stab in my upper midriff, an aching throb in my right thigh, both places where Cyr's mallet had struck. Bones and muscles were aching all over.

A straggler Skurg came blundering after us. I glimpsed the green-glowing goad raised like a saber a few dozen feet away. The Skurg was shy of seven foot, and when I caught the crimson glint in his eye, I knew it could only be our time-old enemy Walleye, come to pay us a visit.

We reached the bridge, our lungs struggling for air. Two triangular-shaped windows leaked in a watery moonlight. I saw the desiccated bodies of more grasshopper shapes—what had once been blackish-green, chitinous bodies of the locust fiends. They were gathered around a semicircle of controls, alien to the touch. Broken glass lay at our feet. I saw a half intact telephone-booth-like tank enclosing a creature of dubious origin—squidish if I were to make a guess, with reptilian tail and desiccated, splayed tentacles which would burn in my memory forever.

I thrust the creature out of my mind.

Skurg Walleye's clomping steps came closer. I ducked back to the left of the low door, fist clenched on my weapon. "Stay put, Areth!" I croaked. "Lure the bastard in here."

She stood frozen for a few seconds. Her face was white, stricken with fear.

When the monster at last ducked in, I leaped up and smashed the mallet as hard as I could on the back of his neck. The place between shoulder blade and spine. The creature sagged back with a moaning cry and Areth came rushing in and kneed him in the nose. She knocked out his yellow teeth. He collapsed with a thud. With husky, banshee yells we both stomped him into the floor, breaking his spine.

Walleye was dead and we could now at least rejoice in a small triumph for the evening.

More footfall echoed from the hallway.

"Let's go!" I grabbed her arm. We fled down the opposite starfish wing that angled toward the airstrip. We took the gangway in huffing strides. On stumbling feet we fled out through the hatch to beetle toward the Daulk fighter for which we so hungered. It was the same ship Skel and I'd scoped out days ago.

I ditched the mallet and we hoofed it into the cramped cockpit. I plopped myself in the pilot's chair. Areth crowded beside me taking the copilot seat.

After a brief scan of the controls I flicked some switches. The craft started immediately. I got it climbing into the air, thankful of the many hours of close attention I'd paid to the nav with Skel, and aboard Goliath with Trix. Even if that seemed a lifetime ago, it was a lifesaver. We got the vessel moving above the airfield. I rained fire down on the running Skurgs even when I saw a huddle of them chasing other miserable shapes on a beeline course to the ships.

There was a mini tactical panel beside the nav controls and Areth stared at it with watery eyes.

"You know how to gun?"

"No, but I can learn."

"Better learn fast."

With tongue clamped between her lips she took over the auxiliary weapons while I worked the main grid. I thrust us up on an a sharp angle to bank low in a breakneck dive to fire down at the gaggle of Skurg pursuing the slaves, leaving a spray of dismembered bodies that were once leather-armored scumbags. It gained the five hunched figures, Krake, Lisse, Somalon and two others, time to scramble aboard the XT6. Kudos to their persistence! They got into the open cargo bay and Krake had the hulk lifting into the air, a rain of fire already streaking from the ships that were just rising from the airfield.

The XT6 roared into the sky only 50 yards up and already she faced lateral and surface fire from Skurg snipers trolling overhead. The XT6 had heavy plate armor but she was slow to move and was heavy of heel. I guessed her impulse thrust was still damaged from the spider weave she'd been wrapped in and she was riding with no shields. I could see the writing on the wall. The XT6 was a sitting duck. Krake and I both knew it.

He leveled her on a collision course with two fighters that had come careening at us. The bogeys banked and split up to avoid collision but Krake's lateral fire caught the second fighter's stern and sent it spinning to the ground.

I swung the Daulk craft around and helped Areth sight on one of the enemy harrying the XT6. The Skurg's shields were overloaded. She blew into a thousand pieces.

Bogeys were all around us. We didn't have enough firepower to defeat the horde. The Skurgs'd put every pilot into the air they could muster. Their rage must have been mammoth at losing half their numbers, let alone a slave revolt on their hands.

Heavy fire came angling from above us. Ion beams sprayed the XT6's midships deck. My heart was in my throat. Twin blasts sent her in a tailspin and she crashed into the cactus plains. Fire erupted from the bridge.

I blinked back wetness in my eyes. More deaths. I tried to stop the tears and shook my head in sick frustration. "Is there no justice in this universe?" I croaked miserably.

"We have to get the hell out of here, Rusco!" Areth cried. "Everyone's dead. One ship against a squadron? Are you crazy?"

She was right. Eight of them, all coming for us.

I tucked tail and resisted the urge to lay fire into any of them. Dead heroes make sad ones and the time for playing martyr was over.

I turned the Daulk craft toward the night sky. I aimed her nose straight at the grinning moon. We flew at maximum thrust. Areth sat ramrod straight beside me, her brow sweat-slicked. Her dark hair was tousled and her fingers desperately worked the auxiliary port gun controls while I manned the starboard gun.

Bright streaks flashed by us, lighting up half the sky. Some caught our hull and I watched our shields dip to 30%. With a grim-lipped curse, I prayed that we'd make it to the varwol threshold. It was a reach of only 5000 miles for a planet of this size and gravitational pull.

We dodged the fire, trying to make as much distance from the planet as possible. But our shields kept dipping with every passing second, and every successful hit. The nav showed we were near a planet called 'Adriak' in the Nefus System. Adriak? What? Never heard of it. The stars wheeled before us. The pale amber planet fell behind as its nearest moon, a mauve disc, grew as we picked up speed through the near sectors of space.

We passed the first varwol threshold. I armed the nav for the nearest target, Perseus Aquis, a handful of light years away. I jammed the hyperdrive slider forward to 'engage'. We hypered out, leaving the Skurgs and their cursed ships a lightstream of dust far behind us.

Areth and I made our exit from the strange, sad world, brooding silently and I thought of Somalon, how he had said he'd be the happiest man alive if he could break out of the Skurg crib.

He hadn't. Nor had the others. All of them—Skel, Krake, Lisse, Comby, Quassa and Baskra. My eyes wetted with fresh tears.

I remembered the prophecy I'd been given by the I-TERA: how they'd all die in space far from their homes. A hollow feeling snaked through me. When I first saw them all down at the beachhead that day long ago coming off the XT6, oozing confidence, I thought they'd escaped the fate that the I-TERA had spelled out for them. But no.

How could a man live in peace with a prescient power like that? Knowing such things every day that would make him insane, he'd want to off himself. I'm glad I no longer had that thing or its power.

I should have gone down with them...but all I had were a couple of busted fingers and ribs. It was not right. My lot was to live on and pick up the pieces...I had to live with the scars and the promise I'd made to Skel. 'To fight the Skurgs. Pick up the torch. *Do the right thing, Rusco.*' It would be a long time before I could ever come close to fulfilling that promise to Skel, or any promise even remotely approaching that magnitude. But it would come. As sure as rainfall I knew that the day would come, and there would be no turning back.

Hours passed. The ship cruised on autopilot, blitzing through the gulfs in blinks of an eye. I lay in Areth's arms, naked, sated, in the back compartment, every bone in my body aching. I was unable to erase memories that tormented me. I'd gotten the girl and escaped death against impossible odds. I'd everything to be grateful for, being alive, but somewhere I felt hollow and empty as a seashell, lost as a street waif scavenging in the rain.

Skel's death was a cruel blow. Certain injustices in the world could never be reconciled.

I knew Cyr's death would bring with it the execrable Moon cult taking over his project and commandeering the underwater cities. They would spread like algae all over the frontier worlds.

Part of me yet hoped it would never come to pass.

In the weeks that followed, I looked back on that desolate place in my mind's eye, remembering every detail, every prickly cactus trembling in the wind, the roaring death fires of the Skurgs, their yellow clacking teeth, the innocent purl of the gold-ridden stream, Skel's disarming grin, his comradely clap on my shoulder, Krake's expert piloting, his boyish charm, Somalon's courage and resourcefulness, Cyr's last stand and his parting blood-wrapped gift of the spinner that had saved our lives.

The lost graveyard of Adriak would always be the final resting place of my friends.

Gy-ar had been eradicated from the face of the worlds. No loss. Oddly the Moon Temple stalkers had somehow melted into the background. No shifty eyes or shadow figures on the periphery of my vision ready to slip a knife in my ribs. No ninja sisters making quick steps in the night shadows, to make secret reports of one Jet Rusco.

Skel's death had left scars on me for life, sent me into a black depression from which I would not recover for a long time. I'd like to say it was the straw that broke the camel's back, the reason I went dark and didn't resurface for many years. The reason I'd turned to a life of crime, into the dark world of the underground, but that would be a lie. An excuse to bury the real reason I did not honor my promise and pick up the torch from where Skel had left off: to drive the Skurgs back into the holes they came from. The reason why I didn't become a greater man.

But that is another story for another time.

CHRIS TURNER

EPILOGUE

Colorful magka birds hoo-hooed in the high mangalorns, ruffling their feathers. All was quiet in the lush forest of Yesma west of the river.

A very bedraggled and white-faced man stumbled over a root and looked up in desolation at the crumpled ruin of his space yacht lying twisted on its side. There was no solace in that crippled hulk. The engines were toast, the instruments were dead. His three crew members were corpses. He had escaped at the last minute, jettisoning the small escape pod before the yacht had gone down, but he had not given himself enough time and the trees had clipped his vehicle. All that was left of his emergency vehicle was a broken hull, which too had crashlanded. He had pulled himself from the wreckage, a miracle in itself. His life intact. His left cheek was burned. His body was covered in welts. He had what he thought a fractured arm. He could only move the small fingers in his left hand painfully. Numerous contusions and bruises did not lift his black mood or despair. At the bank of a small stream he stooped thirstily to slurp some fresh water. His belly growled with hunger. But there was no food to eat but grubs and fronds. What did he know of survival, having lived in luxury surrounded by servants? He bit back his growing hunger and dread. In his nostrils lingered the faint residual of smoke that hung in the air of the fires that he had helped orchestrate.

His head turned.

Low voices. The meaty thwack of machetes on foliage. Tough leafy fronds parted as a small group of commandos approached. He crabbed back in startlement and hope. Only to stare into a ring of khakied figures with unfriendly faces.

Licking lips, he lifted a trembling hand in greeting. "I'll give you gold, jewels, friends," he babbled. "Take me to the nearest city."

Dalree recognized the man for who he was and spat a wad of phlegm at his feet.

"You can keep your gold, 'friend'." He turned with a snarl to the others. "This man—the one we have been searching for—inspired Cyr to burn our forests—drive us into the sea."

Hoarse shouts rose from the four gathered half-track drivers. Razen rose from the huddle to inspect Gy-ar with disdain. There followed grumbles and disgruntled shouts. And so they dragged him none too gently to the ford of the river Umena where the village of Howshous loomed not a mile distant. Tow-haired villagers came to raise fists and hoes at him.

Gy-ar held up a hand. "Wait, please, I beg of you! Before you condemn me, hear me out—" But the villagers would not listen and all set to tear him to pieces.

Dalree shielded him from their grasping hands and hoes. "Wait! This demands thought. We are a civilized people. We rise above the ranks of animals."

A man yelled. "Animals kill predators that invade their territory, threaten their young. Death to those who bring it!"

"True, Dansi. But these are not barbaric times."

"Listen to your kinsman," Gy-ar cried. "He is wise. He speaks reason."

Dalree gave a cryptic smile. "Do not expect mercy from us, Prime Ascendant."

Gy-ar shrank back to his pale-faced, sweaty self.

"This man Gy-ar will live, but not as he has in the past."

Gy-ar's sank to a knee. Even in his wildest imagination he could not guess what the villagers would do to him. In desperation he mustered up defiance from within himself.

"I have many important friends! Powerful allies. They will punish you for this egregious breach of etiquette!"

Dalree shook his head gamely. He looked to the sky with gray, watery eyes. "It has been over a day and a half. No one has come. There are over a million acres in these dense forests. Your luck has run out. No one will find you. Your ship's beacon and your radio are dead."

Gy-ar's shoulders slumped. His lower lip trembled.

"The question is, what punishment would best fit your crimes?"

The old soothsayer, Mayar, the village elder, plodded forth on spindly legs and whispered words in Dalree's ear.

Dalree smiled and nodded. "I thank you, Mayar. Your insight is invaluable. I believe you have solved our dilemma."

With the help of the village craftsmen, the Yesmian rebels created a stout cage of dendron bars and hoisted it high in the mangalorns. Gy-ar was set inside. He looked out between the bars, clutching the wood with white fists and bewildered eyes.

Double ropes slung over two high branches, securing the upper bars. There was no way the Ascendant could get out or upset the cage.

"You will endure many days of sun and wind and rain," Dalree boomed. "This will give you time to contemplate the nature of your evil and the livelihoods you wished to destroy."

A ceremonial fire of green wood was lit in the small clearing, weaving a thick, smoldering smoke.

The fumes wafted up high in the trees and Gy-ar had no choice but to inhale deeply of them. The shaman and village priests danced around the fire, cackling in reverie and rattling their charms and creating old magic to smudge clean Gy-ar's soul. They prayed for the well-being of all and for no more fires or underwater cities to be unleashed upon them.

"Let the smoke be a reminder of what you tried to destroy, Gy-ar!"

"Nooo…!" Gy-ar's wailing cries fell on indifferent ears as he rattled his cage and hurled curses. The dark dendron remained indifferent to his piteous entreaties and coughing.

Dalree looked up and spoke, "A bowl of food and a gourd of water will be lifted up to you twice a day. If what friend Rusco and Skel told us is even half true of your crimes against humanity in faroff worlds, then your punishment is just."

Gy-ar snarled. "Those two will die excruciating deaths at the hands of my Order. The Order of the Moon Temple will prevail!"

"Maybe, but so too will you die. In fact, you will fare worse, because you will live to the endless rise and fall of the sun, a long, drawn-out torment, until you beg for death."

Gy-ar gave a croak of dismay. At last he knew the punishment that the universe had come to roost on him for his impulsive dealings over the I-TERA's recovery, throwing Rusco, the 'Chosen One' to the Skurgs, and his callous disregard of the Screeds of the Masters.

Gy-ar made one last pleading entreaty to the sky.

But Dalree had already made up his mind and turned his back on the Prime Ascendant as he strode away to attend his many duties for the day.

OTHER BOOKS IN THE STARSHIP ROGUE SERIES:

STAR RUNAWAY
THETIS 3
STAR REAPER
STARHUSTLER
STARVENGER

https://innersky.ca/starship

CHRIS TURNER

ABOUT THE AUTHOR

Chris is a prolific author of fantasy, adventure, and science fiction. His writing spans many genres: heroic fantasy, sword and sorcery and speculative fiction.

Browse Chris's books at:

https://innersky.ca/books

CHRIS TURNER

www.ingramcontent.com/pod-product-compliance
Lightning Source LLC
Chambersburg PA
CBHW031028260626
47153CB00016B/640